the
daughters
take the stage

the daughters take the stage

JOANNA PHILBIN

poppy

LITTLE, BROWN AND COMPANY
New York   Boston

Poppy

Hachette Book Group
237 Park Avenue, New York, NY 10017
For more of your favorite series and novels, go to www.pickapoppy.com

Poppy is an imprint of Little, Brown and Company.
The Poppy name and logo are trademarks of Hachette Book Group, Inc.

The publisher is not responsible for websites (or their content)
that are not owned by the publisher.

First Hardcover Edition: May 2011
First Paperback Edition: October 2011

The characters and events portrayed in this book are fictitious. Any similarity to real persons, living or dead, is coincidental and not intended by the author.

Library of Congress Cataloging-in-Publication Data

Philbin, Joanna.
The daughters take the stage / by Joanna Philbin. — 1st ed.
    p. cm.
    Summary: Fourteen-year-old Hudson is a gifted singer/songwriter like her mother, pop sensation Holla Jones, but while working on her debut album, Hudson struggles to convince her mother that she would rather stick with her own intimate style than follow her mother's path to fame.
    ISBN 978-0-316-04909-2 (hc) / ISBN 978-0-316-04908-5 (pb)
    [1. Fame — Fiction.   2. Mothers and daughters — Fiction.   3. Singers — Fiction.   4. Popular music — Fiction.   5. Individuality — Fiction.   6. High schools — Fiction.   7. Schools — Fiction.   8. New York (N.Y.) — Fiction.]
I. Title.
    PZ7.P515Dc 2011
    [Fic] — dc22

                                                                    2010042995

10 9 8 7 6 5 4 3 2 1

RRD-C

Book design by Tracy Shaw

Printed in the United States of America

For Ido

chapter 1

"You can't just sing the song, Hudson. It's not enough to sing the song. You have to *own* it," said Holla Jones as she paced back and forth in front of her daughter, Hudson, on the stage of the Grand Ballroom in the Pierre Hotel. "Own the stage, own the song, and you'll own the crowd. And that, my dear," she said, pivoting to face Hudson, who stood half-hidden behind a curtain, "is how you become a star."

Hudson bit her full bottom lip. She would be playing her first show ever in just a few hours, and already her mom was using the *S* word. Then again, her mom used that word a lot. Actually, Holla Jones was much more than a pop star — she was a treasured piece of American pop culture. For the past twenty years, her songs had become instant hits all over the world. Her concerts sold out in minutes. Her albums went platinum. Her bubblegumpop-with-an-edge sound was copied by artists everywhere. And Hudson knew that she'd been waiting almost fourteen years to teach her only daughter everything she knew.

"So, you walk up to the mic like this," Holla said, taking short, quick steps on her stiletto-heeled booties toward an imaginary microphone at the edge of the stage. "The last thing you want to do is trip in front of an audience before you've even sung a note." She pretended to grab a microphone. "You slip it out of the stand, and then you hold it just a few inches from your lips, and then you back up just a little bit," she said, taking some steps backwards. "Then you say something to the crowd," she went on. "Be witty, but brief. And then, honey, you start to sing," she said, looking over her shoulder at Hudson and smiling.

At thirty-seven her mom was still beautiful, with flawless dark brown skin, lush lips, and straightened toffee-colored hair that fell past her shoulders. Her tight yoga jacket and pants showed off a body that was sculpted to the extreme: carved biceps, a rock-hard stomach, and slender, muscular legs. Her high, regal forehead didn't have one wrinkle, and she moved with a dancer's grace — shoulders thrown back, spine ramrod-straight. Hudson had inherited that grace, along with her mom's sweeping cheekbones and razor-sharp jawline. But her sea green eyes and wavy hair and French toast–colored complexion came from her dad — or at least she figured as much, based on the photos she'd seen of him. Michael Kelly had been Holla's backup dancer on her second concert tour. He was white and preppy-looking, with thick dark hair, a chiseled face, and soulful eyes, like Billy Crudup crossed with Mikhail Baryshnikov. In pictures he stood next to Holla, his head on her shoulder, smiling goofily into the camera. But they'd had a tumultuous relationship, and when the tour ended he broke up with her, just before she learned she was pregnant. He hadn't been

2

heard from or seen since, and Holla, out of pride, had never tried to contact him. Sometimes Hudson wondered if he even knew he had a daughter. Holla didn't mention him too often, and most of the time it was almost as if he'd never existed at all.

"Mom, it's just the Silver Snowflake Ball," Hudson said. "It's not Radio City or anything."

"It doesn't matter," Holla said. "*Every* show is important. Your producer and your record-label executive are coming. They're going to want to see how you'll do this when it's time to go on tour. So come on out here. You can't hide behind those curtains all day."

Hudson stepped out of the wings, still wearing the ripped jeans and black sweater she'd worn to her last final exam. As of today, school was officially over for winter break, and all she really wanted to do right now was go home and take a nap. Besides, she and her mom had already spent hours talking about this, planning this, and rehearsing this. In a million years, she never would have guessed that she'd end up singing at Ava Elting's epic party. She hadn't even been sure that she would go. But then Carina Jurgensen, one of Hudson's best friends and the party planner for the event, had volunteered her as the night's entertainment, and she'd had no choice but to go along with it. Needless to say, Ava had been hoping for the Jonas Brothers or Justin Timberlake or some other big star she thought Carina could get, thanks to her billionaire dad and his A-list connections. But Ava had settled for Hudson. And now she needed to be prepared.

And her mom was right. In just six months her first album would drop, and then she would be playing shows all the time, at even scarier places. She needed to learn how to do this now. And

3

even though she had a feeling that she hadn't quite inherited her mom's performance gene, at least she was getting a one-on-one tutorial that most other beginners would kill for.

"Okay, let's start the track," Holla said. "Jason?" she called out to the wings. "Can we have the music, please?"

Weeks ago, when Hudson was trying to decide on a song for the Ball, "Heartbeat" had seemed like the perfect choice. She'd written it about Kevin Hargreaves, who was four years older, a senior at Lawrenceville boarding school, and basically a complete stranger. But he was a Capricorn, which blended beautifully with Hudson's Pisces sign, and he had deep, bottomless gray eyes that had made her heart pound and her hands sweat every time she'd seen him. Which had been exactly twice — first on the beach in Montauk, and the second time by accident in the Magnolia Bakery near her house. Carina knew him and had practically pushed Hudson into Kevin's face both times. He'd barely made eye contact with her, and had pretty much said only "hey!" while Hudson stared at him, speechless. When she'd heard he was going out with Samantha Crain, a tenth grader at Lawrenceville, she was crushed. She'd gone straight to her piano, and two hours later she'd finished this song — a slow jazz- and soul-inflected number that she sang leaning over her piano, in her deep, smoky voice.

But the song had since gone through a transformation. A few months ago, Holla decided that Hudson's entire sound needed to change, that for the sake of her first album's sales she would need to go bigger, brighter, and more radio-friendly. It wasn't enough to have a small cult following — she needed to fill stadiums. So Hudson let her mom change studios. She let her take apart every track, layering it with digital beats and effects and backup voices. Until little by little, Hudson's music sounded exactly like hers.

Now, as the song came over the ballroom's speakers, Hudson fought the urge to cover her ears. It was bad enough that it sounded fake and manufactured. Now Hudson had to sing to it. She'd never tried to sing without sitting at her piano. She had no idea what she was supposed to do with her hands and arms and feet. Of course, Holla knew what to do.

"So, let's practice those dance moves, honey," Holla said, sidling up next to her. "First is the turn, like this," Holla said, executing a perfect, weightless spin on the toes of her boots. "You try it."

"Mom, I told you, I really don't want to dance," Hudson said.

"You've got to do *something*," Holla insisted. "Come on. Try it. You're such a good dancer."

Hudson threw herself to the left and barely did half a turn.

"You're not trying, Hudson," Holla said. "Come on. I know you can do better than this."

Hudson gazed out at the brightly lit ballroom, filled with tables and chairs yet to be moved out. At least nobody was watching them yet. *How much more fun would tonight be if I could just go to this party like everyone else?* she thought. *Just hang out with Carina and Lizzie and check out people's dresses and scope the room for cute guys?*

"Mom, I really can't do this," Hudson said after trying to imitate her mom's shimmy. "Do I need to dance? Why can't I just sing?"

"Oh, honey, don't be so negative," said Holla. "Don't you know what I always say about negativity?"

" 'Negative thoughts draw negative things,'" Hudson recited.

"That's right," Holla said, flipping her hair over her shoulder. "And you, my dear, are being *extremely* negative about this. Let's play that again!" she called over her shoulder to Jason in the wings.

Hudson waited for the music to begin. *This isn't right,* a voice said inside her. *Get out of this now. People will understand. Even Ava will have to understand.*

"Come on, Hudson, here we go," Holla said. "Let's do the turn, and then a shimmy to the right...that's it."

It was just one night, Hudson told herself. She'd get through this, somehow. After all, she was the child of two dancers. She had to have gotten some of their talent.

But inside, she wasn't so sure. Her mom was the star in the family. And something told her that it was always going to stay that way.

chapter 2

Several hours later Hudson was back behind the same curtain, try-ing not to hyperventilate. On the other side, the Silver Snowflake Ball was in full swing. Butterflies flew around her stomach as she clutched the scratchy silk fabric. At least she knew she looked good. Gino, her mom's hairstylist, had straightened her hair and then curled it into soft waves. Suzette, her mom's makeup artist, had dusted her face with shimmery powder and lined her eyes with a thick purple pencil. Her vintage black silk halter dress felt cool and soft against her skin. She looked like a star. Now all she had to do was act like one. And not pass out.

But first it would help to get a glimpse of her friends. She peeked out from the wings, ready to signal Carina or her other best friend, Lizzie Summers. And there, smack in front of her, was Carina, kissing some guy Hudson had never seen before. He was skinny, with spiky black hair and beat-up Stan Smiths, and he looked nothing like the guys Carina usually liked. It had to be

Alex, the cool downtown DJ Carina had been talking about non-stop for the past few weeks. Normally she would have given them space, but this was an emergency, so Hudson marched right up to them and tapped Carina on the shoulder.

"Sorry to interrupt," she said, "but I think I'm supposed to go on now."

"Oh my God, you look gorgeous!" Carina said, breaking away from the kiss. With her beachy-blond hair, cocoa brown eyes, and freckled nose, Carina usually looked like the picture-perfect surfer girl. But in her emerald green minidress and gold heels, she was stunning.

"Oh my God, I'm so happy I made you do this," Carina said, jumping up and down. Then she remembered that they weren't alone. "Oh, and by the way, this is Alex."

Hudson turned to the guy. He was definitely cute, with large, liquid brown eyes and sharp cheekbones. "Hey, it's nice to meet you," Hudson said. "I've heard a lot about you."

"Hi there," Alex said, shaking her hand. "Um, sorry to change the subject, but is that Holla Jones standing back there?" he asked, pointing into the wings.

Hudson barely turned around. She knew that her mom was hovering nearby.

"Holla's Hudson's mom," Carina told him.

"Wow," Alex said. "This is some school you go to."

As they chatted, Hudson could see that Alex was head over heels for Carina, despite his cool exterior. But she was starting to get more and more nervous. The Silver Snowflake Ball was the most exclusive holiday party in the city. Ava had made sure to

8

invite only the highest-ranking students from all the New York City private schools, and even some boarding schools. Hudson couldn't quite see the crowd below the stage, but she could picture them, milling around, too cool to dance, too jaded to be excited about anyone who'd be performing. She knew that if she didn't do a good job tonight, she'd be the laughingstock of New York. But she also knew that she just needed to get this over with, so she reminded Carina and Alex that it was time for her to start.

"Okay, fine, break a leg," Carina said to her.

As Hudson turned to walk backstage she saw her mom coming toward her. Holla had changed into a tight black top and leather jeans.

"You ready?" Holla asked, reaching out to touch Hudson's curls. "Oh my God, what did Gino do to your hair? It's so…unruly."

"Mom —"

"Are you going to be able to dance in that dress?" Holla asked, looking her up and down with a disapproving frown. "It doesn't look like your hips can move in that. I thought you were going to wear the blue dress with the Lycra in it."

"Mom," Hudson said, feeling her heart rate start to rise. "Everything's fine."

"Now just remember, when you get out there, there's this thing called the fourth wall," Holla said, putting her hands on her slender hips. "It's like an invisible barrier between you and the audience. But you have to break it, over and over. You have to reach out into the audience and let them *know* that you're there —"

Hudson began to tune her mother out as the butterflies flitting around in her stomach turned into baby dragons.

"—and make sure, whatever you do, that you project your voice, even with the microphone, and remember"—she paused for dramatic effect—"Richard is here from Swerve Records. Chris is here. Everyone's watching you tonight. This has to be good."

Hudson nodded. From out of the corner of her eye she saw Ava Elting approaching. "Okay, fine, I have to go," she said, slipping away from her mother's stare just as Ava bossily inserted herself in front of her.

"So are you ready?" Ava asked. She wore her auburn curls piled up on top of her head and an electric purple dress with a side slit that was cut way, *way* too high up her leg.

"Sure," Hudson said, because she knew from the way Ava was looking at her that she didn't have a choice. "Let's go."

"Just remember, it's only *one* song," Ava emphasized. "We don't have time for any more."

"Don't worry," said Hudson. "I wasn't planning to do a full concert."

Ava was oblivious to Hudson's sarcasm. "Good luck!" she called out. Then she strode out onto the stage and right up to the mic, grabbing it like a pro. "Thanks everyone for coming!" she yelled. "And now I'd like to introduce to you the next huge pop music sensation, in her debut performance, the daughter of my really good friend Holla Jones, Hudson Jones!"

"My good friend Holla Jones"? Hudson thought as the applause roared from the ballroom. Ava hadn't even met her mom.

But then the applause started to die, and Hudson knew that it was time to walk out onstage. Her heart began to race. She took her first, tentative steps. *Here we go,* she thought. *You can do this. You can* totally *do this.*

With her eyes on the mic stand, she took the shortest steps she could on her three-inch heels. *The last thing you want to do is trip in front of an audience before you've even sung a note,* her mom had said.

Hudson looked out into the audience and blinked. She'd expected to see Lizzie's and Carina's smiling faces out in the crowd, but thanks to the blinding spotlight, there was only darkness. She couldn't see anything or anyone. She felt her throat tighten but she took the mic out of the stand and took a few steps back. She had no idea what to say.

"Hi, everyone. It's great to see you all here," she half-whispered, holding the microphone an inch from her lips. Her heart was beating so hard she thought it might fly up out of her throat and onto the stage. "This is a song off my first album. It's called 'Heartbeat.'"

She started to turn around, instinctively going to her piano. Then she remembered that it wasn't there. She was all alone. She bowed her head, gripping the mic with her sweaty hand. And when the song finally came blasting out of the speakers, Hudson raised her head to the audience — only to realize that she couldn't remember the song's first line.

The music — the awful, cheesy music — went on, blasting through the speakers. She stared into the darkness. If she turned her head and looked offstage, she knew that she'd see her mom jumping up and down, trying to get her to do some of the dance moves she'd spent so many hours trying to teach her. And she couldn't handle that right now.

Finally, the words came to her, just in time for her cue. She brought the mic to her lips and opened her mouth. The words were there, thank God, ready to be sung. She took a breath...

You can't just sing the song, Hudson. You have to own *it.*

...And nothing came out. She couldn't sing. It was as if she'd been running to the end of the diving board, preparing her body for a perfect swan dive, and then had just come to a dead stop.

She opened her mouth, ready to try again, ready to own that stage even though she was starting to shake and sweat and was pretty sure that she would probably never own a stage as long as she lived...

Nothing. She had no voice.

The music rolled on. She looked out into the darkness. This couldn't really be happening, could it? For a second she floated outside her body and saw herself standing there, mute and sweating. She couldn't see anyone, but they were definitely out there, watching this happen to her, watching her completely freeze up. And she already knew what they were thinking. She could practically feel it.

Her hands shook. Her whole body trembled.

Please, God, this isn't happening, she thought. *This really can't be happening.*

Finally the mic fell out of her slippery hands and hit the stage. *BOOM!* went the sound through the speakers. It shocked her awake. Somewhere inside of her, a loud voice spoke up. And this time it wasn't Holla's. It was entirely Hudson's.

Get out of here... NOW!

So she turned and ran.

12

chapter 3

Alone in the hotel bathroom, Hudson tried to catch her breath. She looked into the mirror above the sink. The perfect waves that Gino had spent an hour making with a curling iron now stuck, deflated, to her sweaty neck. Her kohl eyeliner had bled into Goth-like purple circles under her eyes. One of her gold drop earrings was mysteriously missing. And what was that smell? She sniffed under her arm. *Yuck.*

She turned on the water and splashed her face. *Did I really have to run offstage?* she asked herself, pumping some liquid soap into her hands. *Couldn't I have just walked gracefully into the wings? Or at least just hummed along?* She knew what people upstairs were thinking. And texting. And posting on Facebook right this very minute. The one thing she had never expected people to say about her:

OMG!! Holla Jones's daughter can't SING!

She blotted her face with a towel, trying not to shudder. Maybe it wasn't that bad. Maybe people didn't really care. Maybe it just looked like she'd forgotten something, or like she had to go to the bathroom. *Really* had to go to the bathroom.

She gazed at her clean, bewildered face in the mirror and shook her head. She'd totally screwed up. She'd completely and unforgettably blown it. But had it been all her fault? Holla had turned her into a wreck. For days, her mom had picked apart her voice, her body, her dancing, even her hair — *especially* her hair. And who told her kid when she went out onstage to sing for the very first time that "this has to be good"?

She heard the door to the ladies room creak open.

"Hudson?" said a hushed, familiar voice. "You in here?"

Hudson stepped away from the sink to see Carina and Lizzie stepping hesitantly into the powder room. Both girls looked almost as worried and out of breath as Hudson felt. Lizzie's hazel eyes seemed even larger than usual, or maybe it was that her red curls had been twisted up into a knot, away from her face. Her strapless, smoky blue gown showed off her pale shoulders. Both of her friends looked so pretty.

"Hey, guys," Hudson said meekly.

"Holy *shnit*," Carina said, rushing over and throwing her arms around her friend. "What happened up there? Are you sick or something?"

Hudson hugged Carina and felt the knot in her stomach slowly loosen. "I wish," she said. She stood on her tiptoes to hug Lizzie. "Sorry I'm a little sweaty."

"It's okay," Lizzie said, letting her go but holding her by the arms. "But are *you* okay?"

14

Hudson's face burned. She could barely look at Lizzie. Of the three of them, Hudson was supposed to be the performer, the professional. She stepped back and shrugged. "I just blanked out, you guys. I froze."

Lizzie and Carina traded a look, their faces strained with concern.

Hudson looked down at the moss green carpet. "I got out there and I couldn't do anything. All the stuff my mom's been saying the past few weeks — that I'm singing the wrong way, I'm dancing the wrong way, I'm holding my arms too stiff, I'm not 'selling' the song enough...I couldn't get it out of my head." She glanced up at her friends. "Was it bad? What are people saying up there?"

"Nothing," Carina said, a little too quickly.

"Alex is already spinning some songs." Lizzie brushed some red tendrils out of her face. "People've already forgotten."

"Yeah, I'm sure they have," Hudson said bitterly.

"Look, Hudson, you can't listen to your mom," Carina declared. "She'd drive anyone crazy. She'd drive *me* crazy."

"You were just nervous, that's all," Lizzie said. "I would have had a heart attack up there."

"It's my fault," Carina exclaimed, kicking off her gold shoes and stretching her toes out on the carpet. "*I* made you do this. *I* put you on the spot with Ava. I knew you didn't want to do it. It's my fault. I should be arrested by the friendship police or something."

"No, it's not your fault," Hudson said soberly. "It's my fault."

"How is this *your* fault?" Lizzie asked.

"Because I shouldn't even be trying to be a singer," Hudson said. "Why would I even try?"

"Because you're incredibly talented," Lizzie answered firmly.

"But what good is that if I can't sing on a stage?" Hudson said. *And if my mom is always going to make me do things like her?* she thought, but didn't say.

"If it makes you feel any better," Carina said, "Alex thought you were really cool."

Hudson smiled. "He's cute. My guess is he's an Aquarius. Which would be perfect for you." Hudson loved checking up on whether her friends were compatible with the guys they liked.

"So what are you gonna tell your mom?" Lizzie asked, bringing them back on topic.

"I don't know," Hudson admitted. "If anyone has any ideas, now would be a good time to share."

"You should just come back up to the party," Carina offered. "Just have fun for the rest of the night. Who cares about what happened onstage?"

"I do," Hudson said, walking over to the mirror and giving her damp curls one last shake off her shoulders. She tried to picture walking back into the ballroom upstairs, past all the people who'd just watched her run away. Maybe Carina could do that, but Hudson couldn't.

Lizzie put her arm around Hudson's shoulders. "You're gonna be okay. I promise you."

"Thanks, Lizbutt," Hudson said. "Where's Todd tonight?"

Lizzie opened her purse. "I'm gonna text him now," she said. "He wanted to stay home with his dad tonight. I guess his dad's been really depressed." Todd's dad, Jack Piedmont, had been released on bail after being arrested for allegedly stealing money from the company he ran. Even though Todd was going through the worst time of his life, he and Lizzie still seemed very much together. They'd even dropped the L bomb a couple of weeks earlier.

Carina opened the door. "You're totally welcome to join us up there," she said, wobbling a little on her heels. "If you want to put off the Holla fallout a little longer."

"Are you kidding?" Hudson said as they stepped out into the small, deserted foyer. "She'd find me in five minutes."

Just then, Hudson heard the unmistakable sound of stiletto heels hurrying across a marble floor.

"*There* you are!" yelled a voice, and Hudson whipped around.

It was her mom, running toward her with her arms outstretched and her silky, highlighted hair bouncing softly against her shoulders. "Oh, honey, come *here,*" she cried, throwing her arms around Hudson and pressing her firmly against the collection of necklaces resting against her chest.

Holla's amethyst-encrusted owl pendant dug into Hudson's cheek.

"Thank *God,*" she said, squeezing Hudson so hard she couldn't breathe. "I've been looking for you all *over* this place."

Hudson pried herself away from her mom's embrace. "I just went to the bathroom for a minute. I'm fine."

Little Jimmy, Holla's linebacker-sized bodyguard, caught up to them, huffing and puffing slightly. Behind him was Sophie, Holla's new, perennially frazzled assistant, her Bluetooth still secured to her ear. Hudson gave them both an embarrassed smile. They smiled back, before politely looking down at the gray marble floor.

"Oh, honey, look at you," Holla said tenderly, touching

Hudson's hair and then her cheek. "You're a mess." Holla pushed Hudson's hair off her shoulder. "What happened to your other earring? Did you know that you're missing an earring?"

"Yes," Hudson said.

"Do you want to tell me what happened up there?" Holla asked, her voice softening. "Can you at least tell me that?"

Hudson stared at her mom. *Do you really not know?* she wanted to say. *You drove me crazy.* "I'm not really sure," she finally said. "I think it was just stage fright." She couldn't get into the truth. Not with so many people standing around them.

Holla folded her arms and her expression changed from concerned to controlled. "Go back upstairs and tell everyone it was food poisoning," she said curtly to Sophie.

"*Food* poisoning?" Hudson asked.

"She had some bad sushi," Holla added, ignoring Hudson's question. "And we're all really sorry for the inconvenience."

"Do I say what kind of sushi?" Sophie asked, scrambling inside her purse for her pen and notepad.

"It doesn't matter," Holla said in a clipped voice. "Just go."

Sophie turned on her heel and dashed down the hall, back toward the ballroom. Hudson glanced at Lizzie and Carina. They'd seen Holla flex her amazing powers of spin before, but they seemed stunned. "Mom, are you sure?" Hudson asked.

Holla put her arm around Hudson's shoulder and hugged her again. "Don't you worry about a thing," she said firmly. "Let me take care of this."

Before Hudson could respond, she heard Chris Brompton call out, "There you guys are! We got a little turned around."

She turned to see Chris approaching from the other end of the hallway, followed by Richard Wu, the executive from her record label. In all the chaos, she'd completely forgotten about them. She would have given anything for these men not to have seen her run offstage. Now they were going to comfort her. *Ick.*

"Hudson, you okay?" Chris asked, coming to stand next to her and peering into her face with his bright blue eyes. He wore his usual Levi's and a black button-down, instead of one of his vintage concert T-shirts.

He dressed up for me, she thought.

"Is there anything I can do?" he asked.

Just having him standing next to her was making her feel dizzy. "No, I'm fine," she managed to say. "Just a little" — she glanced at her mom — "food poisoning," she said, wincing at the lie.

"Really?" Chris said, touching her back. "Do you need anything?"

His touch sent a lightning bolt down her spine. She wanted to just look up into his eyes and ask him to hug her, but she restrained herself. "I don't think so."

Richard Wu flipped open his cell phone. Hudson had never seen him without it. "I've got a doctor I can call," he said, already scrolling through his phone. "I think he's an internist."

"She's fine, Richard," Holla declared. "It was just a little bad tuna."

Richard's eyebrows shot up. "Really?" he asked, glancing at Hudson.

Hudson shrugged and nodded.

"Okay." He put his phone away, but he didn't seem convinced.

"I think I should probably get Hudson home now," Holla said. "You girls should go back to the party. Especially since you look so adorable."

"Thanks, Holla," they murmured, visibly uncomfortable.

"You sure, Holla?" Richard asked, scrutinizing Hudson as if she were a jigsaw puzzle he couldn't solve. "We're happy to help."

"I think I just need to take care of my little girl," Holla said sweetly, closing her hand around Hudson's arm. "But I'll let you know how she's doing."

"You got it," Richard said. "Feel better, Hudson."

"Thanks," she said, unable to look him in the eye. "I will."

Chris waved. "I'll e-mail you. Have a great holiday."

Hudson waved back. *I absolutely won't*, she thought.

Holla steered her in the direction of the lobby. "Tell Fernald we're coming out now," Holla told Little Jimmy, who pulled out a cell phone.

"Bye, H," Carina said. "We'll text you later."

"Someone has to get back to her lov-ah," Lizzie teased.

Carina rolled her eyes.

"Have fun, guys," Hudson said as they backed away down the hall. She wondered what they thought of her, going along with such a blatant lie. But they knew the deal: Nobody said no to Holla Jones. She just hoped that they didn't feel sorry for her.

She caught up to her mom as they trotted down a short flight of stairs to the lobby. Behind them, Little Jimmy lumbered, still huffing and puffing. In all the years they'd had a bodyguard, Hudson had never seen Holla actually follow one.

"I want you to look on the bright side," Holla said, leaning in to speak into Hudson's ear. "At least this happened here. And not somewhere important."

"But I thought this *was* somewhere important," Hudson said. "Wasn't that why you said I couldn't make one single mistake? Isn't that why you said 'this has to be good'?"

Holla fixed her almond-shaped eyes on her daughter. "Honey, what are you talking about?" she said, clearly puzzled.

Little Jimmy jogged up next to them. "Looks like we got a crowd," he said, gesturing to the lobby doors.

Outside, through the glass, they could see that a mass of people had formed on the street. Apparently word had gotten out that Holla Jones was at the Pierre. Word always got out that Holla Jones was somewhere. All it took was a call to one of the paparazzi agencies, who usually paid handsomely for the tip.

Holla pivoted on her toes to give Little Jimmy a stony look, and then he ran ahead.

"Mom? Can we talk about this?" Hudson said.

"Later," Holla said firmly. She paused for a moment just inside the doors. Hudson watched her mom form The Face — the cool, tough-as-nails, mysterious exterior that she always showed to her fans. Holla dug a pair of black sunglasses out of her bag and slipped them on to complete the look. Hudson knew their fight was already history.

Hudson let her mom go through the revolving doors first. When Holla emerged on the street, the crowd exploded.

"HOL-LA!" people screamed. "HOL-LA!"

Hudson pushed through the doors and then she was right behind her mom. Several hotel security guards rushed up to the crowd to keep them at bay.

"HOL-LA!" someone screamed. "I LOVE YOU!"

Holla gave the crowd a slight wave and they screamed even harder. Hudson darted over to the far side of the sidewalk, close to the hotel. Crowds always scared her a little. And she was still fuming. How could her mom have said this wasn't important? Hadn't three hundred people just seen the most humiliating moment of her life? How was she supposed to forget about it, when she knew that they never would?

She spotted their SUV down Sixty-first Street and broke into a run toward it, eager to escape the screams. But Holla took her time, lingering near the crowd, deliberately egging them on with her cool detachment. Holla never wanted to sign autographs or shake hands, but she also didn't like to rush past her fans. It was a little game she played with them — not wanting to leave, but not wanting to really do anything with them, either.

Suddenly a girl's voice rose out of the crowd: "I want to *BE YOU, HOLLA!*"

No you don't, Hudson thought, as she reached the car. *I tried it tonight, and it really doesn't work.*

chapter 4

The SUV snaked through the narrow, cramped streets of the West Village, going farther and farther west toward the river. Hudson leaned against the tinted window, listening to Nina Simone sing "Here Comes the Sun" on her iPod. The argument with her mom still hung in the air, but they hadn't said a word since they'd gotten into the car. Instead they sat in silence, Hudson with her iPod, Holla with her knitting needles. Knitting was Holla's new hobby. She liked to make long scarves that neither she nor Hudson would ever wear. Holla claimed the hobby relaxed her, but judging from how fast her hands were working, Holla seemed anything but relaxed.

Fernald, Holla's driver, zoomed right past the front door of their four-story redbrick Georgian-style mansion and turned the corner onto Perry Street. The mansion was more than a hundred and seventy-five years old, and supposedly Edgar Allan Poe had lived in it, once upon a time. But Hudson was pretty sure he wouldn't recognize it now. Holla had gutted the inside, leaving just the staircase, the fireplaces, and the crown moldings. She'd added a yoga studio, a fitness room, an underground parking garage, a screening room, and, on the roof, a swimming pool. *Architectural Digest* had called it "The Queen of Pop's Dream Palace." The only part of the house they didn't show in the magazine spread was the black iron fencing that surrounded it. Holla liked things to be secure, which was good, because every photographer in the world seemed to know they lived there.

As they coasted up to the garage door and waited for it to rise, several photographers leaped out of the shadows and aimed their zoom lenses at the car. They were always there, camped out across the street, ever watchful for an arrival or a departure. Hudson waved at them; she figured it was the polite thing to do. Holla didn't look up from her knitting. She only sighed as they drove past. "What do they think they're getting?" she asked. "The windows are tinted."

Fernald steered their car down the curving ramp and into the garage, right next to Holla's silver Mercedes and black Lexus. Holla owned three cars and didn't drive any of them — not because she didn't know how, but because she couldn't park and walk away. The last time Holla had tried to walk down the street, she'd been mobbed in under five minutes.

"Thanks, Fernald," Holla said when they'd parked.

"You're welcome, Miss Jones," he said.

"And how's your wife doing?" Holla asked. "Does she like the elliptical?"

"She loves it," Fernald said happily, turning around. "I think we've already lost five pounds apiece."

"Great!" Holla said, patting Fernald on the shoulder. "Keep up the good work!" Holla loved to give generous gifts to her staff, even if they did always seem to be tools for self-improvement — exercise equipment, a haircut, a free session of tooth-whitening. Fernald wasn't even overweight — he'd just had a little potbelly — but that didn't matter to Holla.

Hudson followed her mom out of the car and walked behind her on the way to the elevator. She shivered in the unheated space, pulling her unbuttoned coat closer around her bare shoulders. "Honey, just put that on," Holla said, turning around. "You're gonna catch cold."

"I'm fine," she said stiffly.

At the elevator, Mickey, one of Holla's iron-jawed security guards, held the door open for them. "Evening, Miss Jones," he said.

"Evening, Mickey," she murmured in response. Hudson and Holla squeezed up against the wall to make room for Little Jimmy, who jogged toward the elevator, panting. The doors began to close before he got there, but Holla kicked out one leg and forced the doors back with a bang. He scooted inside.

"Thanks, Miss Jones," he said as the doors rumbled shut.

"You know, Jimmy," Holla said. "You're welcome to join me in any of my exercise classes. I'll have Raquel give you a schedule."

"Thank you, Miss Jones," said Little Jimmy, and Hudson could hear the embarrassment in his voice.

Since she was twelve, Hudson had been expected to attend at least two fitness classes a week, which could be anything from yoga to power hula-hooping. Now poor Little Jimmy was going to get roped in, along with the rest of the staff. She just hoped that he wouldn't be caught eating meat or cheese in front of Holla; that would be enough to get him fired. Holla had been obsessed with being "healthy" for years. Diabetes and heart disease ran in the Jones family, so Holla had cut meat, wheat, white flour, and sugar from her diet. This left fish, vegetables, fruit, whole grains, and all kinds of tofu. Naturally, everyone around Holla — including Hudson — was expected to eat this way, too. Even though Hudson could technically eat whatever she wanted when she wasn't at home, she found that she stuck mostly to food that was Holla-approved. Eating anything sweet — even Pinkberry — actually felt a little dangerous.

The elevator opened and they stepped into Holla's spacious all-white chef's kitchen. It was lined with gleaming chrome appliances and glass cabinets, and it had two of everything — two dishwashers, two refrigerators, and two six-burner stoves. Holla's kitchen could feed at least a hundred people, not that they'd ever tried it — Holla didn't usually have parties. The kitchen also doubled as the headquarters for Holla's live-in staff. When they walked in, Holla's blond, rail-thin chef, Lorraine, was rolling out dairy-free pastry on the butcher-block table; Mariana, the curvy Brazilian housekeeper, breezed through with armfuls of fluffy white towels; and Raquel, the sweet-faced and frighteningly competent house manager, polished a stack of silver. There was more staff, of course — a publicist, several yoga and fitness instructors, a business manager, a dog walker — but Lorraine, Mariana, and Raquel were the skeleton crew. There was also Sophie, who'd somehow beaten them downtown from the Pierre and was now sitting in front of a large computer monitor in the corner, reading e-mails. Seeing Sophie, Hudson wondered if Ava had believed the food-poisoning excuse. She walked over to the marble island in the center of the room and grabbed a handful of cut-up raw vegetables. Maybe chewing would relieve some of her stress.

"So?" Raquel asked, looking up from the silver ladle she was polishing. "How did it go?" Raquel had always worn her long, thick black hair in a braid, until the previous month, when Holla had decided she needed a change. She'd sent Raquel off to a boutique salon in SoHo, where they'd given her a layered bob. It still didn't look quite right on her.

"It didn't go so great," Hudson said.

"She had stage fright," Holla said bluntly, removing her leather coat and draping it over a chair.

"Oh," Raquel said, her face crumpling. "I'm sorry."

"It's fine," Hudson said, suddenly mortified. "It wasn't so bad."

"Would you like a little tea?" Lorraine asked gently, putting the kettle on the burner.

"That's okay," Hudson murmured.

"I'll have some," Holla said, brushing a perfect curtain of hair over her shoulder. "And Sophie? What did you say to people?"

"That it was food poisoning," Sophie chirped, avoiding eye contact with Hudson. "From tuna."

"Good," Holla replied.

Hudson felt the staff's eyes on her. It was Holla's lie, but she felt like a liar, too.

"And where are we with the tour?" Holla asked.

"Wembley in London, Madison Square Garden, Slane Castle in Dublin, and Staples Center in Los Angeles all sold out," Sophie read off the computer screen. "Tokyo goes on sale tomorrow. Sydney's still a question mark."

"Hmmm," Holla said. In May, Holla would release her tenth album. This summer would be her fifth world tour. "And where are we with *Saturday Night Live*?"

"You're booked. March seventh."

"Wonderful!" Holla clasped her hands and turned to face Hudson. "Wait — I just had a thought."

"What?" Hudson asked cautiously. She didn't like the way her mom was looking at her.

"What if you did *Saturday Night Live* with me?" Holla asked. "A mother-daughter duet." She looked at Sophie and Raquel. "Don't you guys think so? It would be fun!"

"Are you... are you serious?" Hudson stammered.

"Don't worry, you'll be a pro at this by then," Holla said, accepting a mug of ginger tea from Lorraine. "Oh, Sophie, call them back, would you? Call them back and tell them that —"

"Can I talk to you upstairs?" Hudson asked.

"'Course, honey," Holla said, taking a sip of tea. "You go on ahead. I'll meet you in your room."

Hudson grabbed her coat and walked to the staircase, stomping with barely concealed rage. Forty-five minutes earlier she'd frozen onstage and fled in terror, and now her mom wanted her to repeat the whole thing on live television? Hadn't she seen what had just happened? As usual, her mom was in complete denial of reality, just because she wanted something. She'd have to be honest with her about the real reason she'd run off the stage; she would have to tell her *exactly* how much pressure she'd put on her. And this probably meant having a terrible, earth-shattering fight.

When she reached the third floor she heard the sound of tinkling metal and scuttling paws as Matilda, her brindle-colored French bulldog, ran to greet her.

"Hi there!" Hudson said, scooping the dog into her arms. "How's my little girl?"

Matilda gave Hudson's chin a good licking, and Hudson rubbed Matilda's stubby head. "Mommy totally blew it," Hudson said.

Matilda gave an uncertain snort.

"Nope, it's true," Hudson said, and then put her down. Sometimes she wished she could be Matilda and not have to worry about anything but finding a cozy place to lie down and sleep.

Hudson walked into her room, which was technically a suite. The first room was where she did homework and practiced piano, and the second was her bedroom and closet. It was lucky that she had two rooms because every square inch of both was stuffed. Hudson loved to collect clothes, furniture, albums, Barbies — anything, really. Traveling with her mom on tour over the years, Hudson had been able to find items from all over the world. In the living room were a sheepskin rug from Denmark, a mirrored vanity table from an antiques store in Paris, and a battered leather armchair from a flea market in SoHo. In her bedroom stood a full-length mirror with claw feet; a shabby-chic, whitewashed dresser; and a vintage wrought-iron daybed from London, which was in turn covered with silk cushions from India. She could spend hours at a flea market, rifling through what other people thought was junk. And even though she loved all fashion, vintage designs were her favorite. She liked to think that she was stepping back in time whenever she slipped on clothes from another era.

"Why would you want to have other people's furniture?" Holla would ask, slightly aghast, whenever Hudson lugged home a cool footstool or area rug. Hudson would just shrug and smile. That was the entire point: Other people's marks on her clothes and furniture always made them seem more real.

As Hudson padded across the sheepskin rug, she tried not to look at her most important secondhand item, standing in the corner: a baby grand Steinway piano. It had been her Grandma Helene's. It was the first piano Hudson had ever played, back when she was five. She'd climbed right up onto the bench and started picking out chords by herself as her grandmother watched, amazed. Grandma Helene could play anything by ear, and she'd tried to teach her two daughters, Holla and Jenny, from the time they were little. Neither of them had cared much for it. Hudson, though, was different. She'd gotten all of Grandma Helene's talent, and then some. Grandma Helene became her first teacher, and Hudson was a fast learner. At seven, she learned Beethoven's Moonlight Sonata. At eight, she could play Chopin's Minute Waltz. At nine, she began to write her own songs. Grandma Helene gave Hudson the piano shortly before she became too sick to play it anymore. When she passed away, Hudson had the piano brought to her home and put in her bedroom, where she covered the walls and floor with special sound-absorbing pads. She played every night before she went to sleep, imagining that her grandma was still listening.

"Lizzie writes stories, I surf, and you play piano," Carina would say, and it was true. If she didn't play for a couple of days, Hudson would feel herself start to get anxious, and she would toss and turn in bed at night, thinking about scary things. But as soon as she sat down at her piano and played, all of that would go away. Writing music calmed her down and helped her cope.

But now, as she walked into her bedroom, she ignored the beautiful Steinway. The piano was what had gotten her into this mess in the first place. She wouldn't even look at it, let alone play it.

Hudson unbuckled the straps of her heels and pulled off her dress, then changed into a pair of flannel pajamas. Even with her mom's expensive renovations, the heating system in the old house could be a little funky.

"Honey?" Holla called out from the other room. "I brought you some tea." She walked into Hudson's bedroom and placed the mug on a side table.

"I didn't really have food poisoning," Hudson said.

"I know," Holla said, playing with the chains of her necklaces. "But you've had a rough night." Holla leaned down and straightened some picture frames on Hudson's bedside table.

"And asking me to be on *Saturday Night Live* is gonna make me feel better?" Hudson asked, flopping down on the bed and grabbing one of her silk-covered pillows.

Holla looked at her. "If you're going to make this your career, honey, you have to learn to let things go."

"Right. Like when your whole class watches you blank out,"

Hudson said. "Those were people I *know*. People I go to school with. It wasn't some random audience. And they're not gonna let it go."

"You can't care what people think," Holla said more forcefully. "That's what being an artist means. Do you think *I* ever cared about what people thought?"

"So the solution is for me to do live television," Hudson said.

"You just got afraid up there," Holla declared. "By the time you do the show, that'll be over with."

"What if it's not?" Hudson asked.

"Why do you always have to look on the dark side of everything?"

"And why do you always have to freak me *out* about everything?" Hudson asked.

"What? How did I freak you out?"

"By picking me apart. By telling me I'm doing everything wrong, all the time."

"I was giving you advice," Holla said flatly. "Can't I do that?"

"But ever since I started this album, it's like I can't do anything right. You want me to do things exactly like you."

Holla furrowed her brow, the way she did whenever Hudson said something she thought was ludicrous.

"You changed everything on my album," Hudson went on. "You changed every song."

"Because I wanted your album to sell," Holla replied.

"But those were my songs!"

"So you *don't* want to be a success?" Holla said, letting her voice get loud. "You *don't* want to sell out stadiums and be on the radio and have little girls scream your name when you walk down the street?"

Hudson squeezed the pillow. *Here we go,* she thought. *The unanswerable questions.* "I just don't want to be told over and over that I'm doing something wrong."

"Is that what you think?" Holla folded her arms. "Honey, you are gonna have to get a thicker skin. That's all this business is, you know. Being criticized. For everyone who loves you out there, there's someone who thinks you're awful. But that's not what I was doing. I'm just trying to help you. Who believes in you more than I do? Who's been your biggest champion your whole life? Who got you the best piano teacher in the city? Who put you in dance classes when you were five because you wanted them?"

Hudson picked at a loose thread on her bedspread, waiting for her mom to finish.

"I wish someone had believed in *me* enough to cheer me on," Holla went on. "I had to beg my mother to give me dance lessons. I had to beg her to take me to talent contests in Chicago. I had to do everything myself. My mom didn't care. That's why your aunt Jenny still doesn't know what she's doing with her life. Running around the world, pretending she's some kind of fashion designer —"

"*Jewelry* designer," Hudson corrected.

"Jewelry designer, whatever." Holla snorted. "She could have been dancing *Swan Lake* at Lincoln Center, and now she's flailing around, going nowhere. God knows I tried, but there was only so much I could do, after all." She shook her head, as if the memory of her younger sister was too much. "So listening to you complain

33

about my interest in your career...It just sounds a little ungrateful. And tonight wasn't my fault. You can't pin that on me. I'm sorry you got scared, but that wasn't my fault."

Hudson knew her mom was right. She was trying to blame Holla, when the real problem was that Hudson just didn't have what it took. She'd *thought* she did. She'd thought she could be a musician. But she'd been wrong. How had she ever thought she'd be able to do this? When she could barely talk in class?

"I don't think I can do this," she said. "I want to get out of it."

"*You're* the one who wanted to do this," Holla said. "You're the one who told me you were ready."

"I know," Hudson said quietly. "I've changed my mind." Just saying it was such a relief.

"Honey," Holla said, moving closer to Hudson and taking her hand. "You're just upset. Don't say things you don't mean."

"I do mean it," Hudson said, looking her mom straight in the eye. "I've never meant anything more. I don't want this," Hudson said. "I'm not like you. We both know that."

Holla's face grew serious. She stood up from the bed. "You're making a big mistake. One that you will regret the rest of your life."

"I'm fourteen," Hudson said. "I'll have another chance."

"Not like this," Holla said. "I'm not always going to be able to help you this way. You're throwing away a huge opportunity here, an opportunity other girls would kill for."

But I'm not like other girls, Hudson wanted to say.

"And what are we going to tell your label?" Holla asked, her voice rising again. "That you just want to scrap it all? After we made all those changes?"

34

"Tell them I'm so sorry. Tell them I have stage fright. I don't know. Tell them anything."

Holla tapped her foot on the wood floor. "It's a good thing you're my daughter. Otherwise they would sue you for breach of contract."

"I know I'm your daughter." Hudson sighed. "Believe me."

Holla stared at her for a few more seconds. "I never thought that you'd be the type to give up."

For a second Hudson felt a twinge of sadness, mixed with fear—a feeling of regret before it had actually become regret. "Well, I guess that's who I am," she said, and lay down on her bed, facing the wall.

For a moment there was silence, and then she heard Holla walk out of the room. Hudson listened as the door shut, her eyes still on the wall. It was over.

Hudson lay there, unable and unwilling to move. Outside a car alarm wailed. She shut her eyes and wondered if she could just stay in this position for the rest of her life. *So that's it,* she thought. The album. Her music. Her dream. Everything. It was all finished. She knew that she'd done the right thing, but it didn't feel right. She felt even worse now than she had in the bathroom at the Pierre. But she hadn't had a choice, really, when she thought about it. Tonight had shown her that.

After a few minutes, Hudson got up and walked into the next room. Matilda stared at her from her dog bed, tilting her blocky head as if to say, *That didn't go so well, huh?*

Hudson grabbed her laptop. In times of crisis, she always needed to do two things: text Carina and/or Lizzie, and check the next day's horoscope. First she logged on to signsnscopes.com and checked Pisces for the next day, December 21.

Congratulations! With Uranus, the planet of surprise, moving into your tenth house of career, expect a major work development that will have you smiling!

Hudson closed her laptop. She hated it when she did something to contradict her horoscope. But maybe astrology was just a bunch of nonsense, anyway. According to her chart — the one Aunt Jenny had given her for her last birthday — she was supposed to be incredibly successful. Famous, even. "Almost as famous as your mom," Jenny had whispered, with a wink.

Hudson went back to her desk and got out the chart. It was covered in one of those sheets of plastic used for term papers. The chart was a large circle, sliced into wedges and covered in weird hieroglyphics and waves and cut through with straight lines radiating in all directions. She didn't know enough to actually read charts yet, but she remembered the spot on the circle where her career was. It was a mess of squiggly lines and shapes.

"Whatever," she thought, and put it back in the drawer, shoving it in far enough that she wouldn't be able to look at it again without doing some serious spring cleaning.

Just then her phone, which was still in her purse, on the floor, chimed with a text. She reached down and pulled it out.

It was from Lizzie.

Why'd u leave me w/this??:)

36

Just below the text was a photo of Carina and Alex with their arms around each other at the Ball, smiling and looking goofily into each other's eyes.

Hudson wrote back:

Because I have food poisoning, remember??

Hope you've been throwing up for hours ☺ Lizzie wrote.

U know it.

At least she still had her friends, she thought later, as she climbed into bed. And no matter what happened, that would never change.

chapter 5

Hudson jumped back into yet another *chataranga*, and her elbows buckled as she lowered herself, push-up style, an inch from the floor.

"Now curl your toes into upward dog, and take a deep healing breath," said Niva, Holla's yoga instructor, who paced calmly in front of them. "Reach your heart to the front of the room."

Hudson moved easily into upward dog, balancing her weight on her hands, but reaching her heart anywhere was a tall order. It was Christmas morning, and it was snowing, and she wanted to be lying in bed, smelling Lorraine's vegan chocolate bread pudding as it baked in the oven. Or walking Matilda down the snow-dusted West Village streets. Or exchanging gifts with Lizzie and Carina. (They'd tried once to do "Secret Santa" but the "secret" part had lasted only a few minutes.) Instead she was on a mat, sweating, just inches from her mom, who, several days after their fight in Hudson's bedroom, still seemed to be angry.

"Now curl your toes for downward dog," Niva droned in her ethereal yoga voice.

Hudson grunted a little as she moved back into the pose. Christmas was always a little tricky in Holla's house. It was the one day of the year when all the people who usually swirled around them — Holla's publicist, record executive, and manager, to name a few — went home to pay attention to their own lives and families, and the house was unusually quiet. Sometimes Holla could get her yoga teacher or makeup artist to come over for Christmas dinner, but today it would be only Jenny, Holla's sister. And Hudson knew that this was the real reason she felt a little antsy.

"Feel your limbs get heavy," Niva said as they lay in resting pose at the end of the class. "Feel your arms sink into the floor."

Hudson fluttered her eyes closed. She thought of Lizzie and Carina, who'd been so sweet about her disastrous night at the ball. The next day the two of them had taken her out to Pinkberry for a quick pep talk and reality check. "Nobody even talked about it the whole night, I swear," Carina had said around a mouthful of Cap'n Crunch–topped yogurt.

"Uh, that's because you were on Planet Alex all night," Lizzie had teased, nudging Carina with her elbow.

Now Lizzie was at her grandparents' house down in northern Florida, and Carina was with her dad in Aspen. The city felt empty without them, even though they'd been texting one another the entire week.

"Breathe in through your nose," Niva droned on, her voice getting more and more unworldly. "Let go of all earthly worries…"

Sounds good, Hudson thought, drifting close to sleep, just as the door to the yoga studio opened with a loud *whoosh*. Heavy footsteps shook the bamboo floor.

"Merry Christmas!" said a high-pitched voice.

Hudson opened her eyes and craned her head. Aunt Jenny was standing in the middle of the room, clutching some red shopping bags and looking amazing, as usual. She wore a belted coat of what looked like lavender-dyed rabbit fur, a thick cashmere scarf in deep purple, and earrings that were actually safety pins dripping gold chains. Her cropped hair showed off her beautiful oval face, which was, as always, free of makeup. Her boots were part grandma, part sexy, with pointy toes and stiletto heels, and her nail color matched the inky black of her vinyl bag. Jenny had been the one to take Hudson to her first flea market, and she'd given Hudson her first handbag: a crimson alligator Ferragamo clutch from the sixties. Hudson still had it, but she never left the house with it; she was too scared of losing it. "Oh," said Jenny, letting her shopping bags drop to the floor. "I thought you guys would be done by now. Sorry!"

She was famous for being either too late or too early, and today her arrival had fallen on the way-too-early end of the spectrum. They hadn't expected her until lunch.

"That's okay," Holla said. She slowly sat up. "We're just finishing."

Hudson sat up. "Hi, Jenny!"

"Hey, Hudcap! You look great! Awesome headband."

"Thanks!" Hudson beamed as she got to her feet. She loved her stretchy headband, which was covered with stones that looked like diamonds.

"Sweetie, the *floors*," Holla said.

Hudson looked down, but then she realized that Holla was talking to Jenny. Jenny's spiky heels had made scuff marks on the floor.

"Oh, whoops, sorry about that," Jenny said, examining the heels of her boots with an embarrassed smile.

"Just take them off," Holla said, smiling tightly. "Please. We don't allow shoes in here."

Jenny unzipped her boots and slipped them off. "Sorry, again," she said.

"No problem," Holla said warmly once the boots were off. She walked over to Jenny and the two sisters shared a tepid hug. "How are you?" Holla asked.

"Jet-lagged," Jenny said. "Ever since I got home I've been getting up at the crack of dawn."

"You've gotten taller," Jenny said to Hudson. "When was the last time I saw you?"

"I think just before you moved," Hudson said. She grabbed Jenny's hand. "How's Paris?"

"Incroyable," Jenny said with a smile.

"I want to come visit!" Hudson exclaimed. "Maybe for spring break?"

Jenny's smile faded, but only a little. "Sure."

"Are you hungry?" Holla asked.

"Actually, breakfast would be great," Jenny admitted.

"I'll take you," Hudson answered. She led her aunt upstairs to the kitchen while Holla left them to shower and change.

Hudson made herself a bowl of steel-cut oats while Jenny devoured one of Lorraine's gluten-free muffins.

"So my jewelry studio in Paris was awesome," Jenny said as she pulled off another hunk of muffin. "I shared it with three French girls. They were really mean at first, but then I figured out how to talk to them. French girls definitely make you work for it, but then they open up and they're really cool. I'll miss them."

"So…how's that guy?" Hudson asked, trying not to sound too nosy.

"What guy?" Jenny asked, wiping off her fingers with a napkin.

"The guy you moved there for," Hudson said. "The one you said was The One."

"Oh," Jenny said, grimacing slightly. "Jean-Paul." She shrugged. "It didn't really work out. He was a Capricorn. Totally wrong for me." She waved her hand. "Next time I really need a Sagittarius. Or a Libra. Plus, Paris was different than I thought it would be. I don't know. It was a little cold. I missed New York."

Hudson nodded uncertainly. "So you're not staying there?"

"No," Jenny said, shaking her head. "It's better if I leave."

Hudson ate another spoonful of oats and tried not to worry. One thing was for sure: Her mom wasn't going to like hearing any of this. Jenny had lived in more places for less time than anyone else Hudson had ever heard of. And each time she moved, Holla got more frustrated.

"So you've moved back here then?" Hudson asked.

"Well, sort of," Jenny said. "I still have to go back to Paris and get my stuff. But let's not talk about it, okay? I want to hear all about what's going on with *you*. How are Carina and Lizzie? Are they coming over?"

"No, but they're fine," she said. "They both have boy-friends now."

"Really?" Jenny's eyes lit up. "So now we have to get *you* one."

Hudson shrugged. "You know me. I'm not really into high school guys."

"Smart. Always go for the older ones," Jenny said. "They're the ones who know how to treat you. Then again, Jean-Paul was fifty, and that didn't mean anything." She put down what was left of her muffin. "So how are things with your mom?" she asked in a more serious voice.

Hudson hesitated. She'd learned not to tell Jenny too much about stuff with her mom. "Things are fine," she fibbed, scraping the side of her bowl with her spoon.

"Does she let you do anything?" Jenny asked. "I can tell she doesn't let you *eat* anything," she said, looking at the oatmeal. "But does she let you go anywhere? Or do you still have to be driven around in that car?"

"She's strict," Hudson said simply, hoping to get off the topic.

"And how's your album coming along?"

Hudson stood up quickly. "You know, I think I should proba-bly get in the shower," she said. "I don't like to sit around in wet workout clothes. It's gross."

Jenny stared at Hudson. "I didn't mean to pry, Hudcap. I'm just interested in you."

"I know, but really, everything's fine," she said. "I'll be right back."

In the shower, Hudson lathered her hair, feeling guilty about her rude departure. But there was something about Jenny that made her nervous. Talking to her felt like walking a tightrope — if Hudson told her too much, or said the wrong thing, she would fall, and she didn't know where she might land.

After showering, she dressed in a long-sleeved silver tunic that always made her think of tinsel, pulled on her electric purple skinny jeans, and thrust her feet into some high UGGs. When she walked downstairs, she found that Holla and Jenny had moved into the serene, all-white living room and were curled up on the low, long sofa. A gigantic painting consisting solely of a splash of pink and purple hung on one wall. Candles flickered on the white piano in the corner, and a fire crackled in the fireplace. Holla tried hard to make this house cozy, but it was always a little too big, a little too cold, and a little too white for Hudson to really get comfortable.

"Hey! You're just in time for the trunk show!" Jenny joked. "Sit down and pick something out." Several different racks of earrings and bracelets were set up on the glass coffee table next to an open, velvet-lined display case. The shopping bags Jenny had carried into the yoga studio sat at her feet.

Hudson plopped down next to her aunt. "Those are cool," she said, pointing to a pair of silver earrings in the shape of serpents, with garnets for eyes.

"Try them on," Jenny said, taking them off the rack and handing them to Hudson.

Hudson slid them into her ears. Jenny hadn't been designing jewelry for very long, but she already knew what she was doing.

Hudson grabbed the hand mirror on the table and looked at herself. "Wow," she said, turning her head this way and that, watching the red stones catch the light.

"They're all yours," Jenny said.

"I hope the *InStyle* mention helped," Holla said, leaning back against a pile of throw pillows. She looked relaxed and comfortable sipping from a steaming mug of chai tea, an oversized white blanket over her legs, but Hudson could detect a slight edge in her voice.

"Yeah, it was great, thanks," Jenny said, running a hand through her hair. "Of course, I wasn't really ready to fill orders yet, but it always helps to get your name out there. So, Hudson," she said, turning back to her niece, "do you want those, or do you want to try a few others on?"

"I'll definitely take these," Hudson said, putting down the mirror. "Thanks."

"So... are you moving back here?" Holla asked, taking another sip of tea.

Jenny turned back to her sister. "Yes. Probably right after the holidays. But I spent the time in Paris well, and I made a ton more pieces, and there are a few stores in SoHo now that I think would be just perfect for my stuff. So I'm really excited."

Holla nodded slowly. "And the guy... just didn't work out?"

"No," Jenny replied. "Not so much."

"Well, in that case," Holla said delicately, "I want to propose something."

"What?" Jenny asked, not moving.

"You remember Kierce, my stylist?" Holla asked.

"Uh-huh," Jenny said carefully.

"Well, you know I've always loved your style, and obviously Hudson does, too." Holla chuckled. "And I've been thinking that before I start prepping for the tour next summer, I really ought to try someone new."

Jenny stared at Holla. "You want me to *work* for you?" she asked, baffled.

"Just until you get back on your feet," Holla said.

Jenny just stared at her.

"I think it would be fun," Holla went on. "And honestly, what other prospects do you have right now? What other incredible offers? You've been designing this jewelry for two years, and it's not *exactly* taking the world by storm —"

Jenny's shoulders sagged just the slightest bit at this.

"And I just see you going in circles, honey. I know how talented you are, and instead you're just running around from one city to another —"

"Just stop, okay?" Jenny interrupted suddenly. "Please? Stop."

"What?" Holla asked, sounding genuinely confused.

"That's possibly the worst idea ever," Jenny said. "God, Holla. Sometimes I don't know what planet you're living on."

"What planet *I'm* on?" Holla asked. "While you're running off to Paris to live with some guy you just met? Pretending you're a jewelry designer? Or is it a photographer? Or a handbag designer? I've lost track."

Jenny started pulling the earrings off the racks and placing

46

them in the velvet-lined box. "Right," she muttered. "I forgot. You have all the answers."

"I don't," Holla said. "I just want you to be happy."

"I *am* happy," Jenny shot back. "I like my life. It's exciting, okay? I *like* the way it is."

"Mm-hmm," Holla said. "What's not to like? You get to traipse around Buenos Aires and come home and have me pay your credit card bill."

"That happened *once*," Jenny said, shooting to her feet. She started to gather her things.

"Where are you going?" Holla asked.

"Out of here," Jenny said, grabbing the shopping bags.

"Don't," Holla said. "It's Christmas. Let's just forget it and start over."

"Too late," Jenny said bitterly. She glanced around the room. "Where'd they put my coat?"

Holla pointed to the kitchen. "Back there," she said with an air of defeat.

Jenny leaned down and gave Hudson a hug. "Merry Christmas, Hudcap."

Hudson hugged her aunt back. "Thanks for the earrings," she whispered helplessly.

"Oh, and here," Jenny said, pointing to one of the shopping bags. "These are for you guys." She crouched down and pulled out several presents wrapped in shiny bronze wrapping paper and tied with red velvet bows. She stacked them carefully on the coffee table. "Just a few things from Paris."

Holla eyed the gifts but didn't move to take them. Hudson knew what they were: deliberately out-of-focus photos Jenny had taken and had carefully framed. For Christmas, she always gave them photographs of whatever city she'd just been living in.

"Have them take you down the back way; the front door's locked," Holla said.

"Of course it is," Jenny said, walking toward the kitchen.

They listened to Jenny ask Raquel for her coat and then leave through the service door. Holla stared gloomily into the crackling fire. Several long minutes seemed to pass. Holla's hands tapped out a silent rhythm on the top of the couch while Hudson sat next to her mom in silence. She didn't know what to do. She never did at times like this. "Mom?" she finally said.

Holla swung her feet to the floor and stood up, brushing at her leggings with her hands. "Honey, are you letting that dog jump up onto this couch? I've got hair all over me."

Holla's moment of reflection was clearly over.

"She doesn't even come into this room," Hudson said.

"Well, make sure she doesn't," Holla said. "I'm gonna check on lunch." She padded off in the direction of the kitchen, leaving Hudson alone.

Hudson hugged her knees to her chest and stared into the fire. This kind of fight had happened before, but for some reason she'd felt that Christmas would defuse the normal tension. She was sad for her mom. She knew how much Holla loved Jenny and wanted her life to work out. It wasn't fair for Jenny to always shoot her down. But she could also see how being Holla's stylist wasn't exactly a dream job.

48

And maybe it was better that Aunt Jenny had left. Having her around only made things more confusing. And today, it had made Hudson feel scared. Jenny had turned her back on her dancing talent and had become, according to Holla, a world-class screwup. And right now, as she sat by herself in front of the cold fire, Hudson felt like she was headed for exactly the same fate.

chapter 6

"Is it just me, or did this hallway get longer over break?" Hudson whispered, doing her best not to make eye contact with the cluster of girls standing by the bathroom door. She knew they were staring at her. And whispering. And it was making the walk to the stairwell a little torturous, even though she was sandwiched between her two best friends.

"Don't worry," Lizzie said. "We'll ignore them."

"No we won't," Carina whispered, and then looked over at the girls. "Um, is there a problem?" she demanded, sending the girls scurrying into the bathroom.

"You're making it worse, C." Hudson groaned.

"Well, we have to do something," Carina said. "They can't just think that's *okay*."

Hudson shifted her book bag up her shoulder and headed into the stairwell. The first day back at school had been worse than she'd thought. After Christmas Hudson spent the rest of break holed up in her room reading a stack of fashion magazines and books she'd picked out in the New Age/Self-Help section, with titles like *Falling Down, Getting Up* and *When Bad Things Happen.* She convinced herself that no one would remember the Silver Snowflake Ball by the time they went back to school. The night before school started, she'd even checked her horoscope just to be prepared. She'd read:

> *Tuesday, January 6—Pisces*
> *With Pluto sitting firmly in your seventh house, get ready to be the center of attention! You'll be on everyone's lips— like it or not!*

"Oh, God," she muttered and clicked off before she finished reading. That wasn't good. But still. What were the chances that almost three weeks later, people would still care?

She got her answer as soon as she stepped onto the floor of the Upper School. Ken Clayman and Eli Blackman were leaning against the wall under the bulletin board. Their faces lit up when they spotted her. "Hey, Hudson!" Ken called out. "Did you have any sushi for breakfast?"

Hudson darted down the hall toward her locker, her ears on fire. On her way she passed Sophie Duncan and Jill Rau, who grabbed each other, burst into giggles, and kept walking.

They remember, Hudson thought. *And nobody, nobody, believes it was food poisoning.*

Even seeing her friends for the first time in weeks was no relief.

"You guys, everyone remembers," she whispered to them in

homeroom, just as Ava Elting walked in and sent a searing look at her from across the room.

"No they don't," Carina said. Then she noticed Ava's glare. "Oh, yeah," she said. "They totally do."

"Carina," Lizzie complained.

Todd just gave Hudson a sympathetic smile.

As Madame Dupuis called roll, Hudson focused on a heart she was drawing, over and over, on a page of loose-leaf paper. When her name was called, more whispers and giggles rose from the back of the room.

"Here," Hudson said meekly.

At school she'd always been an object of vague curiosity, a kid other people noticed when she rose her hand in class, or when she wore her feathered headdress to the school dance. She was used to a certain amount of attention because of her mom, and because of her clothes. But that had been positive attention. This was different. Now she felt like a freak.

When it was time for their first free period of the day, Hudson couldn't get down to the library fast enough. "The worst part is, I can't even tell people the truth," Hudson said, still between Lizzie and Carina as they walked down the stairs to the library. "Now everyone thinks I can't sing, and that I made up some excuse to cover it."

"But food poisoning's, like, totally believable," Carina said.

"The point is I should have just told everyone I had stage fright."

"Somehow I don't think that would have gone over any better," Lizzie said.

"And I couldn't have gotten stronger hate vibes from Ava Elting," Hudson said. "She must totally want to kill me."

They walked into the library and Hudson stopped in her tracks. Just inside the doors was an empty table, covered with bags. And in the middle of the table, holding court like its owner, was a familiar black and red Hervé Chapelier bag. Ava's bag.

"Are you sure Ava didn't say anything to you?" Hudson asked Carina. "Like, that I ruined her party or something?"

"Not a thing," Carina said.

Knowing Ava's sometimes-shaky hold on the truth — she'd actually said Todd had cheated on her in order to save face when he dumped her — Hudson was pretty sure that Ava was talking about her behind her back. Especially after that furious look Ava shot her in homeroom. "You guys, let's sit back there," Hudson said. She pointed to an empty table in the corner farthest from Ava's table. It was the least she could do.

"Is Todd coming?" Hudson asked.

"He's coming a little bit later," Lizzie said. Hudson wondered for a moment if everything was okay between them. "So you're still scrapping the album?"

"Yup," Hudson said determinedly. "The record label peeps weren't too happy, but I guess my mom convinced them."

"That's too bad," Lizzie said.

"What do you mean?" Hudson asked.

"Just that you're not going to finish it," Lizzie said, opening her History book.

"Well, you guys saw what my mom did to it. How she totally took it over. It wasn't even mine anymore. Scrapping it was the right thing to do." Hudson took out her Geometry book. "I think I need to forget about music."

"Forget about music?" Lizzie said. "Are you serious?"

"It's the one thing you really love," Carina protested.

"I love other things," Hudson said. "Like fashion. Like astrology." She knew she didn't sound convincing. "Whatever, I'm taking a break. Believe me, it's the best thing for my sanity."

"Speaking of sanity," Carina whispered, tilting her head, "your biggest fan looks just as unhinged as ever."

Hudson looked over. Across the room, hunched over what looked like the *New York Times* crossword puzzle, marking her answers with a fountain pen, was Hillary Crumple. To Lizzie and Carina, Hillary Crumple was pretty much a stalker, blatantly obsessed with Hudson and her mom. They even thought that Hillary had given one of the tabloids Hudson's cell number. But Hudson doubted it. For one, Hillary just didn't look clued-in enough to do that kind of thing. She just seemed a little . . . different. She wore her brown hair tied back in a ponytail, but most of it hung loose and floated, staticky, around her head, despite a few plastic barrettes. She wore acid orange roll-neck sweater had blue waves sewn on the front, and a sequined dolphin jumped through them. Her Chadwick kilt hung to her shins, well past the appointed "cool" length of above the knees. As Hillary filled in another box, unaware of being watched, she made a tiny victory pump with her free hand.

"Wow," Hudson said, genuinely impressed. "She's not even doing that in pencil."

"I don't know," Carina said, eyeing her. "I still think she's the one who gave that tabloid your number."

They watched as Hillary put down her pen, stood up, and walked out of the library.

"Do you think she heard us?" Carina asked.

Lizzie shook her head. "What did they want?" Lizzie asked Hudson. "The tabloids? You never told us."

"Oh, some rumor about my mom dating John Mayer or something." Hudson shrugged. "The usual."

Just then Ava breezed into the library. Her devil-horned knit cap and silver coat were both dusted with snow, and as she sipped from her Starbucks cup, she locked eyes with Hudson and approached the table.

Oh, great, Hudson thought, looking down.

"What?" Lizzie whispered.

"Ava," Hudson said. "Incoming."

"Hi, Hudson," Ava said, coming to stand right next to Hudson's chair.

"Hey, Ava," Hudson said, barely able to look her in the eye.

"Hey, Ava," Carina said.

"Hey, Ava," Lizzie murmured.

"So how was your break, you guys?" Ava asked, popping the lid off her cappuccino. "Did you go away anywhere cool?" Hudson could already smell Ava's Daisy perfume.

"Vail," Carina said.

"Florida," said Lizzie.

"I was here," Hudson said.

"I was back down in Mustique," Ava said, sighing grandly. "It is just sooo beautiful there."

Good to know, Hudson thought. *Now please leave.*

"So, what happened at the Ball?" Ava said, turning to Hudson. "I thought for sure I'd hear from you after...I mean, given your dramatic exit."

Hudson played with the loose spine of her textbook as she felt a blush heat her face. "I wasn't feeling that well," she said, because she couldn't think of anything else.

"Oh, riiiigghht," Ava said, drawing out the word. "I forgot. What was it, again? Some bad tuna?"

Hudson glanced at Carina.

"Have *you* ever had bad tuna?" Carina asked Ava.

"No, but I'm sure it's awful," Ava said, narrowing her big brown eyes. "Almost as awful as not being able to sing."

"I have to go to the bathroom," Hudson said, getting up.

"More food poisoning?" Ava asked with mock sympathy.

Hudson walked past her, toward the door, and out into the hall. *I hate Ava Elting*, she thought, speeding to the bathroom. *I know it's not right to hate people, but she is truly the most evil person on earth.*

Inside the bathroom, she locked herself in a stall and looked at her watch. Ten twenty-five. This was going to be the longest day of her life. She just needed to visualize getting through this, like she'd read over break in one of her New Age books. If you visualized what you wanted, the book said, most of the time you could make it happen. She closed her eyes and pictured herself walking proudly through the school halls, her head held high, immune to the stares and whispers...and then breaking into song when people least expected it...

And then the girls' room door opened.

"I mean, it's one thing to not be able to sing," a girl said in a familiar lockjaw drawl. "But to tell everyone you have food poisoning? I'm just so embarrassed for her."

It was Ilona Peterson, Ava Elting's head henchwoman and easily the meanest girl in the freshman class.

"Oh my God, totally," said Cici Marcus, in her harsh, brittle voice. "Did she really think that people would buy that? *Please.*"

"I think it's kind of awesome," Kate Pinsky chimed in. "I mean, she's had this giant ego ever since fourth grade, and now everyone can see that she's just a big fake."

Hudson felt her stomach shrink into a cold iron fist. Ava had sent the Icks in to talk about her on purpose. And now she couldn't do anything but stand there and listen to it.

A toilet flushed a few stalls away, drowning them out. Someone else was in the bathroom listening to this, too, Hudson realized. This was actually getting worse.

"I mean, talk about negative attention," Ilona went on, not caring about the unknown person in the still-closed stall. "But I guess if you're the daughter of Holla Jones, that's all you know anyway."

"Her music is just soooo cheesy," Cici put in.

The stall door opened with a sharp *thwack.* "Could you guys be *any* more jealous or pathetic?" said a small, squeaky voice. "I mean, listen to yourselves. I almost fell off the seat."

Hudson craned her head to peek through the door crack, but the speaker was out of her line of sight.

"Um, nobody's talking to you," Ilona said icily. "And nobody asked you to eavesdrop, either."

"Yeah," Cici said.

"Well, *I'm* talking to *you*," said the voice, "and if you're gonna gossip about someone you don't even know, *don't* do it about someone who's got more talent and style than the three of you will ever have in your entire *lives*."

Hudson's mouth fell open. *Nobody* talked like this to the Icks. Who was this person?

"And just for your information," added the stranger, "she doesn't have an ego."

"How do you know?" Ilona said thickly. "Hudson Jones would never even *talk* to you."

"Yeah," Cici repeated numbly.

"As if we care what you think," Kate said. "And nice sweater."

Hudson heard them walk to the door.

"I hope *you* guys get food poisoning!" the stranger yelled as they walked out.

Hudson unlatched the stall door with trembling fingers. Whoever this girl was, she couldn't wait to thank her. And promise her eternal friendship, and possibly her firstborn child.

She threw open the door and there, standing on her tippytoes at the sinks, applying sparkly pink lip gloss, was Hillary Crumple.

"Hillary?"

Hillary turned around. "Oh, hi," she said, as if she'd known Hudson had been in the bathroom all along. "How was your break?"

"Uh…my break was fine," Hudson stammered, eyeing the exit.

"Mine, too," Hillary said casually. She turned back to the mirror and spread more lip gloss on her lips. "We just stayed here. It was kind of boring. What did you do? Did you guys go away? I really like your sweater. Where'd you get it?"

"Uh, I don't remember," Hudson said, trying to follow Hillary's line of questioning. "Yours is nice, too."

"Yeah?" Hillary turned back to Hudson and looked down at her sweater proudly. "Thanks. I got it for Christmas. My mom's life coach says that orange is supposed to make you more productive. And blue's supposed to be calming. What's your favorite color?"

Hudson glanced at the door again. "Um...silver?"

"Silver," Hillary mused, capping the lip gloss. "I'm going to have to check with the coach about that one."

"So, Hillary, thanks for what you said," Hudson said. "But you don't have to defend me or anything. It's okay. It's not your job."

"I know," Hillary said, slipping the lip gloss into a side pocket of the boxy pink and blue backpack at her feet. "But you're my friend. And friends stick up for each other."

We're friends? "Right," Hudson said uncertainly.

"And it's not like I'm lying to them or anything," Hillary said, taking a plastic barrette out of her backpack. "*US Weekly* said that you have an amazing voice. Didn't they interview your producer or something?"

"I'm not really sure," Hudson said, running her hands through her wavy black hair. "But thanks again, Hillary. And if you need anything, ever, just let me know."

"Then let's go shopping," Hillary said, turning to the mirror and securing some of her floating hair with the barrette. "Weren't we supposed to do that together? A couple months ago?" Hillary snapped the barrette shut and turned around again. "Do you remember we talked about it?"

"Yeah," Hudson said, feeling caught. She did remember Hillary asking her to go shopping at the Chadwick dance back in the fall. "When's good for you?"

"What about Saturday?" Hillary asked. "I could meet you downtown. Like, in NoLIta somewhere. What's your favorite store?"

Hudson tried to imagine hanging out with Hillary in the chic neighborhood of NoLIta and her mind went blank. "There's Resurrection," Hudson said. "But it's a little expensive —"

"Cool," Hillary said. "Let's meet at noon. That way we can get lunch, too."

"Lunch," Hudson said, trying not to sound surprised. "Great."

"Great," Hillary echoed, hoisting her book bag onto her shoulders. "See you then." A moment later she was out the door, the folded-up *New York Times* sticking out of her book bag.

Hudson washed her hands at the sink, trying to process what had just happened. Lizzie and Carina were probably going to freak out — they were convinced Hillary was dangerous. But Hillary had just chewed out the Icks for her. Who else at Chadwick would have done that? Not even Lizzie or Carina would have been that gutsy. A two-hour shopping date was a small price to pay for that kind of loyalty. Even if Hillary's loyalty felt a little unearned.

She wet the corner of a paper towel and pressed it to her closed eyelids. *Please, God*, she thought. *Don't let me be known as the Girl With the Huge Ego and No Talent*. If only she hadn't run off the stage. If only she hadn't let her mom make up such a goofy excuse.

She wished she could blame her mom, or Carina, or even Ava Elting, but she couldn't. She had no one to blame but herself, and frankly, it sucked.

I hereby promise myself, Hudson Jones, that I will never, ever get up onstage again, she thought as she pulled the girls' room door open. *Ever ever ever.*

chapter 7

"Right up here's fine, Fernald," Hudson directed as the SUV swung over to the curb on Houston Street. Resurrection, the vintage boutique she and Hillary had chosen for their shopping date, was around the corner on Mott Street. But Hudson always preferred getting out of the car at least a block from wherever she was expected to be. It was embarrassing for people to see the SUV dropping her off.

"Just call me when you're ready," Fernald called over his shoulder.

"'Kay," she said brightly, slamming the door behind her. She could have walked over to NoLIta, or at least taken the subway down Seventh Avenue and then the bus along Houston, but Holla didn't like Hudson taking public transportation when she was by herself.

"Do you think I'm going to be kidnapped or something?" she'd asked Holla at the breakfast table, after yet another Saturday-morning power-yoga class. "I don't need Fernald to take me to Mott Street."

"You should see some of the mail I get," Holla had said, sipping her glass of kale juice. She was on one of her monthly juice fasts; she did them religiously to get rid of toxins. "So, I want you home at four o'clock. And two hours of homework this afternoon. Right?"

"Mom," Hudson protested, digging in to her oatmeal.

"Do you want to cram it all in tomorrow night?" Holla asked, squeezing a lemon slice into her drink. "You have to start learning time management, honey. It's absolutely the key to a successful life."

"Fine," Hudson said.

"And this semester we really have to bring up your math grade," Holla said. "Brown doesn't like C's."

"I didn't get a C last semester," Hudson said, carrying her bowl to the sink. "I got a B minus."

Holla threw the lemon slice into her glass and scowled. "Same thing," she remarked.

After waving good-bye to Fernald, Hudson turned south down Mott Street. She'd dressed in her Russian Spy/British Punk outfit — black wool leggings, black knee-high boots, black Russian hat, and a tartan plaid dress with strategically placed tears in the fabric. Her coat was a black trench with a bright red sash — a find from one of the street markets in Rome.

"Just don't let her steal a lock of your hair," Carina had said when Hudson had told her and Lizzie about her shopping date with Hillary.

"Or one of your buttons," Lizzie added. "Voodoo dolls always have buttons."

"Do you guys really think Hillary Crumple has a voodoo doll of me?" Hudson asked them. "That doesn't even make sense."

Far down the street, past the boutiques and espresso cafés housed in the ground levels of old tenements, Hudson could see a tiny figure in a bright pink knit hat and scarf and a gigantic puffy down coat that skimmed the ground. It had to be Hillary. Hudson raised one hand and sped up her walk. She hoped this wouldn't take too long.

"Hey!" Hillary yelled as Hudson approached. "That's such a cool hat. Where'd you get it? Moscow?"

"No. Somewhere around here."

"I love this neighborhood," Hillary said, glancing around. "Every single place down here is cool. You know? No Duane Reades, no Gristedes. Just really cool places. For cool people."

Hudson nodded. "Yeah, pretty much," she said, because she didn't know what else to say.

"I want to live down here one day. It's on my list of things I need to do before I'm thirty. Because that's when you have to get married, and after that, your life isn't fun anymore. Until you get divorced and you get to start over and be single again," Hillary said, pensive. "Or at least that's what my mom's life coach says. So, you ready to go in?"

Hudson looked through the window of Resurrection. Just past the shiny aluminum mannequins decked out in shift dresses from the sixties Hudson could see a saleswoman with ice blond hair. She was already eyeing Hillary with distaste. "Sure," Hudson said tentatively, and rang the doorbell.

The door buzzed and they entered the quiet, dimly lit boutique. Racks of vintage clothing lined the cherry red walls, while long tables laid with scarves and purses and sunglasses filled the interior space. Hudson stood very still and breathed in the scent of old leather and carefully preserved silk. Jenny had brought her here for the very first time, and she'd treated it more as a museum than a store. "Not that I can afford anything in here," Jenny had said good-naturedly as they walked in. "But I use this place for inspiration." Hudson knew exactly what she meant.

"So, I need something for my cousin's bar mitzvah," Hillary said loudly, unzipping her puffy coat to reveal a chunky purple turtleneck. "It's gonna be up in Westchester, at this really fancy hotel. So it sorta needs to be dressy." She darted over to the rack and pulled out a Pucci print dress. "What about this?"

The swirling print in aqua blue and yellow made Hudson squint. "That might be a little too much," she said gently. "You're really into color, huh?"

"I don't know." Hillary shrugged as she put the dress back. "I mean, I may as well stand out in the crowd."

"What about something understated like this?" Hudson said, pulling an ivory silk slip dress with a black ribbon belt off the rack.

Hillary wrinkled her nose. "Ehh. Boring. So what happened at the Silver Snowflake Ball?" Hillary asked, moving back to the racks. "Give me the scoop."

Startled, Hudson hung the slip dress back on its rack. "The scoop?"

"I think you can tell me the real story," Hillary said, rifling through some Bill Blass suits. "After everything I said to those girls in the bathroom."

Hudson picked up a yellow satin clutch purse. "It wasn't food poisoning. It was stage fright," she admitted.

"But how?" Hillary asked.

"What do you mean, *how*?" Hudson asked, putting down the bag.

"How could someone like *you* get stage fright? It doesn't make sense."

"I don't know," Hudson said, examining a rhinestone-encrusted lipstick case. "It just happens to people."

"But you're not just *people*," Hillary said, inspecting a thin alligator belt she'd picked up off the table.

"What do you mean?"

Hillary put down the belt and pointed at the window. "Look."

Hudson looked over. Three photographers stood across the street, half-hiding behind a parked Datsun. They were taking pictures of the store with their zoom lenses.

"They're taking pictures of you, right?" Hillary asked.

"Oh, God," Hudson whispered.

"Do you want me to go out there?" asked the saleswoman.

"No, that's okay," Hudson said. "I got it." She would just give them a few shots and then maybe they'd go away. Her mom wouldn't be thrilled, but Holla knew this happened to Hudson every once in a while.

She walked over to the window and pretended to look at a silk scarf for almost ten seconds, giving them plenty of opportunity to get their shot. It was always a little embarrassing to see photos of herself in the tabloids. Even when they praised her fashion sense as "trailblazing" and "avant-garde." Once one of them had written,

"Move over, Kate Moss! Hudson Jones is the real style icon for teenage girls in the know." When she'd read that, Hudson had been flattered, but it had also made her anxious. Being a "style icon" was way too much pressure for anyone, especially her.

After she'd given the paparazzi at least several good shots, she opened the door to the store. "Okay, guys, thanks so much," she called out. "I don't want the store to freak out or anything."

"Hudson!" they yelled, still shooting. "Step outside!"

"You guys know how my mom feels about this," Hudson said. "Don't make me call her right now."

At that they lowered their cameras and edged away down the street.

When she walked back into the store Hillary was waiting with a smirk on her face and her hand on her hip. "I think we can stop pretending that you're just like everyone else now," she said.

"I was just saying that of course I get nervous being onstage," Hudson said. "Anyone would."

"So why did you say it was food poisoning?" Hillary asked.

Hudson fiddled with the belt of her coat. "That was my mom's idea."

"And you let her do that?"

"Well...she was just trying to be helpful."

"Did you think that was helpful?" Hillary inquired.

Hudson gave Hillary an annoyed look. "Should we try the place down the street? I think they have better stuff for what you need."

"Sure." Hillary zipped up her coat and they walked outside. Hudson tried to think of a way to permanently change the subject.

All this talk about stage fright and her mom was starting to get embarrassing.

Suddenly the SUV swung over to the curb. "Where to?" Fernald yelled through the lowered passenger-side window. He'd been waiting for them to emerge from the store.

"Who's this?" Hillary asked.

"Uh, my driver," Hudson said, blushing again. "That's okay, Fernald!" she yelled. "We're going to walk. We're just going down there." She gestured down the street. "I'll call you, okay?"

Fernald gave her a thumbs-up and then drove down the street, leaving them mercifully alone.

"Wow," Hillary said as they watched the hulking vehicle drive off. "Now I get it. No wonder you freaked out up there."

"What do you mean?" Hudson asked.

"You're so . . . watched."

Hudson thought about this as they passed a woman pushing a baby stroller draped with plastic to keep out the cold. "Well, it's just the way things are," she explained. "There's nothing I can do about it. My mom is really scared about kidnappers and stuff like that."

"But it seems like she's everywhere."

"She's not *everywhere*," Hudson argued.

They turned into another store, which was a large, airy space, painted an industrial white and hung with full-length mirrors. Over the sound system came a familiar pounding song. One of Holla's first hits.

"Uh, right," Hillary said, pointing to the speakers.

"Look, I can't help it if my mom's music is everywhere."

"It has nothing to do with that," Hillary said, unwrapping her pink scarf from around her neck. "I just think your mom kind of rules your life."

Hillary's words stung. "It's a little more complicated than that," Hudson said.

"My mom's single," Hillary said. "So I get it. What's she going to open on Christmas, you know? Who's she going to hang out with on Saturday night?"

"My mom doesn't need me to hang out with her on Saturday night," Hudson said.

"I'm just saying, having only one parent around is hard," Hillary said. "But it's your life, too. And you need someone to step in and show you how to make it your best life."

"Who are you, Oprah?" Hudson asked. "This is my life. There's nothing I can do about it. And up until now, you kind of thought it was cool."

"I *still* think it's cool," Hillary said, following Hudson deeper into the store. "I think *you're* cool. But *you* don't think you're cool. I know you're an amazing singer. I can just tell. So why would you let one dumb night ruin everything?"

Hudson stared at Hillary. It was a good question.

"I read about you dropping your album on PopSugar. That's a really bad idea, by the way. Just so you know." Hillary pulled a black strapless bustier dress with a tulle skirt off the rack. "What do you think of this?"

"Uh, no. And let's please stop the self-help session, okay?" Hudson pulled out a simple black velvet dress with cap sleeves. "Try this."

Hillary examined the dress. "Really?"

"Look, if there's one thing about myself I *do* believe in, it's my taste in clothes," Hudson said, trying not to sound too sarcastic. "Trust me. Try it on."

"Fine," Hillary said, trudging into a fitting room.

Hudson stood there, relieved to be alone for a moment. She listened to Holla's song playing over the speakers, about to end. It had been a huge hit when Hudson had just been born. As with most of her mom's songs, she'd never paid much attention to the lyrics. But now the words jumped out at her.

Oh, baby, you know how much it hurts to let you go
But one day I swear, you're gonna know
That I will love you 'til the end of time...

She'd never thought that not having a father around was weird — lots of kids she knew had divorced parents and lived with their moms. But maybe she and Holla were a little too close. Maybe she *did* need to break away a little bit. Maybe she'd never noticed how much space her mom took up in her life, even when they weren't together.

Hillary walked out of the fitting room. "What do you think?" she asked, twirling around in the dress. It fit her perfectly. Hillary almost looked like Audrey Hepburn.

"I love it," Hudson said.

Hillary stopped twirling and beamed. "Good. I'm gonna take it. But first, I have something to say."

"Oh, God," Hudson said with a smile. "You do?"

"I think you need a life coach."

"What?" Hudson blurted out.

"My mom got one, and it's really helped," Hillary said. "She was a total mess after she and my dad got divorced. Sitting on the couch, eating Rice Krispies treats all the time, watching Animal Planet—"

"I don't need a life coach, Hillary," Hudson interrupted.

"No, but I think you need some help. I think you need to learn how to be Hudson. Not Holla Jones's kid. Just Hudson. And I'm happy to do it."

"Hillary?" Hudson said firmly. "No."

Hillary put up her tiny hand. "Fine, fine. Don't freak out. It was just a suggestion." She headed back into the fitting room, leaving Hudson feeling a little shaken. *Life coach?* She glanced around the store, wondering if anyone had heard them. They definitely weren't having lunch.

She waited as Hillary paid for her dress, and then they walked back outside. "I love it," Hillary said, almost giddy. "Thank you."

"You're welcome," Hudson said as they came to a stop at the corner of Prince Street. "Well, um, I think I have to go do some errands now."

"Okay." Hillary fixed her with a stare. "Are you offended by what I said?"

"Not at all," Hudson said, almost truthfully.

"Okay," she said. She turned this way and that. "Which way is uptown?"

"That way," Hudson said, pointing to Houston.

"Got it," Hillary said, and then she walked up the street. Hudson watched her pink hat disappear up the block. Hillary may have

71

meant well, but she was definitely rude. Hudson still couldn't believe some of the things she'd said. Things that she didn't even want to tell Lizzie and Carina. *Your mom kind of rules your life. You need to learn how to be Hudson.* Who said things like that?

Just then she saw the SUV glide down Mott Street. It was Fernald, circling the block, waiting to pick her up. For a moment she thought about turning the other way and ducking down Prince Street. Suddenly she didn't feel like being under the watchful eye of Holla's staff. But then the feeling passed, and she stepped out into the street and flagged him down, just like she was supposed to.

chapter 8

By late afternoon it had started to rain. Hudson watched people hurry down the street under bobbing umbrellas as they drove along Washington Street, the tires of the SUV making a whooshing sound on the wet asphalt. It was just before four o'clock, so she didn't have to worry about being late. Fernald had taken her up to Carina's apartment, where she'd spent the rest of the day watching *Across the Universe*. She hadn't told Carina any details about her shopping trip with Hillary, except that nothing had been stolen for a voodoo doll.

They finally reached their corner. The rain had cleared out all but the most hard-core photographers, who stood across the street looking miserable in their hooded nylon jackets. She gave them a slight wave as they turned into the garage.

"Hellooo? Anyone here?" Hudson called out as she walked into the brightly lit kitchen. "Where is everyone?"

"They're in the prayer room," said Lorraine, stirring something sludgy and green in a mixing bowl. "Your mom and your record producer."

"*My* record producer?" Hudson asked.

Lorraine nodded. "The one with the gorgeous blue eyes," she said, winking.

Hudson dropped her bag on the kitchen table. Chris Brompton was here. She hadn't been in touch with him since that horrible night at the Pierre, except for one e-mail over Christmas break, when she'd given him a slightly pathetic excuse for stopping work on her album. Something about needing to take a break, to take time to be a kid. She wondered if he'd even believed her. He'd written back, saying that he was disappointed but that he completely understood. The nice, completely mysterious kind of response. But he was there, in her house, right that second. Maybe he wanted to her to reconsider. Or maybe he just wanted to see her again.

She climbed the stairs two at a time. Up on the third floor, tucked into various niches along the wall and protected by alarmed glass, were Holla's numerous awards: Billboard Artist of the Year, Grammy for Record of the Year, People's Choice Award, the NAACP Image Award for Outstanding Female Artist. On the opposite wall hung her framed gold and platinum records. When she was younger, Hudson loved to gaze at these statues and plaques and records, or even ask her mom if she could hold them every once in a while. Now she felt the need to just walk past them as quickly as possible.

Back when she'd bought the house, Holla had been a practicing Buddhist who needed a room for her chanting and meditation. But then Holla had abandoned Buddhism for something she called "nonspecific spirituality," and now the prayer room was just another office. Hudson pushed open the door.

"Are you *kidding* me?" her mom was saying. Holla sat perched on the edge of a white chaise in a snug fuchsia warm-up suit, and she was so absorbed in what she was saying, or who she was saying it to, that she didn't even notice Hudson's entrance. Sitting just a few inches away, at the desk, smiling at her mom in a way that made her heart stop, was Chris Brompton. He looked exactly the same as he had all those days they'd spent together in the studio: shaggy strawberry blond hair, kind but sexy blue eyes, weathered Levi's and short-sleeved T-shirt. Neither of them noticed her for a moment, until Chris glanced over at the door.

"Hey, Hudson," Chris said, getting up from the chair in his easy, laid-back way. "How's it going? Happy New Year!"

"Hi, Chris," Hudson said. Her heart beat rapidly as they hugged. Behind him, on the computer screen, Hudson glimpsed a list of tracks. But she couldn't tell whose songs they were. "What are you doing here?"

"Chris is going to do some work on my album," Holla announced. Her eyes were still glued to Chris's face, and she hadn't moved from her spot on the couch. "I was just so impressed with the work he did on your album, honey, that I asked him to put the finishing touches on mine."

Hudson stood perfectly still. She looked from Holla to Chris and back again. For a moment, she couldn't speak. It was as if a golf ball covered in spikes had suddenly lodged itself in her throat. "On yours?" she asked.

"Well, since you'd decided to put *yours* on the shelf, and he's so

75

good," Holla said, reaching out to give Chris a playful swat on the arm as he sat back down, "I couldn't help myself."

"You couldn't?" Chris asked, laughing. "I'm flattered."

Hudson watched them grinning at each other, trying to absorb this. Chris Brompton had believed in *her*. He'd been *her* producer. Now, just like that, he was gone. The unfairness of it sliced through her. Her mom had thousands of fans — did she really need another one?

"So, Chris just had a brilliant idea," Holla said to Hudson. "You want to tell her?"

Chris swiveled around to the computer. "Okay, listen to this." He clicked on one of the tracks.

From the first sped-up, over-synthesized beat, Hudson knew exactly what it was: her song "Heartbeat." The song she'd tried to sing at the Silver Snowflake Ball. "What about it?" she asked, fighting off a sense of panic.

Chris paused it and turned back around. "It's a really good song, Hudson. I always thought it was your best. And, well" — he looked at Holla — "I think it would be perfect for your mom."

Hudson blinked.

"Only if you're okay with that, of course," Holla said, still smiling at Chris. She padded over to the desk. "I don't want you to feel weird about it."

"But... don't you have songs already?" Hudson asked.

"Chris doesn't think I have a single. *Do* you?" she asked him, with mock seriousness.

"Not like this one," Chris confessed, running a hand through his hair. "Of course," he said, turning to Hudson, "if you're not cool with it, it's no big deal."

Hudson couldn't move. *Of course* she wasn't cool with it. Did he even have to ask? Why didn't he know that already? It was her song. One of her favorites. Even though her mom had ruined it. And now he wanted to give it to someone who'd never liked it that much in the first place? "I thought you didn't like my music," Hudson managed to say.

Holla raised an eyebrow. "Honey, I *love* your music," she said. "Which is why I think this song — tweaked, of course — would be perfect for me."

"But it's *my* song," Hudson argued.

Holla stood and wobbled on her feet, as if she'd lost her balance, then caught the back of Chris's chair.

"You okay?" Chris asked, leaping to his feet and taking her arm.

"Yes, yes, I think so," Holla said, touching her forehead. "It's just this juice cleanse. It always makes me a little light-headed."

Chris led Holla over to the window seat and carefully patted her arm, as if she were a delicate thing that might break. "That better?" he asked. "Do you need some water?"

"That would be great," she said.

"You got it," Chris said.

As soon as he left, Holla looked up at Hudson. "So, you were saying?"

Hudson gathered herself. "I was just saying that it's my song," she said.

"So?" Holla said. "Are you saying you've changed your mind about the album?"

"No."

"So you just don't want me to have it," Holla prompted.

"I...I didn't say that," Hudson stammered.

"Then you just want it to go to waste," Holla said.

"No, but..."

"Honey, what's the matter? You're going to get all the royalties. I thought you'd be thrilled to have one of your songs actually out there instead of on a shelf gathering dust."

As usual, her mom had found the one point that Hudson couldn't debate. She looked at the framed cover of *Vanity Fair* on the wall, the one her mom had posed for years earlier. THE PRINCESS OF POP, it read. Her mom stood on a beach in a ballgown, wearing a tiara. And in her arms, naked and squirming, was Hudson, just a year old. Her mom looked so pretty, so happy. Overjoyed about her new little girl. The little girl who now was being petty and trivial and hopelessly stubborn. "Fine," she said. "You can have it."

Chris walked back into the room with a glass of water.

"Really?" Holla asked, suddenly contrite. "Are you sure?" She took the glass from Chris and sipped from it.

"Yeah," Hudson said. "Why not?"

"Thank you, honey," Holla said. She got up and gave Hudson an overpowering hug. "I'll do it justice. I promise. Now, you have some homework to do, right?"

"Uh-huh," Hudson said.

"Thanks, Hudson," Chris said. "You might have just given your mom her next hit."

"Awesome," she said as she backed out of the room. She grasped the banister as she walked down the stairs, trying to keep her feet moving, one in front of the other.

This had to be a joke. All her mom had done before now was

tell her how unmarketable her music was, and now she wanted to record one of Hudson's songs because she needed a single? She should have just said no. Carina and Lizzie would have just said no. It was just one stupid syllable. But, as usual, something inside of her had just shut down. Whenever she got angry, or hurt, she couldn't speak, couldn't fight back. It was like being caught in a sandstorm that blotted out words and sight and thought. And the only way out of it all was to just say *Fine*.

When she got to her room, she pulled out her iPhone. She needed to text Lizzie and Carina. They would be on her side. They'd understand. They always did. But she stopped, her finger poised over the screen. Her friends would ask why she hadn't fought back. Carina would go on and on about Hudson's inner bee-yatch. Lizzie would just say *Why didn't you say no?* And Hudson wouldn't have an answer. *Because I didn't feel like I could? Because it's my mom and she gets everything she wants?* Those weren't good enough answers.

She threw herself on her bed and buried her face in a cushion. Carina was right: She needed to find her inner bee-yatch, ASAP. But she had no idea how. This was who she was: Sensitive. Sweet. Nice. More at home by herself at her piano than in a crowd. The exact opposite of her fiery, vocal, afraid-of-nothing-and-nobody mom. She would never be any different, and she couldn't hope to be. Because how did people change who they were?

She sat straight up.

Maybe a person *could* change who she was.

If she got a life coach.

chapter 9

"Your mom wants your song?" Carina asked incredulously as they walked up the street toward school. "But she told you your stuff sucked. That day in the studio. I was there!"

"I know," Hudson said simply as they reached the school doors.

"I don't get it," Lizzie said. "After everything she said?"

"She's a Leo with an Aries rising," said Hudson.

"What does that mean?" Lizzie said.

"That it's not that surprising," Hudson said, pulling the doors open.

"But you didn't have to say yes," Lizzie said as they walked into the school lobby. She pulled off her knit hat and shook out her red curls.

"And what about your inner bee-yatch?" Carina cried, blowing on her cold fingers. Carina was always losing her gloves. "What happened to her?"

"Maybe Hudson doesn't have an inner bee-yatch," Lizzie said to Carina.

"If you don't start saying no to your mom, like, *now*, then things are just gonna get worse," Carina said.

"You guys, I *know*," Hudson said as they passed the library. "That's why I've decided to get a life coach."

"A life coach?" Carina asked, crinkling her brown eyes. "Are you kidding?"

"Lots of people use them," Lizzie pointed out. "It's like a therapist who actually does stuff."

"Who are you getting?" Carina asked. "Please tell me it's not some kooky astrologer."

"Heeeyy, guys!" called a lilting voice behind them on the stairs. "Wait up!"

They slowly turned around to see Ava Elting climbing the stairs with the Icks. She'd traded her devil-horned hat for a black stocking cap with orange and red zigzagging lines around it, like the ones on an EKG machine. Her nails had been painted a deep sky blue, and she wore a skinny lavender scarf that barely covered her long neck. "Did you guys have a good weekend?" Ava asked. "I had the *best* time. I went up to Vermont to go snowboarding. I even got a private lesson from this guy who used to be on the Olympic team."

"That's nice," Lizzie said in a way that said she couldn't care less.

"So Hudson, I saw that you've pulled your album," Ava said, sidling up to her on the stairs. "That must have been such a hard decision for you."

Ilona and Cici snickered quietly. Kate supplied the deathstare.

"It wasn't that hard," Hudson said, trying to reach the top of the stairs as quickly as possible. "I'm just really busy with school right now."

"Was it because of what happened at the Ball?" Ava pressed. "I hope not. Considering it was just food poisoning and everything."

Hudson pursed her lips. "No. It had nothing to do with that."

"I just think it's a shame that things aren't working out," Ava replied. "I mean, that must be a lot for you to live up to. *I'd* crack under the pressure."

Just as Hudson began to get angry, she turned and saw Hillary walking up the stairs behind them. She sported her usual messy ponytail, and pieces of brown hair fell against her forehead. Her square pink and blue backpack was strapped to her back, and today her sweater was a blinding shade of tennis-ball yellow. "You guys go ahead," Hudson said. "I'll see you in homeroom."

Ava reached the door to the Upper School, grinning triumphantly. "See you later, Hudson," she said, giggling, and pulled the door open. The Icks followed, each of them giggling as well.

"Where are you going?" Carina asked, but Hudson was already descending the stairs toward Hillary, eager to put the Ava encounter behind her.

"Hey, Hillary!" she called out. "Can I talk to you for a second?"

Hillary pushed some hair out of her eyes. "Sure," she said in her tiny voice. "Those are really cute earrings."

"Thanks." Hudson fell into step beside her on the stairs. "So I was thinking about what you said the other day. About the life-coaching thing. I think I need to do it. I think I *have* to do it. So... can you still be my life coach?"

Hillary stopped climbing the stairs. Her thin legs were bare despite the freezing weather, and her kilt hung unevenly below her knees, as if she'd misbuttoned it. "If I do this for you," she asked in a low, portentous voice, "can I ask you for something?"

"Sure, what?" Hudson said.

Hillary crossed her arms. "Will you go with me to my cousin's bar mitzvah on Saturday?"

Hudson paused. This was a curveball. "But…but I don't even know your cousin."

"I know," Hillary said, unfazed. "I just want you to go with me. My friend Zoe was supposed to, but now she has to go to New Jersey for her grandma's birthday or something like that. So can you go? Please?"

"But…but why do I have to go with you?" Hudson asked.

Hillary hesitated. "Because there's going to be this guy there that I like."

"Oh," Hudson said, surprised. She hadn't thought Hillary even cared about guys yet.

"And I need someone to be with me when I talk to him," Hillary went on. "And tell me if they think he likes me back. He's my cousin's friend — my older cousin, Ben — and he's a sophomore —"

"A *sophomore*?" Hudson asked.

"And they're starting this band and he plays saxophone and he's on the chess team and, well, I think he likes me, but I really need a second opinion."

"Oh. Okay." Hudson tried to imagine a sophomore really liking Hillary, but she found it a little hard to swallow. "I'll go."

"Just don't tell anyone, okay?" Hillary asked, her voice rising with panic. "Because everyone'll think it's just some stupid crush. You promise?"

"I promise," Hudson said. "But…can you still be my life coach?"

"Oh, sure," Hillary said. She started taking the steps two at a time. "But first we have to figure out a life goal. You always have to have a life goal when you're being life-coached. So what do you want to change about your life?"

They reached the fourth floor and walked into the crowded Middle School hallway. It had been only a year since Hudson had gone to school up here, but it already felt like a million years ago. Several eighth-grade girls stared at her with undisguised worship. "Well, it's like you said," Hudson told her, "I need to be my own person. And I really don't want to say 'fine' anymore."

"What do you mean?" Hillary asked.

"I mean, I'm always just saying 'fine.' When I really want to say anything *but* 'fine.' Do you know what I mean?"

Hillary nodded. If she thought Hudson didn't make any sense, she didn't say so. "Okay. First step, then: I want you to write down everything you're afraid of. All your fears." She reached into her boxy backpack and took out a pencil with a heart eraser stuck on the end of it. "Here," she said, taking out a piece of loose-leaf paper and scribbling something on it. "Take this." She handed it to Hudson. At the top of the page she'd written HUDSON'S FEARS.

"Wait," Hudson said. "Fears? Do you mean like earthquakes?"

"Just write down everything you think of."

"But why do I have to write them down?"

"My mom's coach says that once you write down your fears,

they lose their power over you," Hillary said, sticking her pencil back into her backpack.

Hudson couldn't help but feel a little disappointed. This was life-coaching? She'd assumed that Hillary would just rattle off more of her blunt insights and then offer some concrete, practical solutions. Writing down random fears wasn't going to change anything. But she didn't want to be late for homeroom, and most important, she didn't want to be rude. "Okay, fine," she said, putting the piece of paper in her backpack. "I'll let you know what I come up with."

When she slipped into her seat next to Carina and Lizzie in homeroom just before the second bell, Carina looked up from her Spanish homework, which she was frantically finishing. Spanish was Carina's least favorite subject.

"What was that about?" Carina asked.

"I just went to see my life coach," Hudson said.

"Hillary?" Carina shouted. "Your *stalker's* your life coach?"

"She's not my stalker," Hudson said.

Lizzie looked up from her copy of *This Side of Paradise*. "Well, she is an odd choice, you have to admit," she said.

Later, during her study period, Hudson took out her math notebook and uncapped her favorite Bic liquid gel pen. She read the words *Hudson's Fears* over and over. She'd never thought of herself as someone who had lots of fears. So now she wondered, *What am I afraid of?* She started to write.

getting a C in geometry
getting a B in everything else
Not getting into Brown or, well, anywhere

Something bad happening to Lizzie and Carina
Roaches, waterbugs, and snakes (ugh...)
Plane turbulence ☹
Not being liked
Small planes (except for Carina's dad's plane,
  which isn't that small, but it still counts)
Cute older guys who are really smart and like
  good music, and who I become friends with
All cute guys
Class presentations
Lunar eclipses (especially in Virgo)
Getting caught eating junk food in front of
  my mom
Being laughed at (too late for that ☺*)*

Later, as they waited for Bio to start, she took out the sheet and wrote more. And then she added some more fears during lunch. Before she knew it, she had four loose-leaf pages, all of them covered in fears. She was stunned. She'd had no idea that she was afraid of so many things. It was amazing that she'd even made it to ninth grade.

She folded up the pages and stowed them deep in the middle of her Geometry notebook. She didn't even want to show Carina and Lizzie. She was sure that neither of them was afraid of half as many things as she was.

At the end of the day, Hillary accosted her in the lobby as she was leaving.

"So, did you make your list?" she asked, eyeballing Hudson's bag.

"You don't have to see them, do you?"

"No," Hillary said. "Just tell me about one of them."

Hudson tried to remember one that wasn't completely embarrassing. "I think I said I was afraid of eating junk food in front of my mom."

"Great!" Hillary said, almost jumping out of her bluchers. "Okay. I want you to go home tonight and have pizza for dinner."

"What?" Hudson asked, stupefied. "I can't do that."

"Why not?"

"Because it's dairy. And white flour. And possibly nitrates."

Hillary shook her head. "But do you *like* pizza?"

Hudson nodded. "Yeah. I love it."

"Good," she said. "Then have it tonight. It's just for tonight."

"Wait," Hudson said, shifting her book bag to her other shoulder. "How is eating a pizza going to help me be my own person?"

Hillary folded her arms and cocked her head. "I know what I'm doing, Hudson," she said bossily. "Trust me."

Hudson walked out of the lobby and caught up with Lizzie and Carina, who were on the corner talking. "Can you guys come over for dinner tonight?" she asked them.

"What's up?" Lizzie asked.

"Are you guys having flaxseed tacos again?" Carina asked, wrinkling her button nose.

"No, I'm having pizza," she answered. "And I need you guys to help me."

chapter 10

Lizzie, Carina, Todd, and Hudson sat in a circle on the sheepskin rug, staring intently at the black cordless phone in Hudson's hand.

"If you're gonna do it, you gotta do it now," Lizzie urged, stretching her long legs out on the rug. "It's six forty-five. You said dinner was at seven, right?"

"On the dot," Hudson said. She pressed the Talk button on the phone so that they could hear the low hum of a dial tone, and then she pressed it again so that the phone hung up. It was the fourth time she'd almost dialed. In her dog bed in the corner, Matilda lifted her head and looked at Hudson like she was certifiably nuts.

"Okay," Carina said, taking charge. "What's the worst thing that can happen? It's *pizza*. Your mom's not going to throw you out of the house. Right?"

Hudson didn't say anything.

"Right?" Carina asked, less confidently.

"Carina's right," Todd said. "Pizza's loads healthier than a lot of other stuff you could be eating. There was a guy in my class in London who only ate Curly Wurlys and Aero bars for every meal."

"What's a Curly Wurly?" Carina asked.

"It's basically chocolate-covered caramel," Todd answered. "It's amazing."

"But why do they call it a Curly Wurly?" Carina asked, giggling.

"Let's get back to the pizza-ordering," Lizzie broke in, twisting her hair into a bun on top of her head. "Just do it. Nothing bad is going to happen. And for the record, having pizza more often wouldn't kill you."

"What do you mean?" Hudson asked.

"Just that you're always eating so healthy," Lizzie said gently. "It's like you're always trying to eat the *right* thing."

"Yeah, like if there's a choice between a burger and a salad, you'll always eat the salad," Carina added. "Because it's the right thing."

Hudson looked at Todd.

"I really don't know," Todd said, shrugging. "But I'll take everyone's word for it."

"Well…" Hudson argued. "Isn't that how we're supposed to be?"

"We're not supposed to be perfect, H," Carina said. "That's the worst thing you can be. Perfect."

Hudson knew Carina was right. "Okay. Here goes." She pressed the Talk button again. This time she dialed the number she'd written down on a piece of paper.

A man picked up. "Ray's!" he yelled into her ear.

"Hi, I'd like to order a large plain pizza, please," Hudson said carefully, as if she were speaking another language. "Or do I say cheese? Is cheese extra cheese or is it just plain?"

"What?" the man said.

"Nothing," Hudson said. "I'll just take a plain pizza. For delivery. Seven-fifty Washington Street."

"Large plain — you got a doorman or a buzzer?" he yelled.

"A buzzer," she said.

"Fine. Twenty minutes."

Click.

Hudson hung up the phone.

"Good for you," Lizzie said, reaching out and grabbing Hudson's arm. "I'm proud of you."

"I still don't know why Hillary wants me to do this," Hudson said.

"I do," Lizzie said. "How are you ever going to start living your own life if you don't even eat what you want?"

"Yeah," Carina said. "Maybe Creepy Crumple is onto something."

"Dinnertime!" Lorraine yelled over the intercom in Hudson's room.

"Don't worry, H," Todd said, helping her to her feet. "I think you're going to do just splendidly with this junk food."

"Thanks, Todd," Hudson said. He was so adorably English sometimes.

The three of them walked down the stairs to the kitchen, while Hudson thought about her friends' advice. She couldn't help it if she was used to eating healthfully. It was the right thing, after all. But the right thing for whom? It was hard to know sometimes. Her mom always prided herself on being the healthiest person she knew. Maybe even the healthiest person in America. But maybe being the healthiest person in America wasn't so healthy, Hudson realized. Maybe the point was to be healthy, but to not let it rule your life.

Hudson led the way into the kitchen and they took their places around the empty table.

"Remember," Carina said, sipping from the glass of triple-purified water at her place setting, "no matter what happens, it's just pizza."

Behind them, Hudson heard the elevator door rumble open, and soon Holla strode into the kitchen in a shiny silver trench coat, with Sophie in tow. "I'm meeting him tonight at the Rose Bar," Holla said, speaking into her cell phone. "I'll let you know what he says." She clicked off. "Sophie? Get us that sofa near the fireplace. And let Mr. Schnabel know we'll be there if he wants to join us."

Holla unbuttoned her trench. Instead of her usual studio uniform of warm-up suit and ponytail, she wore a black sweater with a deep V-neck and blue jeans tucked into knee-high leather boots. Her hair was down around her shoulders and curled at the ends. It was Hudson's favorite look for her mom — smart and elegant, but casual.

"Hi, everyone," she said, smiling at her daughter's friends. "I didn't know Hudson was having guests tonight." Even though Holla liked her privacy, she never seemed to mind when Hudson had her friends over.

"It was sort of a spur-of-the-moment kind of thing," Hudson said. "Mom, this is Todd."

"It's a pleasure, Miss Jones," Todd said, standing up and offering his hand.

"You can call me Holla," her mom said, shaking Todd's hand. Hudson could see that she thought Todd was cute. "So nice to meet you. Hello, girls," she said, leaning down and giving Carina and Lizzie each a hug and a kiss.

"Hi, Holla," Lizzie said.

"Hi," Carina murmured.

"Oh, it feels good to be home," Holla said, tossing her trench coat over the back of one of the bar stools by the island. "Another long day of mixing."

"So...how's it going?" Hudson asked. She never knew how exactly to talk to her mom around her friends. Lizzie and Carina were always a little uncomfortable around her, which made Hudson uncomfortable, too.

"We're getting a lot done, and thank God Chris is on board," Holla said as she scooted into the booth next to Hudson. "I realize now I should have had him this whole time." She looked at Hudson and frowned. "What if you got some bangs? I think they'd look cute on you. Don't you guys think?" she asked Lizzie, Carina, and Todd.

"So, Todd is a writer," Hudson said, changing the subject before they could answer. "Just like Lizzie."

"Oh?" Holla asked as Lorraine brought her a tall glass of ice water with lemon.

"His story is up for best short story at the entire school," Hudson said.

"Really?" Holla said, smiling as she sipped her water. "That's wonderful. What's it about?"

Todd blushed. "It's not really anything," he said, waving it off.

"It's about Lizzie," Carina said, smiling.

Hudson was relieved to see her friends relaxing in front of her mom.

"Really? So are you guys dating?" Holla asked.

"Uh, yes," Lizzie said shyly.

"Ohhh, that's so cute," Holla said. "Is there anyone in Hudson's life? She doesn't tell me a thing."

Hudson gulped and looked down at her plate. "Mom, please," she said under her breath. Bangs were one thing to discuss in front of her friends. Her love life was another.

"Everything's ready!" Lorraine called over from the island. "Come and get it!"

Hudson shot up from her seat and walked to the kitchen island, where Lorraine had set out a buffet.

"Baked tofu with sea-vegetable slaw," Lorraine said, gesturing to a platter heaped with what looked like stringy black seaweed. "Plus, sesame broccoli and wild rice with beet chutney."

"Where's the pizza?" Carina whispered desperately.

"Just take some," Hudson whispered back, spooning giant gobs of wild rice onto her plate, and even some of the sea-vegetable slaw. "It's hijiki."

"Hi-*what*-ee?" Carina whispered back.

"It's not bad." Hudson went back to her seat and politely began picking at her food.

"Did Hudson tell you guys that I'm singing one of her songs?" Holla asked between tiny mouthfuls of wild rice.

Her friends nodded as they pretended to eat. "H is really talented," Carina said.

"I know," Holla said. "And at least now the world is gonna have a chance to see that."

Hudson gripped the fork tighter as she swirled food around

her plate. She knew that her mom meant this as a compliment, but inside she felt like cringing.

"Honey?" Holla asked. "What's wrong? You love hijiki."

"I'm just not in the mood for it tonight," Hudson said.

"Well, is there something else you'd rather have?" asked Holla. "How about a crispy seitan sandwich?"

There was a buzz at the back door. Hudson, Lizzie, and Carina all sat up. The pizza had arrived.

"Are you expecting something?" Raquel asked Holla as she walked out of the kitchen to the back door.

Holla shook her head. "No, I don't think so."

Raquel went to the elevator as Lizzie, Carina, Hudson, and Todd exchanged urgent looks. *This is it*, Hudson thought. *The moment of truth.*

Raquel returned, carrying a pizza box. "Did somebody order a *pizza*?" she asked, scrunching up her face in horror.

The smell of melted cheese and oregano filled the room, answering her question.

"I did," Hudson said, springing out of her chair. She ran to the back door to pay the delivery man. When she returned, her mom was staring at the pizza box with undisguised fury. Carina and Lizzie and Todd looked down, inspecting their plates. Even Lorraine looked terrified. But the room smelled delicious.

"Hudson, you're being rude to Lorraine," Holla said evenly.

"I know," Hudson began. "But I just felt like having pizza tonight."

"Throw it out," Holla said to Raquel. "And sit down and finish your dinner," she said to Hudson. "I don't know what kind of point you're trying to make, but this is ridiculous."

Carina glanced up from her plate and gave Hudson a meaningful eyebrow raise. Hudson understood. She couldn't back down. Her heart pounding, she opened the pizza box and grabbed a thin, greasy slice.

"Hudson," Holla said. She sounded like she was struggling to stay even-tempered. "What are you doing?"

Hudson took a gooey, cheesy bite. "Yum," she couldn't help saying. She couldn't remember the last time anything had tasted this good to her.

"Do you know how bad that is for you?" Holla asked.

Hudson swallowed. "That's really good." She turned to her friends. "Want some?"

Carina and Lizzie and Todd all nodded eagerly.

"Go ahead, you guys," she said. "Have some." She walked the pizza box over to the table and held it out.

Carina quickly grabbed a slice. Then Lizzie did. Then Todd. Now all four of them were eating pizza and licking their fingers.

Holla watched them for a moment, her brown eyes glittering with anger. Finally, she picked up her fork and knife and sliced into her tofu. Lorraine and Raquel went back to quietly moving around the kitchen.

Hudson couldn't believe what she was doing. She was eating three of her mom's most hated food groups — dairy, wheat, and grease — right in front of her. And Holla wasn't stopping her. As soon as she finished the first slice, she reached for another with her greasy, cheesy fingers. So did Carina and Lizzie, and even Todd. Before long, they'd eaten the entire pizza. The empty grease-streaked box lay open on the kitchen counter. Hudson still stood next to it. She'd been too scared to sit down next to her mom, afraid that Holla might rip the slice right out of her hands.

"Can we be excused?" Hudson asked, finally daring to look at her mother.

Holla chewed her food and stared at her plate. "Yes," she said quietly. "And please get rid of that."

Without a word, Hudson took the pizza box into the hallway near the elevator and threw it into one of the recycling bins. As she clamped the top onto the bin, a thrill went through her. *I did it!* she thought. Maybe her "point" had been ridiculous, but she'd definitely made one.

She walked out to the hallway, where her friends were waiting for her.

"Oh my God, your mom was shooting dagger eyes at us," Carina whispered as they walked up the stairs.

"Are you okay?" Lizzie asked.

"I'm great," Hudson said, grinning. To Holla, food was a very big deal. Food was control. And Hudson had just taken control in Holla's house, for the very first time.

chapter 11

The next morning Hudson walked downstairs very, very quietly. She hadn't seen Holla since the pizza showdown the night before, and she wasn't sure what to expect. Hudson knew that she was in uncharted territory here.

She placed her book bag on a chair in the hall and walked into the kitchen to grab something to eat, steeling herself for a confrontation. But instead of Holla at the kitchen table, Chris Brompton was sitting there, reading the *New York Post* and sipping a soy cappuccino, like he enjoyed breakfast at Hudson's house all the time.

"Oh, hey, Hudson," he said, putting down his coffee. "'Morning." He got up out of his seat halfway and then just stood there awkwardly. Instead of jeans he wore long plaid swimming trunks and a burgundy T-shirt that read BONDI BEACH.

"What are you doing here?" Hudson asked. She glanced at the kitchen clock. It was quarter to eight.

"Oh, your mom just wanted me to come take one of her yoga classes," he said with a sheepish smile. "I'm just booting up with some caffeine." He held up his cup and took another sip, which left foamed soy milk all over his upper lip.

Lorraine walked into the kitchen. "Anything I can get you, Hudson?" she asked.

"I'll just have this," Hudson said, opening the refrigerator and grabbing an orange.

Lorraine retreated into the pantry, leaving them alone again.

"So, yoga, huh?" Hudson said, starting to peel her orange. "You better be careful. It's not for beginners."

"I can handle it," Chris said, sitting back down. "And I hope you're not weirded out by anything. You know, about me working with your mom."

"No, I think it's great," she lied, tearing off a hunk of orange peel. Even though she was still annoyed with him, being this close to him again, all alone, brought her back to that dizzy, exhilarated feeling she had when she worked with him in the studio. Or used to have, in the days before her mom had barged in. He'd made her feel so talented, so special, so seen.

"Just so you know, I was really surprised when you wrote me that e-mail," he said, looking straight at her. "About quitting the album. You're an amazing talent, Hudson. I hope you know that."

"Then why were you okay with changing it all?" The question had just slipped out.

"What do you mean?" Chris's laid-back smile dissolved into a frown.

"When my mom came in and changed every song, you seemed

totally fine with it." She stared right into his eyes. "Why? If you thought I was so talented?"

Chris looked dumbfounded. He stared into his cappuccino, then stirred it with his spoon. "Just because I respect your mom's talent and opinion doesn't mean I don't believe in you," he said. "And I think your mom happened to be right."

So he had no real answer, Hudson thought. Only an excuse for her mom. Chris had completely gone over to the dark side. "Well, I guess I better be going," she said, just as her mom walked into the kitchen.

"Well, good morning," Holla said, glancing first at Chris and then at Hudson. Her canary yellow yoga top looked beautiful against her dark brown skin, and was cut short to reveal her formidable six-pack. "And you actually made it," she said to Chris.

"I know," Chris said, sitting up straight. "My friends would never believe this."

"Hi, Mom," Hudson said.

"Hi, honey," Holla answered warmly. "You sleep okay?"

"Great," Hudson said. Her mom didn't seem to be the slightest bit angry. Or maybe she just didn't want to show it in front of Chris.

Holla fixed her gaze on Hudson's feet. "They let you wear those boots to school?" she asked, pointing at Hudson's Russian Spy/British Punk knee-high boots. "What about the ankle boots? The heels are so much lower —"

"I gotta go," Hudson said, backing out of the kitchen. "I'll see you later."

"Bye, Hudson," Chris said, waving.

"Bye, Chris," Hudson said tonelessly.

"Get ready to have your butt kicked," she heard Holla tease Chris as she walked out to the hall, grabbed her book bag, and pushed the elevator button with a sick feeling in her gut.

They're into each other, she thought. She'd seen that look on her mom's face before, and heard the way Holla's voice went up an octave whenever she was around someone she liked. And Chris was just her type: young, hunky, and boyishly handsome. Just like Hudson's dad.

But instead of feeling angry, she felt oddly Zen about it all. Her crush on Chris Brompton was officially over. She'd asked him straight-out why he'd caved so quickly to her mom's demands, and instead of being honest, instead of just saying that he liked her mom, that he'd wanted to date her, he'd talked about "respecting her opinion." *Whatever,* Hudson thought as she got into the elevator. She'd done the right thing, backing out of that album. Except she wanted that feeling back — that feeling of being talented, of being special in her own right. And now it seemed like she would never feel that again.

*

A few hours later she and Lizzie and Carina headed to the library for their free period.

"You don't have any proof," Lizzie said definitively, toying with the chain link wristband of her watch. "All you know is that he was there for yoga."

"Yeah, like six hours after they hung out at some bar the night before," Hudson said.

"He's probably terrified of her," Carina said. "I thought she was going to murder us all last night. Good job, by the way. You totally rocked that pizza thing."

"Thanks," Hudson said. "But it just makes me sad, you know? Like, I'll never have that again. Someone who made me feel the way he did. And now he's going to be my stepfather."

"He's *not* going to be your stepfather," Lizzie said.

"You think that every time your mom gets involved with someone," Carina said. "And, well, you know what usually happens."

Hudson *did* know. Her mom's relationships never lasted long. The men Holla picked always seemed so enamored of her. Until something changed. Sometimes she found out that they were still married, for example. And sometimes, the guys would start to retreat, as if a few weeks of constant togetherness were all they could offer. And every time, Holla would be destroyed. Her last boyfriend had been twenty-six and a sound engineer, and even though Holla had dumped him, and not the other way around, she'd come to Hudson's room every night, crying, for a week straight.

"You just need to focus on school right now," Lizzie said as they took a seat at one of the library tables. "We all need to."

Lizzie was right; Miss Evanevski had just warned them of a quiz the next day in Geometry. But just as Hudson pulled out her notebook she spied Hillary across the room, sitting at a table, alone, and wearing a bulky knit sweater with blue and purple sequined butterflies on it. She was doing the *New York Times* crossword again.

"I'll be right back," Hudson said, getting up.

"Tell your life coach you had *two* slices," Carina said, a proud grin on her face.

Hudson walked over to Hillary's table and slid into the seat across from her. "So guess what? I did it. I ordered a pizza."

"But did you actually eat it?" Hillary asked, her pen poised in the air.

"Yep! Two whole slices!"

"Great," Hillary said, capping her pen. "Did it taste good?" Hudson noticed the magenta plastic barrettes clamped firmly on either side of her head, and wondered if Hillary's mom still did her hair.

"It tasted amazing," Hudson whispered. "Of course, my mom was a little annoyed, but it was worth it."

"Good," Hillary said. "You passed the first test. I'm really proud of you."

"So, e-mail me the details about the bar mitzvah," Hudson said, getting up from the table. "I gotta go study for a Geometry quiz."

"Uh, we're not finished yet," Hillary said. "Sit down."

Hudson sat down. "There's more?"

"Of course there's more," Hillary said. "You didn't think that was it, right? A few slices of pizza and you're your own person?" Hillary stared at Hudson and pursed her lips as she thought. "You said you have a quiz?"

"Yeah," Hudson said, playing with her silver hoop earrings. "Geometry, aka hell."

"Good. Don't study for it."

"*What?*" Hudson said so loudly that the librarian sitting nearby put her finger to her lips.

"Don't study for it," Hillary repeated.

"But I can't not study for it," Hudson said. "I'll fail."

Hillary shook her head. "You may not get an A, but you won't fail."

"I'll barely get a C."

"And that would ruin your month, right?" Hillary challenged.

"Can I ask what the point of this is?" Hudson said, trying not to be annoyed.

"The point is to know that if you do get a bad grade, you can *survive* it," Hillary said, reclipping one of her plastic barrettes. "This is step two. You have to stop being afraid of bad grades. And I can tell that bad grades really freak you out."

"Is that a bad thing?" Hudson asked. "I mean, I'm not going to ruin my life just because I have a fear of bad grades."

"But you're living your life in *fear*," Hillary said. "You need to show yourself that getting a not-so-great grade isn't the end of the world. And you are *not* going to mess up your transcript with one quiz."

"I'm sorry, Hillary," Hudson said. "But I have to study."

"Then just do an hour," Hillary shot back. "Study for it for one hour. That's it. No more."

"Fine," Hudson said reluctantly as she got up to leave.

"You just said 'fine' again," Hillary pointed out.

"Whatever," Hudson said grouchily, walking back to her friends. Eating pizza in front of her mom was one thing. Now Hillary might be going a little too far.

*

That night, at her desk, Hudson checked her antique French boudoir clock. She'd been trying to solve sample Geometry problems for the past fifty-eight minutes, and by now her stomach was clenched into a knot. Geometry tended to do that to her. In class, finding the area of this triangle and that polygon made perfect sense, but as soon as she faced a problem on her own, everything she knew just melted away like snow. She looked at the answers Miss Evanevski had given them. She'd only gotten one on the first try. To make matters worse, she couldn't stop picturing Chris and Holla in some kind of romantic clinch. They were probably out together right this minute, drinking champagne out of glasses they clinked together like cheesy honeymooners. Ugh.

She eyed her piano across the room. Whenever she'd been stressed about something in the past, she'd sat down at it. Maybe she just needed to play right now.

She walked over and carefully lifted the heavy lid from the keys, then sat down on the polished bench. Her book of Chopin nocturnes still leaned against the sheet-music stand. She breathed in the smell of polished wood and touched the soft, velvety keys. Over the years she had spent hours here every night, first practicing the classics and then writing her own songs. Music had been the only thing she thought about. Until lately. She hadn't played in almost a month. As soon as she'd decided to turn her love for music into a career, everything had changed.

She decided to play an old game. She closed her eyes and tried to clear her mind. When a song appeared, she didn't question it or try to think of another one. She just started to play and sing the words.

Birds flying high you know how I feel
Sun in the sky you know how I feel

She finished the song, then sat quietly on the bench, just breathing. The knot in her stomach was gone, and her lungs were no longer tight. *Thank you, Nina Simone,* she thought. She felt exhilarated and relaxed, like she'd just dived into the Atlantic with Carina in the middle of summer and bodysurfed for an hour. How had she gone so long without playing her piano? No wonder she'd been feeling so anxious lately.

She closed the lid and went back to her desk. Her math notes were still spread all over the place. She'd done only four of the eight practice problems Miss Evanevski had given her, but she closed her textbook and got ready for bed. Hillary was right: She could survive one stupid quiz. She was sure of it.

*

"H, you okay?" Lizzie asked from beside her as she got out her protractor and graph paper. "You look like death."

"Yeah, I'm fine," Hudson said, taking out her pencils. She'd decided not to tell her friends about this latest life-coaching move from Hillary. "Just a little nervous."

She'd barely thought about the quiz as she sat through English and History. But as soon as she walked into Geometry, everything changed. All around her, people were studying — frantically. They sat bent over their books, working out problem sets, erasing and starting over. Hudson sat down, her heart pounding in her chest as if she were about to bungee jump without a cord. She'd been *crazy* not to study. And now she was going to pay the price.

"Hey, relax," Carina said, leaning past Lizzie. "You know this stuff. You're gonna be fine."

I would if I'd studied last night, she thought.

Miss Evanevski placed the tests on people's desks. "Okay, you can start," she announced to the room.

Hudson turned the test over. It was five problem sets. She scanned the pictures of circles and rays and shaded triangles and her mind went stubbornly blank. She was going to fail this quiz, and it was going to be long and drawn out and painful.

She worked through the first problem, the pencil slipping around between her sweaty fingers. Somehow she came up with an answer, but she had no idea if it was right. She moved on to the next one. Then the next one, and then the next, letting herself erase and start over only once for each question.

"Time!" Miss Evanevski called.

Breathless, Hudson looked up at the clock, sure that there was no way forty-five minutes had passed, but they had. People put down their pencils and protractors. Hudson looked down at her graph paper. It was covered with frantic scribbling. She was sure she'd failed.

"All right, hand them over," Miss Evanevski said, pacing through the room, collecting the quizzes. She smiled encouragingly at Hudson as she gestured for her quiz.

Hudson placed her paper in Miss Evanevski's carefully manicured hand. *There's no turning back*, she thought.

"That wasn't so bad," Carina said as they walked out of the classroom.

Hudson didn't say anything. She could imagine the big red F on her quiz already, throbbing like a cheap neon sign. But by the time she'd gotten to her locker, she felt oddly okay. The world hadn't ended. She was still basically herself. And whatever her grade ended up being, she knew that she would probably survive it.

A small note was sticking out of one of the air vents of her locker. She yanked it out and opened it.

You rule!

HC

"What's that?" Carina asked.

"Just a note from my life coach," Hudson said, stuffing the note in her bag.

"Is that stuff actually working?" asked Lizzie.

Hudson opened her locker. She felt anxious and exhausted from the Geometry test. But she also felt brave, and that was something she hadn't felt in a while.

"I think it actually might be," she said, and slammed her locker closed with a smile.

chapter 12

The next day in Geometry, Miss Evanevski passed out the corrected tests. "All in all, everyone did well," she said, placing Hudson's quiz facedown on her desk. "Though there were a few surprises."

Hudson turned over the quiz. In bright red marker, at the top, was her grade: 77. A C plus.

"Yes!" Hudson said out loud. She hadn't failed. It was a miracle.

Miss Evanevski gave her a quizzical look from across the room. Hudson immediately got rid of her smile.

"And let's go through it, shall we?" Miss Evanevski said, giving Hudson one last weird look.

"I got a C plus," Hudson confided to Hillary later that morning, in the library. "I didn't fail!"

"Told ya," Hillary said. "Congratulations on completing step two."

"So what's step three?" Hudson asked.

Hillary pulled two lipsticks out of her square backpack. "Before we get into that, which one do you think I should wear tomorrow?" she asked, uncapping them. "This one's Frisky Fuchsia and this one's Blushing Berry."

"Wait. Tomorrow?" Hudson asked cluelessly.

"The bar mitzvah!" Hillary said, slightly annoyed. "You're still coming, right? You have to tell me what Logan thinks."

"Oh, right," Hudson said, drumming her fingers on the library table. "Hillary, don't read too much into this, but my mom can be a little weird about me leaving the city," she said. "Especially with people she doesn't know."

"What about summer camp?" Hillary asked. "Haven't you ever been to camp?"

Hudson shook her head. "My mom says there are too many crazy people in the world. But she lets me go to my friend's house out in Montauk. That's about as close as I've gotten to camp."

"Well, no one's going to kidnap you at my cousin's bar mitzvah," Hillary snapped. "I promise. Just ask her."

"I'll try, Hillary," Hudson said, "but I can't promise anything."

"That's why you're doing all this stuff," Hillary said. "We're trying to help you become your own person, remember?"

That night, when she was finished with her homework, Hudson got up from her desk and sat down at her piano. Holla was still at the studio, recording with Chris. Just thinking about them together in the studio made Hudson feel weird, almost as if they were at a party she hadn't been invited to. She needed to distract herself. She closed her eyes and a song popped into her head — an old Fleetwood Mac song she'd always loved. Tentatively, she touched the keys, and then she started to sing.

For you, there'll be no more crying
For you, the sun will be shining

A knock on the door made her stop.

"Honey?" Holla called, opening the door a tiny bit. "Can I come in?" She stepped into the room lightly, with a dancer's grace. She looked impossibly sleek and thin in an off-the-shoulder electric green top, black denim leggings, and ankle boots, and her hair fell in soft waves to her shoulders. "Did you have dinner?"

"Yes," Hudson said.

"Finish your homework?"

"Uh-huh."

"Great." Holla headed to Hudson's walk-in closet. "You mind if I borrow something?"

"Go ahead," Hudson said. She needed to ask Holla about the bar mitzvah, so it could only help to let her mom peruse her wardrobe. "How was your day?"

"Long. And that new guy from the record label has to second-guess everything. As if I've never done this before." Holla walked out holding a hanger. "What about this?"

Hudson stared at the orange sherbet–colored cotton shift dress. It was from the line Tocca had put out in the mid-nineties. But Hudson had worn it only twice because it was so short. "Um, that's a summer dress," she said.

"I'm wearing it inside," Holla said casually, folding it over her arm. "And how are you doing, sweetie? How's school?"

"Okay."

"How's Geometry?"

Hudson took a deep breath. "It's fine, Mom." She didn't want to tell her about the C plus.

Holla glanced at Hudson's piano. "What are you doing?"

"Just playing a little."

"Well, keep going," she said, perching on the arm of Hudson's battered leather armchair and crossing her legs. "You know how much I love your voice."

"That's okay," Hudson said. "My voice is kind of weird tonight."

"No, go ahead," Holla urged. "I want to hear. I think it's great you're playing again."

Hudson knew exactly what would happen if she started to sing, but there didn't seem to be any way out of it. "Okay."

She found the opening chords and started playing.

For you, there'll be no more crying
For you —

"Honey, *fuller,*" Holla cut in. "Don't rush it. Fill out the word. *Youuuuuuu.*"

Hudson stopped playing and swung the lid closed over the keys.

"What?" Holla asked. "What happened?"

"Nothing," she said.

Holla frowned. "I just want you to get the most out of practicing. And correct phrasing is very important. Why do you have to be so sensitive? Don't you think I know a little bit about this?"

"My friend wants me to go to a bar mitzvah tomorrow," Hudson said, changing the subject. "Can I go? It's in Westchester."

"Westchester?" Holla asked, wrinkling her nose as if she'd just smelled something bad. "Where in Westchester?"

"Larchmont, I think."

Holla shook her head as if this were utterly ridiculous. "What friend is this?"

"Her name's Hillary Crumple," Hudson said. "I kind of owe her a favor. Fernald can take me in the car, and I'll be back by five."
And I promise, nobody's going to kidnap me, she wanted to add.

"I'll have Little Jimmy go with you," Holla said. "I don't need him at the studio."

"I don't need a bodyguard to go to a bar mitzvah."

Holla walked to the door and paused with her hand on the knob. "Fine, Hudson," she said. "You can go, but Fernald will take you there and bring you home. And there's something I'd like you to do for me."

"What?"

Holla shifted the dress on her arm. "I'd like you to check in on your aunt. Maybe spend the day with her on Sunday? I know she's finally back from Paris. For good this time," she added. "And I'm worried about her."

"So why don't you just go over there and see her?" Hudson asked. "I'm sure she'd love it."

"No, she wouldn't," Holla said, in a way that implied she'd given all of this a great deal of thought.

"I'm sure she's sorry about Christmas. You should just call her."

Holla shook her head. "Will you just do me that favor, please?" She walked over to Hudson and kissed the top of her head. "You're my partner in crime. You know that."

"Holla? Where'd you go?"

The voice calling from outside Hudson's bedroom door was unmistakably familiar. And unmistakably male.

"Are you up here? Where'd you go?"

Hudson's pulse raced. It was Chris.

Holla went to the door and opened it a crack. "I'll be down in a second," she said.

"Chris is here?" Hudson asked.

"Oh, we're just going to do some more work," Holla said matter-of-factly. "We'll be up in the office if you need us."

"Mom?"

"Yes?" From the way her face was glowing Hudson could tell that her mom had already fallen in love. "What, honey?" she asked. "What is it? You look so worried."

"Nothing," Hudson said. "I'm fine."

"Thanks for the dress," Holla said, and then she was gone.

chapter 13

"Okay, there he is," Hillary said, smoothing the front of her velvet dress and smacking her fuchsia-painted lips. "He's over there, checking out the dessert table."

Hudson looked across the spacious pink and blue–lit banquet hall, past the tables dressed with kelly green tablecloths and imitation roulette wheel centerpieces, and past the band onstage grinding out a cover of "Hey Ya!" For most of the ceremony, which had taken place at a synagogue a mile away, and then for most of the delicious meal they'd just eaten, Hudson had been waiting to spring into action as Hillary's wingwoman, on alert for Logan the Mysterious. But Hillary had refused to point him out. Whenever Hudson asked, Hillary would whisper, "You can't look now. He's right *there*."

But now Hudson could see two boys checking out the dessert buffet. One was tall and skinny, with a mop of curly brown hair and a dark blue suit that seemed a little short at the ankles. He kept trying to shake a sliver of chocolate frosting off the cake knife, but he wasn't having much luck. The boy next to him was shorter and stockier, with whitish blond hair. He was heaping his plate with everything on the table — brownies, cookies, and slices of three different cakes. "Which one is he?" Hudson asked.

"The cute one!" Hillary said.

"They've got their backs turned."

"The blond one!" Hillary exclaimed. "The other one's my cousin Ben. You met him at the synagogue."

"Oh, right," Hudson said, vaguely remembering Ben in the lineup of Hillary's extended family.

"Okay, I'm gonna go talk to him. How's my hair?"

Hudson looked at Hillary, who was still patting her hair and her dress. She looked good. Someone had mercifully whisked all of Hillary's flyaway hair into a neat, chic bun at the top of her head, and the black velvet dress looked perfect on her, even though she'd chosen to wear a strand of big white pearls with it. "You look great," Hudson said. "Go get 'im."

"Uh-uh, I'm not going alone," Hillary said, grabbing Hudson's hand. "Let's go."

As the two of them marched across the banquet room, Hudson tried not to be embarrassed. She never liked approaching guys. That was Carina's thing. Hudson's thing was to wistfully stare at them and wonder about them and look up their astrological signs. But never guys her age. To her, it was hard to get excited about a guy who was just doing homework every night.

The boys turned around and watched them approach. The tall, skinny boy — Hillary's cousin — smiled and waved at them with his fork. He looked shy and a little bit awkward, as if he were still getting used to being so tall. His blond, stocky friend didn't smile at them or wave at all. He was definitely cute, and he knew it. He had narrow, smoldering eyes, and he stared at Hudson in a familiar, unblinking way that she had seen before. *Uh-oh,* she thought, her heart sinking. *He likes me.*

"Hey, nerd," Hillary said to the tall, skinny boy, carefully ignoring his friend. "What are you guys doing?"

"Just having some cake," Ben said, just as a glob of it fell off his fork and onto the floor.

"This is my friend Hudson," Hillary said. "You guys already met."

"Hi," Hudson said.

"Oh, uh, hi there," Ben said, momentarily distracted by the cake on the carpet but smiling at her anyway.

"So...are you gonna go up there and jump on the bass?" Hillary said, pointing to the stage. "Ben's starting a jazz band," she explained to Hudson. "He's really good."

"Not really," Ben said shyly, waving off Hillary's compliment.

"This is my friend Hudson," Hillary said to the other boy. "This is Logan."

"Hey," Logan said, taking a bite of brownie with studied mellowness.

"Hi," Hudson replied, careful not to meet his gaze for too long.

"Are you guys looking for a singer?" Hillary blurted.

"We haven't started yet," Ben said, looking at Logan. "We're still trying to figure out what kind of jazz band we're going to be. It might just be drums, bass, and sax."

"Well, Hudson sings," Hillary said. "And plays piano. She almost did her own al —"

Before Hillary could say *album* Hudson clamped her hand around Hillary's arm. "I just sing a little," she said, shooting Hillary a quick warning glance.

"Yeah?" Ben asked. "What sort of stuff do you sing?"

Hudson smiled. "A lot of stuff," she said. "Mostly my own songs."

"She has an amazing voice," Hillary said. "You should *totally* audition her for your band. You don't want to do that awful coffee-shop jazz. That stuff is just noise. Ugh."

Just then the lead singer's voice rang out over the sound system. "All right, people! It's that time we've all been waiting for — when you get up here and show us what *you* got!"

They all looked to the center of the room. The rest of the band had cleared off the stage, and a projection screen was being lowered from the ceiling. As the lights dimmed, Hudson realized what was happening. It was karaoke time.

"Okay, who wants to go first?" the lead singer yelled again with an almost diabolical smile. "Come up here and pick out a tune! And then be the star of your very own music video!"

On the dance floor, kids milled around, wondering who would be the first to go.

"Perfect timing," Hillary said to Hudson. "Go up there and show everyone what I'm talking about!"

"*What?*" Hudson asked, clamping down on Hillary's arm even tighter. "You're joking, right?"

"I'm dead serious," Hillary said. "We were just talking about your great voice."

"Um, can I speak to you for a second?" Hudson asked, yanking Hillary aside.

"So what you do think? Is he into me?" Hillary asked as soon as they were alone. "I could feel him looking at me. You know, when I talked."

"I really don't know," Hudson fibbed. "I'd have to see you guys together more. But what are you doing? Why are you trying to make me sing?"

"Because this is the perfect step three," Hillary said. "Singing in public. This is your biggest fear. You can tackle it right now!"

"I'm not tackling any fears today," Hudson said, trying not to snap. "I came here to be your wingwoman."

"And I hate to criticize, but you could be just a little more talkative around Logan," Hillary said. "I can't do all the work."

Hudson took a deep breath. "Well, I really don't want you to mention the album to people."

"Fine, but those guys wouldn't know your mom if she fell on them. They're total nerds. The only TV they watch is the Discovery Channel."

"And I'm not singing here. No way."

"It's karaoke!" Hillary said, loud enough that Ben looked over at them. "Nobody expects anyone to be good."

Hudson met Ben's eye and he politely looked away. The group of seventh-graders had started edging closer to the stage. Hillary's cousin Josh, the boy being bar mitzvahed, was being pushed to the front of the dance floor. Hillary was right: How serious could this be? "I'll do it if you do it," she dared.

Hillary snorted. "Of *course* I'm doing it," she said. "Watch me."

With that she yanked her arm free and charged through the crowd. "I'll go!" she yelled. "I'll go!" Hillary almost knocked her own cousin down as she ran up to the stage.

"We have our first performer, everyone!" the lead singer shouted with glee into the mic. "What's your name?" He tipped the mic to Hillary.

Hillary grabbed the mic. "Hillary Victoria Crumple," she said, matter-of-factly. "Just start the first song. I'll sing anything."

Hudson watched with amazement as Hillary positioned herself in the center of the bright white spotlight. Hudson hadn't seen this kind of confidence and flair since the last time she'd seen Holla in concert.

"This is dedicated to my cousin Josh!" Hillary shouted into the mic. "And my friend Hudson!" A moment later a familiar beat started to play.

"Oh, God, no," Hudson said under her breath. She knew what the song was, and it was the worst song Hillary could have picked. And when Hillary began to chant into the mic in a wobbly, screechy voice, Hudson's blood ran cold.

I wanna hold 'em like they do in Texas plays
Fold 'em let 'em hit me raise it baby stay with me

She snuck a look at Ben and Logan, who didn't move. The kids on the dance floor seemed shocked speechless. But that wouldn't last. Pretty soon they were going to be snickering, if not all-out laughing. *I have to save her,* Hudson thought. *Before she makes a worse spectacle of herself than I did at the Silver Snowflake Ball.*

She began to push through the crowd. A few boys had already started to laugh. Finally she made it up to the stage, just in time to join Hillary for the chorus. Hudson threw her arm around Hillary and kept singing. All she was thinking about was trying to drown out Hillary's voice, or at least trying to make it sound like it was on-key. She didn't dare look down.

Until, toward the end of the song, she finally did, and saw that everyone was dancing. A middle-aged man with a paunch — somebody's dad — stood beside his chair, clapping his hands over his head. An elderly woman with wispy white hair did the twist on the dance floor. Even Ben's brother and his friends had stopped snickering and were jumping up and down in time with the beat.

Hudson looked over at Hillary, who was grinning, as if to say, *Isn't this great?*

When the song was finally over, the lead singer pounced on them with the mic. "That was fan-TAS-tic! What's your name?" he asked, tipping the mic toward Hudson.

"Hudson," she said, still out of breath.

"Let's hear it for Hudson and Hillary, everyone!" he cried.

Everyone clapped, hooted, and hollered. Hudson linked arms with Hillary and, grinning crazily, they both took a bow.

"That was amazing!" Hillary said as soon as they'd jumped down from the stage. "We totally killed!"

Hudson felt someone tap her on her shoulder. She turned around to see Ben staring at her with a radiant, awestruck smile. "Hillary was right," he said. "About your voice."

"Thanks."

"I hate it when she's right," he joked.

"Me, too," she joked back.

He ran a hand through his unruly hair. "So...this might be kind of sudden, but...would you be into being our lead singer?"

Hudson blinked. *Yes*, a voice inside her said. *Say yes.* "I'd love to," she said.

"Cool. Just come over tomorrow for rehearsal. Around two." He looked at Hillary. "I bet Hillary will want me to pay her a commission or something."

Hillary sidled up beside them. "What's going on?" Hillary asked.

"Hudson's gonna be our lead singer," said Ben. "Turns out you've got an eye for talent, Hil."

"Um, *obvi*," Hillary said.

Ben glanced at the stage, where his brother was trying to sing an Eminem song. "I think I better get over there. Before the girl he likes never speaks to him again."

As he gave them an awkward wave and headed back toward the stage, Hillary started jumping up and down. "God, I love it when I'm right about stuff!" she shrieked. "You're going to be their lead singer!"

"But I can't do this," Hudson said, suddenly panicked. "I don't even live up here. How am I going to be the lead singer of a jazz band? Here? When my mom will barely even let me off the block?"

Hillary shook her head. "Don't you get it? This is just what you need! A second chance to do what you really want to do. And your mom has nothing to do with it!"

Hudson watched Ben onstage, backing up his brother on the Eminem song. The two of them looked so goofy that she had to

121

smile. Singing up there had been fun, and now she had a feeling that being in a simple high school band might be even *more* fun. She wouldn't have to worry about concerts or clothes or *Saturday Night Live* appearances. Music would be fun again. And wasn't that what all this was about — fun?

Still, there was one last thing she had to do. She dashed back to her table, fished her phone out of her bag, and wrote a quick text.

Just got asked 2 b the lead singer of a bnd. Up in Larch-mont. Yay or nay?

The answers came back right away, first from Lizzie, and then from Carina:

YAY!!!

With a smile spreading across her face, Hudson put the phone away and walked back to Hillary, who was at the dessert table, piling her plate with cookies. She was sure now. This was fate.

"I'm in," Hudson said to her. "As long as you don't tell Ben anything. You know, about my mom."

Hillary looked up. "No way," she said. "And you better thank me when you win your first Grammy."

chapter 14

The next morning Hudson sat bolt upright in bed and rubbed her eyes. She'd told Ben that she would be back up in Larchmont by two o'clock for rehearsal. But she'd also promised her mom that she'd see Aunt Jenny today. *Oops*, she thought. And it was already nine o'clock.

She grabbed her iPhone and texted her aunt.

Brunch at 11?

A moment later, Jenny wrote back:

Come over. 421 E. 76th Street.

Phew, Hudson thought. She would just be able to pull this off.

She showered and dressed in what she called her Seventies Urban Princess outfit: slim-fitting gray wool pants, an oversized cashmere cowl-neck sweater, and vintage platform boots. She drew back her curtains and looked out at the cloudless blue sky. The sidewalks were deserted — even the patch of sidewalk across from their house was empty of photographers. It had to be freezing outside. Hudson ran back to her closet and grabbed the thick black cape she'd picked up in Covent Garden during her mom's last tour and pinned it at her throat. Hopefully this wouldn't be too over-the-top for Larchmont.

When she opened her bedroom door she was surprised to find a big shopping bag waiting for her. There was a note pinned to the handles:

Honey plz bring this for Jenny. I thought she'd like it.
Mom

Hudson reached into the bag and pulled out the present: a thick white throw blanket, wrapped in red ribbon. It was exactly like the one they had in their living room. Hopefully Jenny wouldn't remember. Her mom meant well, but sometimes she could be a little dense. Hudson stuffed it back in the bag.

Soon she and Fernald were driving uptown. The few people out on the streets were bundled up with scarves wrapped over their mouths and noses and walked, heads bent, into the wind. Hillary had decided to spend the night in Larchmont after the bar mitz-vah, so Hudson would be going up herself. Which meant that she'd be taking the train alone.

At Jenny's building, Hudson hopped out of the car with the shopping bag and the wind hit her face like a bunch of knives. "I'll text you in a bit!" she yelled to Fernald, her eyes watering from the cold.

He waved back to her, trusting as usual. Hudson felt a stab of guilt when she thought about her plan to elude him later — she'd need to get rid of him before she left for the train — but she pushed it aside.

Standing outside and shivering she pulled out her phone and called Carina.

"What are you doing today?"

"Staying the hell indoors," she replied. "It's like five below out."

"Can you come with me to Larchmont for my first band rehearsal?"

"*Larchmont?*" There was a long pause. Hudson could practically see Carina biting her lip, trying not to say no. "Sure," Carina finally said. "Just tell me where and when."

"Grand Central, one o'clock. Let's meet under the clock. We're taking the train."

Then she called Lizzie, who signed on right away. "As long as we're back by five," Lizzie said. "I'm trying to finish a story tonight."

"No problem." Hudson clicked off and went to Jenny's door. Thank God for her friends.

Jenny's building had no doorman, only a buzzer. Hudson rang the bell and a few seconds later the front door unlocked with a loud buzz. She pushed her way into a dingy, dim vestibule, then walked through another set of doors. There was no elevator, only a set of stairs. From above she heard a door open. "I'm up here!" Jenny's voice called. "Fourth floor!"

Hudson climbed the stairs, and when she turned the corner,

slightly out of breath — her platform boots didn't make it easy — Jenny was waiting for her at the door. "Hey, stranger!" she said, beckoning Hudson inside. "Come in and warm up!"

Jenny was more casual today in hole-ridden jeans, a faded red T-shirt, and a fuzzy Mr. Rogers–esque cardigan in a pale shade of yellowish brown. Hudson gave her a hug, and then walked inside. Her apartment was small, just one room, but, like Hudson's room, it was stuffed with eclectic pieces: a small chandelier suspended over a blond wood farm table and chairs, a Tiffany lamp on a skinny-legged end table, a beautiful red and purple dhurrie rug that stretched across the floor. But the two windows faced a brick wall, and it was so dark inside the apartment that it could have been nighttime.

"I haven't had a lot of time to finish decorating," Jenny said. "I've been so busy."

"That's okay," Hudson said, looking around. "It actually looks really cool in here."

"Do you want some tea?" Jenny asked. "I got the most amazing Earl Grey tea from this little tea shop in the Marais. And there's a French bakery around the corner from here that makes semi-decent croissants." Jenny put the kettle on to boil, then put the croissants on a plate and carried them to the table. "What's that?" she asked, pointing to the shopping bag.

"It's for you. From my mom."

Jenny gave Hudson a suspicious look. "What is it?"

"A housewarming gift," Hudson said, giving it to her.

Jenny reached into the bag and pulled out the throw blanket, letting it fall to its full length. "Isn't this the one you guys have in your living room?"

"Yes," Hudson said awkwardly. "I guess she thought you'd like it."

Jenny carefully spread the blanket over the back of her shabby chic–style couch. "Well, this time, I have to hand it to her. It's beautiful. Tell her I said thank you."

"I think she feels bad about Christmas," Hudson offered.

"So do I," Jenny said. The kettle began to whistle, so she slipped into the tiny kitchen and turned off the gas. "Every time I tell myself not to lose it, but she's just impossible to be around sometimes. You were there. You saw it." She poured the water into two mugs. "She just does that to me."

And me, too, Hudson thought. "I think she just worries about you."

"I know, but I like my life. I'm happy," she said, bringing the mugs of tea to the table.

"I think she just feels that you're a little..." Hudson let her voice trail off, aware that she was on dangerous ground.

"Lost?" Jenny said with a smile. "Look, I know I don't have Holla's discipline. Hardly anyone does. But I think I do okay." They sat down and Jenny stirred her tea, lost in thought. "She always wanted to be famous. That was always her thing. Did I ever tell you that?"

Hudson shook her head.

"She'd even talk about herself in the third person. She'd interview herself, pretend she was on Barbara Walters or something."

Jenny smiled as dunked her tea bag in and out of the mug. "I remember the day she won her first talent show. I was six, she was eleven. She sang and danced to some Madonna song. She was even better than Madonna."

"I'm sure," Hudson said, picking at her croissant.

"And I just wasn't like that," Jenny added. "I didn't need to be famous. I liked to dance. I was good at it. But when I blew my audition for the Martha Graham Company —"

"What? You blew an audition?" Hudson asked.

"Yep," Jenny said, taking a careful sip. "Just froze up. Forgot my routine. I practiced for weeks, and then when the time came I just stood there like an idiot, while a whole tableful of people stared at me."

"Why'd you freeze up?" Hudson pressed, clutching her mug.

"I'm not sure," Jenny said wistfully. "I was so self-conscious. At that point Holla was huge. She'd already won her first Grammy. She'd just had you. And there I was, trying to make it as a dancer. It was a lot of pressure."

Hudson stirred her tea, listening.

"When Holla heard what had happened, she called the company and talked them into giving me another chance."

"She did?" Hudson asked.

"I said no," Jenny said, looking down into her mug.

"Why?"

"Because I don't think I really wanted it. And I knew that no matter what, I would always be compared to her. How are you just a dancer when your older sister's insanely famous? You know what I mean?"

Hudson nodded. She knew exactly what Jenny meant, but she didn't want to say anything.

"The same thing happened with your father," Jenny said.

"My father?" Hudson asked, her curiosity piqued.

Jenny looked guilty. "I suppose you haven't heard a lot about what really happened with him," she said. "But I don't think he could handle it, either. Your mom's fame. Always being linked to someone like that. And your mom isn't exactly easy to deal with, either. But that's another story."

Hudson put down her mug. "Do you know where he is?" she asked, looking down at the table, trying to sound casual.

Jenny shook her head. "I heard he was in Europe for a little while, but now, I don't know. He was the type of guy who liked to stay under the radar."

Hudson let this sink in. She wondered if Jenny had ever seen him.

"But saying no to that audition was the best decision I ever made."

"But you loved dancing," Hudson argued.

Jenny gave Hudson a gentle smile. "I love a lot of different stuff. I'm an air sign. And you, my dear, are all water. Very creative, very sensitive."

"Yeah, so far it's been great," Hudson said wryly.

"Well, don't be surprised if you end up more famous than your mom. I told you it's in your chart, right?"

Hudson smiled weakly. "Too bad I pulled the album."

"What?" Jenny asked. "What happened?"

"The same thing that happened to you. Right before Christmas, I was supposed to sing at this big dance, and I froze up. Right there onstage. In front of three hundred people."

"Was your mom there?"

Hudson nodded.

"What'd she do?" Jenny asked, slightly horrified.

"Told everyone I had food poisoning—what do you think?" Hudson said, with an ironic smile. "But before it happened, she was driving me crazy. I was doing *this* wrong, I was doing *that* wrong. I needed to learn all these dance moves, and sing to this track. And before that she made my producer change my entire sound. To hers."

Jenny listened with a somber look on her face.

"So I just decided, forget it. It's not worth it. No matter what I do, it'll never be right for her. She wants me to *be* her."

Jenny put her hand on Hudson's wrist. "You can be whatever you want, Hudson." Her brown eyes were soft but also battle-scarred, as if she were a fellow survivor of something.

"But I've been thinking…what if I just joined a regular high school band? No record deal. No concert dates. No promotion. Just playing a couple shows here and there and jamming. Just for fun?"

Jenny raised one eyebrow. She seemed to sense that this wasn't exactly hypothetical. "I'd say it sounded great," she said. "Not everything has to be so serious, you know. You're allowed to have fun in your life."

Hudson glanced at her watch. It was almost twelve thirty. She needed to go meet her friends at Grand Central. "I have to go. I told my friends I'd meet them."

Jenny smiled knowingly. "Your friends, or your band?"

Hudson smiled back. "You should come over to the house sometime. My mom really does feel bad. She loves you. She really does."

Jenny rolled her eyes. "Sometimes I think we're just not meant to be friends."

"Maybe we can throw a little birthday party for you next month," Hudson said, undeterred. "Your birthday's February seventeenth...what about that Saturday night? The twenty-first?"

"Whoa," Jenny said, holding up her hand. "Are you sure that's a good idea?"

"Of course," Hudson said, getting to her feet. "I'm sure she'd want to do it."

"We'll see," Jenny said, hugging her niece good-bye. "I'm always here for you, you know. And it looks like I'm actually staying here for a while. So come hang out with your crazy aunt."

"I will," Hudson said as she left.

Downstairs, in the dim vestibule, Hudson remembered what she had to do. She called Fernald.

"Hey, Fernald, I think I'm gonna be staying here awhile," she said lightly. "Jenny'll drop me home in a cab." Her heart raced with the lie.

"Sure thing, Hudson," he said, before she clicked off.

She had no idea how she was going to do this every time she had rehearsal, but she told herself she'd worry about that later.

chapter 15

"If my dad could see me right now he'd freak," Carina said, settling into her seat across from Hudson and pulling a warm chocolate-chip cookie from a brown Zaro's bag. "But this definitely beats reading *Macbeth* all day."

"When was the last time we were on a train together?" Lizzie said, taking her battered copy of *Nine Stories* out of her purse.

"Sixth-grade field trip to D.C.," Hudson said. "Remember when Eli threw up in the club car?"

They burst out laughing as a bell sounded and the doors shut. They'd chosen a group of four seats that faced one another in the back of the train, and Carina propped her Chuck Taylors up on the cracked Naugahyde seat next to Hudson.

"Yeah, I remember," Carina said. "Some of it got on my foot."

"Ugh!" Lizzie yelled.

The train lurched forward, and soon they were rolling along

through a dark tunnel. Hudson still couldn't believe what they were doing, but being with her friends made her less anxious.

"Thanks so much for coming with me, you guys," Hudson said. "Who knew that doing karaoke at a bar mitzvah could be so eventful?"

"What'd you sing?" Lizzie asked, putting her book away.

"'Poker Face,'" Hudson said. "But it was a duet. With Hillary."

Carina crumpled the brown bag. "*Hillary?*" she asked. "Your stalker Hillary?"

"She's not my stalker," Hudson said.

"Are you guys becoming friends now?" Lizzie asked warily, looking over the top of her book.

"She asked me to go and I went," Hudson said. "She's a little weird, but she's actually really cool."

"No one with that kind of backpack can be cool," Carina said.

"Be nice, C," Lizzie said, nudging her in the arm.

Suddenly the train shot out of the tunnel and into sunlight. Hudson looked out through the smudged window. They were on a track above Park Avenue, passing through Harlem. The cloudless sky glowed a deep cornflower blue, and sun glinted off the windshields of parked cars below. She'd never seen the city from this angle before.

"Wait," Lizzie said, pulling one unruly curl behind her ear. A moment later, it sprang back again. "Do the guys in the band know about your mom?"

"It never came up. And as long as they don't ask, I'm not telling them."

"But don't you think they'll find out?" Carina asked. "You're in the tabloids, like, once a month."

"These guys don't read *US Weekly*," Hudson said. "They're into jazz and the Discovery Channel."

"But you don't have to be looking for info," Carina said. "All they have to do is see a photo of you somewhere —"

"And then I'll tell them," Hudson interrupted. "It's not the end of the world if they find out. But right now, it feels good to just be... nobody."

"And you're definitely not telling your mom," Lizzie prompted.

"No." Hudson played with her cowl-neck collar. "She'd never understand why I'd choose a high school band in the suburbs over Madison Square Garden."

"Is this guy at least cute?" Carina asked. "What does he look like?"

"Curly hair. Tall. Skinny. He's really nice."

"Sounds like a dork."

"He's not a dork," Hudson said.

"And there's nothing wrong with a dork," Lizzie said. "Todd's kind of a dork."

"Todd is definitely *not* a dork," Hudson replied. "And how's Alex?"

"Oh, I found out his birthday," Carina said. "It's September twenty-fourth."

"A Libra," Hudson said approvingly. "That's just what we want. His air balances out your fire."

"I wish you could figure out if he's compatible with my dad," said Carina. "Alex is supposed to come over for dinner next week.

And something tells me they're not gonna bond over music and subtitled movies."

"Don't even expect it to go well," Lizzie put in. "Todd's polite, he's a writer, he calls people 'sir,' and my dad still doesn't know his name. He calls him Brad. It's like he's mentally blocked him out or something."

"It's so funny; I think my mom would love for me to go out with someone," Hudson said, yawning. "That way she could tell me how to do that, too."

Lizzie and Carina laughed.

As they crossed the bridge into the Bronx, Hudson felt herself start to get drowsy from the gentle rocking of the train. A short time later, Hudson felt Lizzie's foot nudge her leg. She opened her eyes to see bare trees and power lines and a church steeple whizzing past the window. "I think we're the next stop," Lizzie said, as Carina rubbed her eyes.

The train began to slow down, and they passed a white sign that said LARCHMONT in big black letters. A few moments later they screeched to a stop. "Let's go," Hudson said, getting to her feet. The doors opened and they stepped out onto the platform as a gust of wind seeped in underneath her cape. "Hillary gave me directions. She said it's a quick walk."

"Uh, no," Carina said, heading for the line of black cabs waiting by the platform. "This may be the suburbs, but we're still taking a cab."

They got into a cab, gave the driver the address, and pulled out of the train station parking lot. Soon they turned onto a picturesque main street with an old-fashioned movie theater and a barbershop.

"This place is so cute," Hudson said. "Can you imagine living up here?"

"It's too quiet," Carina said bluntly.

"Our lives would be so different," Lizzie said. "We'd have to learn how to drive. And go to a school with a football team. And there would be cheerleaders."

"Cheerleaders," Hudson said, trying to picture it. "Do you ever think that we're gonna end up total weirdos, growing up in the city? Not driving, not going to football games and stuff like that?"

"I think if we end up total weirdos, it's gonna be for other reasons," Lizzie said.

They turned off the main street onto a rural road. "So I hope this isn't Silver Snowflake Ball, the Sequel," said Hudson.

"But do you know if this band is any good?" Lizzie asked. "You're so talented, H. It'd be good to know if they're up to your standards."

"You sound a little like my mom," Hudson said.

"No, seriously," Carina said. "How do we know that these guys even know how to play music?"

"Well, I guess we'll find out," Hudson said.

They passed several three-story homes, Victorians mostly, until they turned into a gravel drive. The half-melted remains of a snowman stood frozen on the front lawn. Beyond it was a Victorian shingle house. It looked old and friendly. A gray Ford Windstar was parked in the driveway. A few bikes lay on their sides in the snow.

They paid the driver and walked up the steps to the house. "Can you imagine having a front lawn?" Carina asked in a whisper as Hudson rang the doorbell.

"You have, like, three of them," Lizzie said.

"I mean, *all* the time," Carina said.

Hillary opened the front door. She wore jeans and a surprisingly muted navy blue sweater. It was the first time Hudson had ever seen Hillary in pants. And in a sweater that wasn't a blindingly bright color.

"Oh, hey," Hillary said, blinking her yellow-green eyes. "I didn't know you all were coming."

"I asked them to come for moral support," Hudson said. "You know Lizzie and Carina. You guys remember Hillary."

As they stepped into the house there were murmured greetings.

"Everyone's downstairs in the basement," Hillary said, leading them past a bench covered in coats and scarves and mittens. Hudson heard the whirring, tumbling sound of a dryer in the distance and, upstairs, the muffled blare of a TV. Hillary pulled Hudson aside. "Logan and I have been talking this *whole* time," she whispered excitedly into her ear.

"That's great!" Hudson said encouragingly.

"I really feel like he's *this* close to asking me out," Hillary said excitedly. "Should I have a date planned or should I leave it up to him?"

"I think we should just leave it up to him," Hudson said. "And by the way, you look really nice."

"Thanks. Do you guys want something to eat?" Hillary asked her friends in a louder voice.

"Sure," Carina said, going straight to the fridge and opening it. "Are these enchiladas?" she asked, taking a Tupperware container from the fridge. "Score."

"C, put that back," Lizzie said.

"No, she can have some," said a voice, and Hudson turned to see Ben walk into the kitchen. At first Hudson barely recognized him. He looked so different than he had the day before. Then Hudson realized that he was wearing clothes that fit: dark jeans, a black T-shirt that read STOP THE ROBOTS, and a pair of wire-rimmed glasses that were a little too square-shaped to be cool. "Hey, Hudson," he said shyly. "Nice...cape."

"Hey, Ben," Hudson said. "These are my friends Carina and Lizzie. They came with me for...well, because they'd never seen Larchmont." She quickly unpinned her cape and took it off.

"Oh, hey," Ben said, awkwardly shaking their hands. "Nice to meet you."

Hudson watched Carina and Lizzie size him up. Lizzie was always polite, but sometimes Carina could take her time. "Nice to meet you, too," Lizzie said.

"You sure I can eat these?" Carina asked, popping the lid off the Tupperware.

"Oh, sure. My mom would be flattered. Does anyone want something to drink?" he asked.

"Water would be great," Hudson said. She tried to imagine her mom making enchiladas — at least, with real cheese. It was impossible.

"So, lemme ask you something, Ben," Carina said, folding her arms and walking away from the Tupperware. "What *exactly* are your plans for this band?" She sounded just like she had the day they'd barged into Andrea Sidwell's photo studio to find out about Lizzie's modeling opportunities.

"My friends are a little protective," Hudson explained.

"No, I get it," Ben said, going straight to the sink to get Hudson a glass of water. "I saw you sing. You don't want to be around a bunch of deadweights." He grinned and pushed his glasses up the bridge of his nose. "Well, we're definitely not deadweights."

"No, it's not that," Hudson said, feeling the heat in her face.

"I think, Marina —"

"It's *Ca* -rina," Carina interrupted.

"Carina, I love jazz," he said. "Are you into jazz?"

"Uh, no," Carina said decisively. "But Hudson here is. Actually, she's got her own unique style. It's like a cross between Nina..." Carina turned to Hudson. "Nina, *who*?"

"Nina Simone," Hudson said. "Nina Simone and Abbey Lincoln. And a little bit of Julie London."

"And Lady Gaga," Ben said with a smile. "Let's go down to the basement. That's where we're all set up. And you can see for yourself if we're up to your standards." As he made his way out of the kitchen he stumbled on a broom handle but caught himself.

Hudson saw Carina almost giggle. "Be nice," she whispered.

"I am!" Carina whispered back.

Hillary tagged along. "Logan looks really cute today," she whispered to Hudson. "And we talked for, like, three whole minutes."

"Then I'm sure he's really into you, Hil," Hudson said.

Hillary wrinkled her nose. "You sure I look okay? Do you think I look too boring?" she asked, yanking on her sweater.

"I think you look perfect," Hudson said, making Hillary beam. "Very agnès b."

"Who's agnès b.?" Hillary asked.

139

"Oh, just...no one," Hudson said, knowing that Hillary probably wouldn't have heard of the super-influential French designer from the eighties. "So, have you guys picked a name?" Hudson asked Ben as she followed him down a back hallway.

"Right now we're the Stone Cold Freaks," Ben said. "But that's just temporary."

Thank God, Hudson thought. Hudson and Carina and Lizzie all flashed looks at one another.

"And I have to tell you, the other guys aren't *mad*," he said, looking over his shoulder, "but they're a little weirded out. They knew we needed someone on piano, but they didn't know we were gonna have a lead singer. I spoke a little too soon."

Hudson cast a worried look at her friends.

"But don't worry. Let's just play one of your songs," he said, pushing up his glasses again. "And if it's as good as Hillary says, then great."

"No problem," she said cheerfully. So this was going to be more like an audition after all. In that case, she was extra glad she'd brought her friends.

Then Ben opened the door to the basement stairs, and she heard the music. Or at least what sounded like music. Someone was pounding mercilessly on the drums while a saxophone whined and warbled over the beat. Hudson knew that this was supposed to be the kind of hectic, free-form "coffee-shop jazz" that Hillary had referred to at the bar mitzvah. But this wasn't even that. This was just noise.

"Yikes," Lizzie said under her breath.

"Oh, God," Carina whispered. "It's *this* kind of jazz?"

"Just hold on, you guys," Hudson said as they walked down the stairs behind Ben. But she felt something inside her deflate and sink to the ground. The Stone Cold Freaks definitely weren't the studio band she'd used to record her album.

They reached the bottom of the stairs and walked into the basement, which had been converted into an old-fashioned rec room. There was a Ping-Pong table, a refrigerator, an upright piano, and a brown and pink plaid sofa that faced an old-fashioned wall-unit TV. Brown acoustic paneling covered the walls. And in the corner were the other Stone Cold Freaks — Logan sitting in a plastic folding chair, playing his sax, and behind him a freckled boy with bright red hair pounding his drum kit. Hudson almost had to plug her ears.

"Hey guys, Hudson's here," Ben said, waving at the two of them to stop. "Hudson, you know Logan. And this is Gordie," he said, waving to the redheaded guy on drums. "These are Hudson's friends Marina and —"

"Lizzie," Lizzie said.

"And it's *Ca*-rina," Carina said.

"Hi, guys," Hudson said, waving.

Ben turned to face her. "Wait. What'd you say your last name was?"

Hudson thought fast. Jones couldn't be a more common last name, and from what Hillary had said about Ben and his friends, they probably wouldn't make the Holla connection if she just told the truth. "Jones," she said.

"Hudson Jones," Ben said, oblivious. "So, guys, Hudson writes her own stuff. Right, Hudson?"

"I do," she said, feeling her heart start to race. What if they didn't like her music? She noticed Logan looking at her with a very different expression than yesterday; he seemed to be scowling.

Ben pointed to the upright piano. "Go ahead," he said. "Do one of your songs and we'll join in."

Hudson glanced at her friends. This was definitely an audition. Carina gave her a small thumbs-up as she sat down on the couch. Lizzie winked at her. "Okay," Hudson said, swallowing.

I can do this, she thought as she sat down on the creaky old piano bench. She touched one of the keys. The piano was horribly out of tune.

"Whenever you're ready," Ben said. "Just go for it."

Hudson looked down at the keys. Her heart was beating in her chest like she was about to run a marathon. This wasn't like jumping onstage with Hillary and singing a silly karaoke song. This was real. This was supposed to be good. And on top of that, she could practically feel Logan's scowl burning into her back. *I am going to make this guy like my music*, she thought. *No matter what.*

"Okay, this is a song called 'Heartbeat,'" she said. Her fingers found the familiar chords on the piano. *Go ahead*, she thought. *Just sing the first line. That's all you need to do.*

Her voice wavered at first. She hadn't tried to sing this song since the Silver Snowflake Ball. For a second she was back there, onstage, in front of all those people, knowing that her mom was just a few feet behind her in the wings, watching...

And then she remembered: *Nobody knows who I am.* Something inside of her swung open, like a gate being unlocked. She sang the first two lines.

I love the way you talk to me on the line
I love the way you tell me that you're mine

Before she knew it she was singing it the way she had the day she'd written it, slowly and passionately and smokily, letting her voice wrap around each syllable.

And then Ben started to play his bass — *thump a thump a thump a thump* — setting the perfect rhythm. He was good. She could tell right away.

Then Gordie started on drums, nothing too hard or distracting, just following Ben's lead.

Then, at the bridge, Logan blasted his sax, making Hudson jump. It was way too loud, and all over the place, like a manic foghorn.

When she was done, she sat and faced the keys for a moment, letting herself settle. Finishing a song was always a little like coming out of a trance — time would jump forward again and she'd suddenly become aware of her surroundings. The room was eerily quiet. That usually meant one of two things: People either loved the song or they hated it.

She turned around. Gordie sat with one hand still touching a cymbal, faintly smiling. Ben rested his bass on the floor and was blinking busily behind his glasses, his Adam's apple jumping up and down. Even Logan looked semi-impressed as he cradled his sax. Carina and Lizzie sat on the couch, clutching each other's hands. Even Hillary, standing against the wall, seemed to be moved.

"Did you really write that?" Ben finally asked.

"She totally did," Carina asserted from her spot on the couch.

"Wow," Ben said. "Can you give us a minute?" He glanced at his bandmates.

"Sure." Hudson practically leaped to her feet. "We'll just go upstairs."

Hudson took the stairs two at a time, with Hillary, Lizzie, and Carina behind her. "I knew it!" Hillary said when they got upstairs. "You blew them away!"

"Really?" Hudson asked.

"You *crushed* it!" Carina said, hugging Hudson.

"That was incredible," Lizzie said. "I got chills."

"They're totally going to want you," Hillary said.

"You think so?" Hudson asked.

Hillary nodded.

For the first time, Hudson realized that she didn't just *want* to be the lead singer of the Stone Cold Freaks. She *needed* to be.

Just then she heard the creak of Ben's feet on the stairs. "Hudson?" he called out. "Can you come down here?"

Hudson and Hillary exchanged a worried look. "Just go," Hillary said, swatting her on the arm.

Hudson walked back down the stairs. The Stone Cold Freaks had assembled themselves on the plaid couch. Gordie was smiling, but Logan's eyes were on the muted TV.

"So," Ben began, grinning, "can you come up for rehearsal on Wednesday? Around four thirty?"

"Really?" she cried, hopping up and down. "Yes, I definitely can!"

"Okay then," Ben said. He stood up and held out his hand. "Welcome to the Stone Cold Freaks."

She shook his hand, said good-bye, and then walked back up to the kitchen, not even feeling the stairs underneath her feet. She'd sung that song in front of total strangers, and they'd loved it. They'd loved it so much they'd asked her — for real, this time — to front their band.

She said good-bye to Hillary, and thanked her for everything, and then she and Lizzie and Carina walked out to the gravel driveway in the freezing cold, where they waited for the cab they'd called.

"You did it!" Carina squealed. "How do you feel?"

"I don't know why, but I'm more psyched about this than I was about my album," Hudson said. "Isn't that weird?"

"Maybe this is what you were supposed to do all along," Lizzie said, as a bright green cab turned into the driveway. "Maybe this is going to be more fun than your album."

"Maybe," Hudson said. "But first I really need to change their name."

chapter 16

That night Hudson sat at the kitchen table, picking at a plate of mushy boiled dandelion greens and feeling giddy. She was the lead singer of a *band*. *Outside* of the city. She had a whole new life. A life that her mom had no clue about. Hudson glanced over at Holla, who was across the room giving Sophie a list of orders. She almost felt a little guilty, but it was also undeniably thrilling.

"Tell them I want to be at the final callbacks," Holla said, pulling her sweaty hair up into a ponytail. She yawned slightly into her hand. "The last time I let Howard do it he picked the laziest dancers I've ever seen."

"You got it," Sophie said.

"Why is this so hard?" Holla grumbled. "Why do I have to do everything myself, all the time?"

Sophie stared at her, biting her full lips. "I'm not sure," she said helplessly.

"That's it 'til tomorrow," Holla said, turning back to the kitchen table. "You can go home now."

"Thanks, Holla," Sophie whispered as she began to gather her things from the computer desk. So far Sophie seemed to be dealing well with Holla's exacting demands, but Hudson was pretty sure she wouldn't last through the spring. Most of Holla's assistants quit — or were fired — after three months.

Holla walked over to the kitchen table and slid into a chair. Even though Hudson could see she was exhausted, her mom's posture was perfect. Lorraine placed a hot plate of mushed green vegetables in front of her. "It's always the same, every tour," Holla said to Hudson. "All these last-minute dramas. You're coming with me this summer, right?"

"Uh-huh," Hudson said. It seemed odd for her mom to ask, since that was what she did every time.

"So, honey, how was Jenny?" Holla asked. "And please, sit up straight."

"Jenny was great," Hudson answered, sitting up. "She loved the blanket."

"Really?" Holla asked, and Hudson could see the sudden interest in her eyes. "You guys spent an awfully long time together. What time did you get back here? Five thirty?"

Hudson remembered her lie to Fernald. "You know, I think she feels really bad about the fight you guys had," she said, ignoring Holla's question.

"She does?" Holla asked, putting down her fork. "What'd she say?"

"Just…well, that she feels bad," Hudson improvised. "I think we should do something nice for her. Just to let her know there are no hard feelings."

Holla zipped up her workout jacket. "I've done a lot of nice things for her, baby. It only makes things worse."

"I know, but maybe just this once we could do something to really show her that we're her family," Hudson said. "Like throw her a birthday party. Invite her friends. Sort of a welcome back to New York. Maybe then she'll stop running off all the time."

Her mom chewed her food slowly, considering this. "Where?"

"What about here?"

"*Here?*" Holla asked. "Why does it have to be here?"

"It doesn't," Hudson said. "It just might be more personal that way."

Holla sipped from her glass of coconut water. "Does she hate me?" she asked suddenly, the space between her eyebrows creased and her lips pressed together. "Just tell me the truth. I can handle it. Does she hate me?"

"She doesn't hate you, Mom."

"Because I promised Grandma that I would take care of her, that I would watch out for her," Holla said, her eyes growing soft and shiny. "We all knew that she was wild. And maybe I made it worse, being so successful, so quickly…Maybe it's my fault…"

Hudson touched her mom's arm. "It's okay. She's your sister. She loves you," Hudson reassured her.

Holla patted Hudson's hand, and just like that, the moment of insecurity passed. Her face hardened again, ever so slightly, and she picked up her fork. "Then let's plan it. But you make sure that she's okay with it. If I present it to her, she'll just say no."

"Fine." Hudson pushed the food around on her plate. "What if I go over to her place and hang out with her again? Like, Wednesday afternoon?" It was the perfect alibi for her Larchmont rehearsal date.

"Sure. And I'd like you to come down to the studio this week and give me some feedback. On your song."

Hudson stopped pushing a clump of dandelion greens around her plate. "Okay," Hudson said, too surprised to say anything else. "Let's do Thursday."

"Thursday it is," Holla said. "And honey, please sit up straight."

*

The next day Hudson was on her way out of Geometry class when Miss Evanevski said, "Hudson? Can you wait a moment?"

Hudson gave Carina and Lizzie a glance that said *Not a big deal, I'll meet up with you in a second* and whirled around. "Is something wrong?"

"I just wanted to discuss your quiz from last week," Miss Evanevski said. Hudson's Geometry teacher was tall and fragile-looking, with a pointy chin and a permanently disappointed expression, which intensified when she said, "I was a little alarmed to see your grade."

"I know," she said. "I'm sorry about that."

"Do you need some extra help?" Miss Evanevski sat down at her desk. "I'm happy to refer you to a tutor."

"It was just a onetime thing," Hudson explained.

Miss Evanevski frowned. "I'm supposed to inform your

parents if you get less than a C minus on a test," she said. "But this is so out of character for you, Hudson, that I'm tempted to call your mom anyway."

"Please don't," Hudson said. "Believe me, it won't happen again."

Miss Evanevski picked up a red pen and started shuffling piles of tests on her desk. "Why are you so sure?"

"Because I just decided not to study for it, sort of as an experiment," Hudson said, before she realized how that sounded.

Miss Evanevski frowned. "Experiment?"

"Well," Hudson said, "it's all part of my life-coaching."

"Your what?" Miss Evanevski asked, alarmed. "You're seeing a life coach? Are your parents aware of this?"

"Please," Hudson pleaded. "It's really nothing. Forget I said anything. I promise I'll study next time. You know I always do."

The sound of a footstep behind her made Hudson turn, and there on the threshold stood Ava Elting. From the smug smile on her face Hudson knew that she'd heard the entire conversation. "Oh, sorry," Ava said, tucking one of her auburn curls behind her ear.

"No, we're done, Ava. What is it?" Miss Evanevski said, beckoning her into the classroom.

Hudson headed for the hallway, her face burning. Of course Ava Elting had overheard. She replayed everything that she'd just said in front of Miss Evanevski. The C plus on her quiz. The life coach. It was hard to know which was more embarrassing. Both were enough ammunition to keep Ava busy for weeks. As Hudson passed her, she stared straight ahead and averted her eyes.

She sped down the hall to History and sat down next to Carina, Lizzie, and Todd.

"What was that all about?" Lizzie asked.

"I got a C plus on our last quiz," Hudson said, "and now I think Ava Elting knows that I have a life coach."

"Oh, jeez," Carina whispered.

It didn't take long for Ava to unleash this new tidbit. When Ava walked into History she took a seat right behind Hudson.

"So, is everything okay? I couldn't help overhearing that you're seeing a life coach," she drawled, making Hudson's stomach turn over.

"Uh-huh," Hudson said over her shoulder, holding her breath.

"I'm just soooo surprised," Ava went on. "I thought you were so together. At least, it seems that way. But I guess nothing is ever quite as it seems, is it?"

Hudson froze. Out of the corner of her eye, she could see Carina and Lizzie listening to this, too.

"Just so you know, I'm always, always here for you," Ava said. "I wouldn't want you to end up on *E! True Hollywood Story.*"

Hudson whirled around. "Don't you have more important, interesting things to think about than *my* life?" she asked.

Ava blinked her large brown eyes, as if she couldn't believe what she'd just heard. "Uh, *yeah,*" she finally said with her famous smirk. She tossed some of her auburn hair over her shoulder as she stood up. "I was just trying to be nice." Then she walked over to another empty chair as Mr. Weatherly sat on the edge of his desk.

"All right, people! Who wants to tell us about Alexander the Great?"

Hudson's heart pounded in her chest; she couldn't believe what she'd just said. Carina nudged Hudson's arm. "*You* are my new hero," she whispered.

Hudson knew that things with Ava probably weren't over. But she'd finally said exactly what had been on her mind. Maybe getting angry every now and again wasn't such a bad thing. Especially if it meant making Ava Elting get up and move seats in class. Maybe Hudson would never quite have an inner bee-yatch. But she could stick up for herself when the time came, and that was all that really mattered.

chapter 17

Hudson leaned back against the vinyl seat with her book bag on her lap and felt the wheels of the three thirty-five train roll underneath her. She'd told Fernald to drop her at Jenny's straight from school, and as soon as he'd driven away she'd taken the subway to Grand Central. She'd jumped on board just in time and scored a row of three seats all to herself. Looking at the cracked seats she wished Hillary or Lizzie or Carina could have come. Tonight it would just be her and the Stone Cold Freaks. *Note to self,* she thought. *Must change that name.*

At Larchmont she got off the train and got into a cab. As they pulled into the gravel drive at Ben's house, Hudson noticed that there were more cars in the driveway this time — a beat-up maroon hatchback and a forest green Saab. A couple of bikes lay on their side near the steps to the front door. Logan's and Gordie's, she assumed. She hoped Logan wouldn't still be acting weird. She'd tried to think of something to do or say to get him to like her but

the things she'd thought of — bringing him cookies, or maybe g‑
ting him an iTunes gift certificate — just seemed a little despera‑

She paid the driver, then walked up the steps and rang the be‑
The door opened and Hudson was greeted by a woman in her mi‑
forties with shoulder-length, softly layered brown hair and Ben‑
large brown eyes.

"Mrs. Geyer?" Hudson asked, remembering Ben's mom from
the bar mitzvah.

"Call me Patty," she said, extending her hand. "Come on in,
Hudson."

Hudson shook her hand. "It's nice to see you again," she said.

"You can leave your coat right there," said Mrs. Geyer, pointing to the bench in the entryway, which was again covered in coats
and scarves. "You want some hot chocolate? Something to warm
you up?"

"Hot chocolate would be great," Hudson said, following her
into the kitchen.

"Hope instant's okay," Mrs. Geyer said, putting a kettle on the
stove. "I know we're not supposed to be drinking stuff like that,
but sometimes it's just so much easier."

"Yeah, I know," Hudson said. She didn't think her mom even
had Hershey's chocolate in the house, let alone instant Swiss Miss.

"You know, I saw you sing with Hillary," she said. "You really
are very talented."

"Thank you," Hudson said.

"And there's something so familiar about you," Mrs. Geyer
said. "Maybe it's your voice. But you remind me of someone." She
shook her head and shrugged. "So, you live in the city?"

"Yep," Hudson said, starting to get nervous. She scanned the kitchen for a cast-aside *US Weekly* or *Life & Style*. But before Mrs. Geyer could question her further, Ben walked into the kitchen. Or rather, tripped into the kitchen, over a hockey stick that lay diagonally on the ground. "Oh, hey, Hudson!" he said, grabbing a chair to steady himself.

"Honey," Mrs. Geyer said.

"Good news," Ben said, straightening up. "We have our first show. This Friday night."

"*This* Friday?" Hudson asked.

"Well, it's not really a show," Ben said, taking off his glasses and blowing on them to clean them. "It's my friend's birthday party. I told them we'd play at it. It's just at her house."

"Ellie is going to *love* you guys," said Mrs. Geyer, handing Hudson a mug of Swiss Miss.

"Are you sure we're ready for that?" Hudson asked as she followed Ben down the stairs to the basement. "We've barely had a rehearsal."

"Yeah, it'll be great," Ben said casually. "No worries."

"Okay," she said, unconvinced. He may not have been worried, but she was. And who exactly was Ellie?

When she reached the basement, she realized that the show was going to happen a lot sooner than Friday — it was about to happen now. There, draped on the pink and brown plaid couch and sitting cross-legged on the floor, were four girls and four guys. All of them seemed to be Ben's age. Two of the girls were identical twins. A couple of the guys watched the TV on mute. The rest seemed to be watching Gordie and Logan, who were in the middle of another experimental jazz set. Gordie wailed on his drum kit while Logan blasted away with his sax. Hudson didn't know how anyone could listen to them for long. She didn't want to say anything, but she thought that they definitely needed some quality rehearsal time before they played for a group.

"Okay, guys, Hudson's here," said Ben. "Everyone? This is Hudson Jones, our new lead singer."

"Hi, everyone," Hudson said, waving shyly.

"Hey," one of the girls said, getting to her feet. "I'm Ellie. It's my party on Friday. Oh, and don't worry — we have a piano. You guys are gonna be great." Ellie was Asian-American, and she had a friendly way of leaning in close when she talked. Her black hair splashed against her shoulders, and she wore an adorable purple ruffled blouse that Hudson immediately wanted to borrow.

"Thanks," Hudson said. "Are you guys here for our rehearsal?"

"Yeah, but we all promise to be super-quiet," Ellie said, dropping back down to the floor. "Okay, everyone," she announced to the group. "Time to zip it."

"Hudson, we definitely want to do the song you sang the other day," said Ben. "But we thought we'd just practice a few covers, too. Anything you want to start with?"

Hudson sat down at the piano. She could still feel the group of kids behind her, staring at her. She wished Ben had warned her about having an audience. This didn't seem fair. But then she reminded herself: *Nobody knows who you are.*

Gordie waved hello from behind the drum kit, and she waved back. Logan kept his head down, and busied himself by fidgeting with the keys of his sax. She couldn't tell if he was ignoring her.

"Let's do 'I'll Be Seeing You,'" she suggested. *At least it has lots of saxophone in it,* Hudson thought.

"Cool," said Ben.

She started playing, and when Logan joined in, his sax was so loud that it almost drowned out her voice. Hudson did her best to sing over him, but it wasn't easy.

"That was awesome!" Ellie yelled out when they were done. "You guys have to do that one!"

They followed with "Fly Me to the Moon," "At Last," and "Feeling Good," which Logan almost entirely blotted out with his sax. But Ben was phenomenal. He never missed one beat, and seemed to have practiced all of these songs for hours. Finally they ended with "My Baby Just Cares for Me," which had only a small part for Logan to ruin.

"That was soooo good!" Ellie said as the rest of the kids clapped. "Hudson, you have an amazing voice!"

"I told you, right?" Ben asked.

"Thanks," Hudson said, feeling herself turn red. Receiving praise always made her uncomfortable. When she happened to catch Logan glowering at her, she felt even more awkward. "But I probably should try to make the six-oh-seven train."

"Ellie can take you," Ben said, getting up. "She's got her license. She's a junior."

Hudson turned to Logan. "Good rehearsal," she said to him, smiling.

"Yeah," Logan replied, barely looking at her. Then he got up and went to sit down next to the twin girls, as if Hudson were no more than a stranger.

Yep, he hates me, Hudson thought as she followed Ben and Ellie out the back basement door. There was probably nothing she could do about it, but it gnawed at her, like one of her geometry problems.

Outside it was already dark, and a big frosty full moon hovered above the trees. Hudson craned her head back to look up at the night sky. "Wow," she said. "You can actually see stars."

"Uh, yeah," Ellie said, laughing, as she opened the door to her Saab.

"You can never see stars in the city," Hudson said. "There're too many lights."

"We could use a few more lights up here," Ben said, crawling into the back and flipping the seat back up so Hudson could sit in front.

Hudson got into the car and shut the door. She had never been driven by someone who was so close to her age. For a moment she was almost scared, but then Ellie turned the key in the ignition and expertly backed out of the driveway.

"What?" Ellie asked, catching Hudson watching her.

"I don't know any kids in the city who drive," Hudson observed.

"It kind of comes in handy up here," said Ellie, pulling out onto the street. "What part do you live in?"

"The West Village," she said.

"Cool," said Ellie, nodding with approval. "My dad works in the city. We go in once in a while, to shop or go to some restaurant that's way overpriced. Where do you go to school?"

"Chadwick," Hudson said. "Same place Ben's cousin Hillary goes."

"I've heard of that school." Ellie wrinkled her nose, as if she smelled something bad. "Isn't that where all those celebrities' kids go?"

Hudson started. "Um, I guess so," she said carefully.

"Wait," Ellie said. "Ben, didn't you ask your cousin once who went there? Who did she say again?"

"I can't remember. And I think you just missed the turn," Ben said, sitting forward. "It's back there."

"Oh, great," Ellie said, pulling over and then making a U-turn. "Um, how long have I lived here?" she joked. "Earth to Ellie."

Hudson smiled. She liked Ellie more and more. But she wondered if Hillary had ever told Ben who she was. It sounded like she had, a long time ago. What if he remembered?

"Where do *you* guys go to school?" Hudson asked quickly, before Ellie could return to her line of questioning.

"Mamaroneck High."

"It's in the next town over," said Ben.

"Do you guys have a football team?" Hudson asked.

"Of course," Ellie said. "Why?"

"That's something else we don't have," Hudson said.

"It's really not that great," Ben put in. "I'd rather go to Chadwick any day. At least there are cool music clubs downtown."

"Ben is *really* into jazz," Ellie said, as if Ben weren't in the car.

"I think that's great," Hudson said. She looked at Ben in the rearview mirror. He smiled.

"No. *Really* into it," Ellie repeated.

"Better watch out," he joked. "I'm pretty serious about this."

"Good," Hudson said, smiling back at him.

They pulled into the train station parking lot. A few people stood huddled on the platform.

"Thanks for the ride, Ellie." Hudson got out of the car and wrapped her scarf over her face. It was so cold her nose felt like it might fall off.

Ben got out of the backseat and moved to the front. "So be at my place by six o'clock Friday night," he said. "And Hudson?" Ben stuck his head out of the passenger side window. "You were awesome tonight."

"You really were," Ellie said.

"So were you, Ben," Hudson said. "I'll see you Friday."

She walked up the steps to the platform, touched by how nice they'd been to her. But she had to wonder if they would have been so nice if they'd known who she was. She remembered the way Ellie had wrinkled her nose as she said *celebrities' kids*. Eventually they were going to figure out who she was. But by then, she hoped, they'd be able to see her the same way as they had tonight: a shy girl with a big voice who loved jazz and Nina Simone. A girl, Hudson thought, watching Ellie's car drive out of the lot, who felt like she might just have a career in music after all.

chapter 18

"I just want you to be honest," Holla said as the service elevator creaked on the long ride up to the recording studio. "It's your song, so I want your true reaction."

"Sure, Mom," Hudson said uncertainly, shifting her book bag onto her other shoulder. No matter how often Holla said she wanted Hudson's "true reaction" to something—whether she wanted to know if her hands looked "veiny" or if the dance routine for a certain song was too *Solid Gold*—Hudson never told her mom what she didn't want to hear.

"I think you're going to be very proud," Holla said, taking off the black oversized sunglasses she'd put on to walk past the photographers and fans who'd been waiting outside the recording studio. "Chris thinks it's gonna be huge." She smiled nervously as she put the glasses in her ostrich-skin shoulder bag. "We'll see."

Hudson glanced at Little Jimmy and Sophie, and for a moment they made sympathetic eye contact with her. They, too, knew how

Holla felt about other people's opinions, even when she'd asked for them.

"And how's Jenny?" Holla asked.

"Jenny?" Hudson asked, momentarily thrown.

"You were with her for hours yesterday," she said. "Did you run the party idea past her? Does she want to do it?"

With a start, Hudson remembered lying about seeing Jenny so she could go to Larchmont for band rehearsal. "Oh, yeah, she thinks it's a great idea."

"And February twenty-first is fine with her?"

"Yup," Hudson asserted, as brightly as possible. Hadn't Jenny actually said that the other day? She couldn't remember. She needed to text her.

Hudson followed the group through a pair of glass doors into the studio's reception area, past the lounge and the kitchen, and down the hallway to a door marked CONTROL ROOM 2. Holla opened the door.

"Hey!" Chris said, standing up from behind the wraparound sound console. "Welcome back, Hudson!" He wore a blue knit hat that made his eyes seem extra vivid, and a T-shirt with Jimi Hendrix's face on it. He started to hug her, but then gave her a high five instead. "Thanks for coming down."

"Hey, Chris," Hudson said, feeling, as usual, a little awkward around him. "How's everything going?"

"Great. I can't wait for you to hear the song," he said. "Oh, this is Liam, the sound engineer," he said, gesturing to the older man sitting in a chair. He had big, sad eyes and a mustache, and seemed eager to get started. "Liam, this is Holla's daughter, Hudson. I used to be her producer."

"Hi," Liam said tersely, then went back to studying the knobs and dials of the immense console.

"Okay, who has a coconut water?" Holla asked, putting down her bag.

Chris opened a mini-fridge in the back of the room and pulled out a blue can. "Here you go, madam."

Holla popped open the can and gave him a meaningful smile. "*Merci*," she said with a giggle and took a couple of sips. "Okay!" she said sharply. "I'm ready. Let's do this." She turned to look at Hudson. "Remember, tell me what you think. Okay?"

Hudson nodded earnestly and Holla walked out. Hudson went to the couch in the back and dropped her book bag to the floor. She sat on the couch and spread her coat over her legs, staring at Chris as he manned the sound console. She still got a weird feeling about him and her mom. They were spending hours together in this tiny room every day. Then he was coming over at night. And he seemed extra amped-up right now, as if he were on his best behavior.

Chris leaned close to the intercom and said, "Okay, Holla, how are you doing in there?"

Through the glass they watched Holla walk into the vocal booth next door. She slipped on a pair of headphones and gave Chris a thumbs-up.

Chris turned around and looked at Hudson, his blue eyes sparkling. "Just wait, you're gonna love this," he boasted, and then turned back around. "And uh one," Chris said into the intercom. "Uh, two. Uh one, two, three, four..."

Liam hit a button and Hudson's song poured out through the speakers. It sounded even worse. They'd added even more tracks to it, which Hudson hadn't thought was possible. There were more crash cymbals and kick-drums, and now a chorus of digital voices screamed "Hey!" on every fourth beat. At one point, Hudson thought she could hear a sampled car alarm. *Oh, God,* she thought, hugging her knees to her chest. *How do I tell my mom that this is good?*

Through the glass she watched her mom in her stretchy purple sweater and yoga pants, swaying to the music.

And then Holla closed her eyes, tilted her chin, and started to sing.

Oooh, I love the way you talk to me on the line
Ooh, I love the way you tell me that you're mine
I love the way you won't let me go
And now I love that I'm telling you so...

Hudson had experienced many surreal moments in her life — being mobbed with her mom by screaming and crying Japanese girls in Harajuku, Tokyo; racing a Big Wheel through the winding tunnels below Madison Square Garden; being photographed by a cell phone camera in her dentist's waiting room — but this topped them all. Her thirty-seven-year-old mom was singing a song about a sixteen-year-old boy. A boy Hudson had once had a crush on. And she was practically writhing as she was doing it. She hugged her knees in tighter, cringing even more. The four-minute song seemed to last a lifetime.

"Perfect!" Chris yelled into the intercom when Holla was done. "That was just perfect!"

"Really?" Holla asked excitedly. She pulled off her headphones, looking flushed and giddy. Then she left the booth.

Chris swiveled around in his chair to face Hudson. "What'd you think?" he asked, his face bright with pride. "Sounds pretty good, huh?"

Hudson swallowed. "Yeah!" she chirped.

Holla bounded into the control room. "Phew!" she cried out, striking a dramatic pose, with the back of her hand pressed against her forehead. "So it was okay?" she asked Chris. "I didn't go too high at the end?"

"It was amazing," he said. "And someone else liked it, too." He jerked his thumb in Hudson's direction.

"You did? You liked it?" Holla asked, her brown eyes filled with delight.

Hudson bit her lip. "You guys really put a lot of work into it," she said carefully.

Holla's eyes narrowed, catching Hudson's hesitation. "What do you mean?" she asked, stepping closer to Chris.

"I just think it sounds a little ... busy," Hudson said delicately.

Holla and Chris traded quizzical looks. "Busy?" Holla repeated.

"Forget it," Hudson said. "It's great. I'm sure it'll be a big hit."

"Wait, hold on," Holla said, holding up a hand. "You don't get away that easy. Explain what you mean."

"Um, just that it ... well ... it just doesn't sound like ..." Hudson let her voice trail off as her mom continued to stare. "Can I talk to you in private?"

Holla looked at Chris and the sound engineer. Without a word they got up and went to the door. Sophie and Little Jimmy followed. The door shut behind them.

Alone with Holla, who seemed to be growing more annoyed every second, Hudson tried to figure out how to tell her mom the truth. "Your voice sounds great, Mom," she began, "but there's too much going on. He's done too much to the backup track. It's too layered. All the sampling... it just sounds a little cheesy."

At the word *cheesy*, Holla raised an eyebrow. "Sounds like you hated it."

"I didn't hate it," Hudson said. "I'm just saying that it could be better with less going on in it. That's all."

Holla nodded, seeming to mull this over. "Well, you haven't wanted me to do this song ever since we asked you about it," Holla said. "Admit it. You've had a problem with this from the beginning."

"You said you wanted my opinion, just now, in the elevator," Hudson said, getting angry. "And I'm giving it to you. I'm not trying to be mean or anything."

"This is supposed to be my next single," Holla said, her voice starting to get louder. "How could you tell me it's bad?"

"Because I'm just trying to be honest."

"Well, Chris seems to think it's great," Holla pointed out.

"Of course he does," Hudson muttered.

"What does that mean?" Holla asked.

"It means you're totally dating him," Hudson blurted out. "Right?"

Holla's angry expression lifted. "So that's what you're mad at me about? Chris?"

"I'm not mad," Hudson said.

"You're *always* mad," Holla spat. "You never like anyone I date. It's like I'm living with my mother."

"Maybe I'm just not looking forward to when you guys break up and you're in my room sobbing every night," Hudson said, letting her own voice get loud. "Since we all know *that's* coming."

Holla's eyes darkened, and she pointed to the door. "Go home," she said in a withering voice. "Right. Now."

Hudson picked up her book bag and went to the door. "I'm sorry," she mumbled as she reached for the knob.

"Just go," Holla repeated.

Hudson opened the door. Sophie, Chris, Liam, and Little Jimmy stood in the hallway, studying the carpet. She knew that they'd heard everything. Chris looked up at her. "Hudson?" he asked carefully, as if she were a mental patient who might have a seizure any moment. "Is everything okay?"

Hudson shook her head and trudged past him. As if she were going to pour her heart out to him, of all people. She pulled out her iPhone as she reached the elevators and typed two words:

Pinkberry. NOW.

*

"You did the right thing, H," Lizzie said a half hour later, digging her spoon into her cup of pomegranate Pinkberry topped with mochi. "You said how you felt. Your mom asked for your opinion and you gave it. That's all you can do."

"But what's the point if all she's gonna do is freak out?" Hudson took a bite of her yogurt with blueberries and let it melt on her tongue.

"It was a trap," Carina said, finishing her cup. "Whenever someone says they want your 'honest opinion,' it always, always means they don't."

Thankfully Carina had been hanging out at Lizzie's place, which made the Pinkberry on Columbus and Seventy-fifth Street superconvenient. Hudson looked out the window at Fernald in the black SUV, double-parked in front of the store. "But seriously, you guys," she said, cupping a blueberry with her spoon. "The song was awful. She needed to know. And then all that stuff with Chris..." She paused. "Obviously, I know we were never gonna be together or go out. And I feel dumb that I even had a crush on him. But why does *she* have to have him? Why does she have to have *everyone* love her, all the time? It's not fair."

"But that's the deal," Carina said, tossing her empty cup into the trash. "She's, like, the biggest star in the world."

"Do you think she *is* gonna end up in your room sobbing?" Lizzie asked, her hazel eyes locked on Hudson.

"I don't know," Hudson said, taking another small bite of her tart yogurt. "Maybe Chris is different. Maybe he's the one who'll really love her for who she is." She pushed the container away. "I'm just so sick of it. At least those guys get to leave one day. I'll never get to leave. I'm gonna have to deal with this the rest of my life."

Lizzie leaned closer and took Hudson's hand. "You're your own person, H. Really. Your mom has nothing to do with you." She chuckled. "I mean, believe me. I know how hard it is."

Hudson nodded. "But you had Andrea. I don't have someone

like that. I just have *me*. And I don't know if I can do it all on my own."

Lizzie and Carina put their hands on top of Hudson's. "Yes, you can," Carina said. "We know you can."

Hudson squeezed her friends's hands. She thought she might tear up for a moment so she pulled her hand away. "So, I forgot to tell you guys that we have a show. Tomorrow night. Up in Larchmont."

"You have a *show*?" Carina gasped. "Where?"

"At some girl's house. Her name's Ellie. She's really nice."

"Can we come?" Carina asked.

"We *have* to come!" Lizzie said. "Can I bring Todd?"

"Can I bring Alex?" Carina asked.

"You guys — I don't even know these people," Hudson hedged.

"And neither will we!" Carina cried. "Come on, you have to let us come."

Hudson tossed her melted Pinkberry in the trash. "Okay, fine. Let me check with Ben and I'll let you guys know."

Later, after she'd dropped Carina and Lizzie off at Lizzie's house, Hudson thought about what Lizzie had said in Pinkberry. She tried to imagine a world in which Holla didn't exist. Where she'd never seen billboards of her in Times Square or heard her songs as background music in taxicabs and restaurants and boutiques. Where she'd never seen her mom mobbed by fans screaming her name. It was impossible, like trying to imagine a world without sunlight or water. Her mom would always be there, taking up all the space in the room. Lizzie was wrong: Holla would always have *everything* to do with who Hudson was.

169

Later that night, as Hudson did her homework, she got an idea. Her mom was still at the studio, and probably would be for hours. So she picked up the phone and dialed.

"Hunan Gourmet!" said the voice on the other end of the line.

Hudson scanned the menu on her laptop. "Order for delivery, please," she said. "The chicken lo mein and the moo shu pork. With extra brown sauce."

Hunan Gourmet had a reputation for being the most organic and non-MSG Chinese takeout place in the West Village, but still, it was Chinese food. And Chinese food was very much not allowed in the Holla Jones Diet Plan. Ordering it felt like the ultimate way to rebel, and after Hudson's fight with Holla, it just felt like the right thing to do.

When it arrived, she pulled off the plastic tops, trying not to freak out about oozing toxins. Then she sat at the kitchen table, alone, slurping up her lo mein. Some of it was a little too salty, and some of it was too spicy, but most of it was delicious. To her credit, Lorraine didn't say a word. She just stood at the island, darting sly smiles in Hudson's direction as she chopped up some kale.

chapter 19

The next afternoon Hillary planted herself next to Hudson at the lockers. She wore a somber black sweater, and the absence of color made Hillary's skin look even paler than usual.

"How was rehearsal the other night?" Hillary asked.

"Great!" she said, deciding not to mention Logan and his angry glares. "And we have a show tonight. Wanna come?"

"I can't. I have to do something with my mom," Hillary said, her arms folded in front of her. "I'm so annoyed. But can you do me a favor? Can you ask Logan about me?"

From the little interaction she'd had with Logan so far, Hudson already knew that this wouldn't be easy. "I'll try," she said.

"Just mention my name, and maybe that I wish I could be at the party, and just see what he says. And watch his facial expression. Even if he's trying to play it cool, you'll be able to tell from his face."

Hudson pulled out her Geometry book. "I'll keep that in mind, Hil."

Hillary beamed. "Great!" she said. "And then tomorrow we can maybe go shopping again?"

Hudson needed to get to class. "Sure," she said. "Meet me at Kirna Zabete in SoHo. Noon."

As she watched Hillary walk away, Hudson wondered if it was a good or bad thing to be so superconfident. On one hand, people like her mom and like Hillary never let the word *no* stand in their way. But sometimes that meant that they also set themselves up for disappointment. Hudson wasn't sure, but she had the distinct feeling that Hillary was going to be headed for some real disappointment as far as Logan was concerned.

*

After giving Carina and Lizzie directions to the party in Larchmont and making plans to meet them at eight, Hudson left school and made the trip home to change. As Fernald navigated the traffic down Fifth Avenue, Hudson looked at the brittle winter sunlight slanting through the branches of Central Park and realized that she would need another alibi to get out of the house for the night. She still hadn't seen her mom since yesterday's fight at the recording studio, and with any luck, Holla and Chris would have plans tonight. Still, Hudson would have to say something to Raquel, so she thought quickly.

Jenny. She needed to ask her about the birthday party, anyway. She picked up her phone and called her aunt.

"Jenny?" she asked. "It's Hudson."

"Hey, Hudcap," came her aunt's cheery, but tired, voice over the line. "How's it going? I've missed you."

"So, I talked to my mom about that birthday party we'd like to throw you," she said. "My mom really wants to do it."

Jenny laughed. "Well, considering my sink just exploded and Barneys just told me they don't want to carry my line and I had the world's worst date last night," she said, "I'd say a party sounds kind of nice. But I'm gonna be out of town. Remember Juan Gregorio?"

"Who?" Hudson asked.

"The guy from Buenos Aires. He's invited me down for the week of my birthday. I think he misses me."

"Oh," Hudson said.

"So just tell her I can't do it the twenty-first. I'd call her myself, but I don't want to look pushy."

"Yeah, no problem," Hudson said. "And if my mom calls you tonight, will you say I'm with you?"

"O-kay," Jenny said cautiously. "What is it?"

"It's just this band I'm in. We have our first show tonight. Not at a club or anything. It's just a high school party. She still doesn't know about it."

"No problem," Jenny said. "I'll tell her. I hope it's going well."

"Okay, thanks!" Hudson said. "And let's hang out again soon!" *Thank God for Aunt Jenny,* she thought as she pressed the End Call button. She'd really lucked out when her aunt came home from France.

Back at home, Hudson showered, dried her hair, and put on her Leather Milkmaid dress, designed by Martin Meloy. Martin Meloy wasn't her favorite, since the whole debacle with Lizzie and his ad campaign, but she still loved the dress. She topped it off with a beat-up boy's motorcycle jacket she'd scored at a flea market in Florence and then slipped on her stretchy, rhinestone-covered headband for a little sparkle. This was going to be her first show, and she wanted to look good for it.

When she slipped downstairs, she almost walked right into Raquel, who was holding a tall, spindly orchid. "You look nice," she said. "Where are you going?"

"Aunt Jenny's taking me to a Broadway play," Hudson said, heading to the elevator. "We're having dinner before."

"Does your mom know this?" asked Raquel.

"I think so," Hudson said, trying hard to look Raquel in the eye.

"Just be home by eleven thirty," Raquel said, continuing past her down the hall.

Hudson gave Fernald the address of a restaurant on Forty-third and Sixth, which was about halfway between the theater district and Grand Central.

"Aunt Jenny will bring me home in a cab later," she told him as she got out.

Fernald nodded and she slammed the door. Then she ran down Forty-third Street, straight into the wind, amazed at how good she was getting at this. And she almost wanted to laugh. Probably every kid in Larchmont wished they could be in the city on a Friday night. And here she was, lying through her teeth so she could flee to the suburbs.

Ben had texted her that he and his mom would be waiting for her at the train station. As she stepped onto the platform at Larchmont, she saw his mom's car parked under a street lamp and recognized Ben's tall, lanky frame when he stepped out of the front seat. "Hudson!" he yelled. "Over here!"

She waved and ran to the car, relieved to see them. She still wasn't used to taking the train by herself.

Mrs. Geyer waved at her from behind the steering wheel. "Hi, Hudson!" she said.

"Thanks for picking me up," she said as she slipped into the backseat.

"How was your train ride?" Mrs. Geyer asked. "Does your mom know you're up here?"

"Oh, yeah," she said, trying to sound convincing. "She wanted to thank you for picking me up."

Ben got back into the passenger seat and closed the door.

"Because she should really have my phone number," Mrs. Geyer said. "Do you want to give it to her?"

"I'll give it to her later," Hudson said. "She's out right now."

This seemed to be enough for Ben's mom. They drove out of the parking lot and then turned in the opposite direction from town. "It's so quiet up here," Hudson marveled.

"*Too* quiet," Ben said. Hudson could see that Ben had tamed his hair with some kind of product, because it wasn't as springy as usual. He'd also switched his glasses for contact lenses, and she could smell some kind of spicy, musky scent that might have been aftershave.

"Ben thinks it's boring up here," said Mrs. Geyer, fiddling with the radio. "He'd love to live down in the city. What do your parents do in the city?" Mrs. Geyer asked.

"Mom," Ben objected. "Don't be rude."

"I'm not being rude, I'm just making conversation," Mrs. Geyer said.

"Well, it's just my mom and me, and she kind of...works from home." Hudson paused. "She's in the arts."

"Hmmm," Mrs. Geyer said as they turned into a driveway. "So she's a painter? Or a writer?"

"Kind of a cross between the two."

Mrs. Geyer drove up to what Hudson assumed was Ellie's house. It was a modest Tudor-style home with a stained-glass window in the front door. There were lights on in the windows downstairs, and already Hudson could see kids inside, milling around.

"All right, I'll come by to get you around eleven," Mrs. Geyer said. "Hudson, is that good for you? Or should we get you to the train a little earlier?"

"I'm getting a ride back to the city with my friends," she said. "But thank you."

"Have fun tonight," Mrs. Geyer said. "Ben, don't forget your bass."

"I know, Mom." Ben sighed.

Hudson and Ben got out of the car. He pulled the case containing his electric bass from the trunk, and as Mrs. Geyer pulled out of the driveway, he rolled his eyes at Hudson.

"Your mom's really cool," Hudson said. "I wish my mom was half as cool as that."

"She's okay," Ben said. "She's not that into this band thing. To her it's like this big distraction from what I should be doing."

"And what's that?" Hudson asked.

"Being on the chess team. Being on the physics team. Trying to get into MIT," said Ben. "Or Harvard. Or Johns Hopkins. Those are the only colleges that are officially approved."

"Really?" she asked.

"Both my parents are professors. And look at me. I'm, like, genetically engineered to be in a science lab somewhere, studying genomes or writing software."

Hudson laughed.

"But this is who I really am," he said, shaking the case of his bass. "I got big plans for this group. Just so you know."

"So I hear," she said, smiling. "What's your big plan?"

"That we play at Joe's Pub," he said simply, as if this were the most logical thing in the world. Joe's Pub was a famous club and cabaret space in New York. It booked all kinds of acts — jazz and pop and rock and even stand-up comedy — and everything from up-and-comers to the seriously famous.

"Joe's Pub?" Hudson asked.

"My dad took me there a couple of years ago," Ben went on. "He loves jazz. He's the one who got me into it. He gave me all his old John Coltrane and Miles Davis CDs. My mom wants to kill him." Ben smiled to himself and kicked at the gravel in the driveway. "So he took me to Joe's Pub to see Bill Frisell, who's probably the greatest jazz guitarist of all time, and I had kind of a flashforward. I could just see myself doing the same thing, onstage there one day." Ben chuckled. "*Obviously* I know it's a long shot. Not to mention my parents would completely freak out if I actually got that far. But if I did play there, one day, then maybe my *not* doing what they want wouldn't be so hard for them to take."

Hudson listened, remembering the conversation she'd had with Richard Wu just a few months earlier. She'd wanted to book a show at Joe's Pub. Naturally, Holla had changed his mind about that. She'd wanted someplace bigger, more of a real concert hall, like Roseland. Hudson hadn't even fought her on it. "So you think that would do it? Playing at Joe's Pub?"

Ben shrugged. "It's just my goal right now. And maybe I could make it happen. The whole trick to this business is connections. That's how anyone gets anywhere. It's, like, ninety percent connections. I went to camp with this kid whose dad was some big-shot music exec guy. He could totally help us."

"I think it has a little more to do with talent," Hudson argued.

"Well, maybe," Ben said. "But what about all those kids who become movie stars because their parents are? You think they got the job just because of their talent?"

Hudson didn't want to answer that. "Look, if you *are* that serious about doing this, then what about changing the name?" she asked. "The Stone Cold Freaks isn't doing us justice. What do you think of...the Rising Signs?"

Ben didn't say anything.

"I'm kind of into astrology," Hudson explained.

"The Rising Signs," he murmured, looking off into the night. "That's kind of cool."

"Let's run it past Logan and Gordie and see what they think."

"The Rising Signs," Ben repeated as he leaned down to pick up his case. "Nice one."

They walked into Ellie's house, and as Ben stopped to chat with some friends, Hudson stepped slowly into the living room. She didn't usually go to parties alone, much less parties thrown by people she barely knew. Groups of girls walked past her, laughing and talking. All of them wore jeans and oxford shirts or sweaters.

Hudson looked down at her poufy leather and hot pink silk dress and felt a little self-conscious. A couple of girls eyed her dress from across the room. Hudson waved at them. They waved back, hesitantly, but kept talking. Hudson walked over to the piano and dropped her bag. At least she could hide out here for a while.

"Ooh, Hudson!" Ellie cried, coming toward her. She was more dressed up than her friends were, in jeans and a camisole lined with sequins along the neckline and straps. "Great dress! I love it!"

"Thanks," Hudson said, relieved. "And happy birthday."

"Hey, can I ask you something?" Ellie said in a low voice. "Ben just told me you're really into astrology."

"A little, yeah."

Ellie leaned closer, practically whispering. "Could you find out if me and this guy are compatible?" She nodded her head at Logan, who was walking toward them with his saxophone case.

"Him?" Hudson pointed. "Logan?"

"We sort of hooked up last weekend," Ellie admitted. "And I *think* he likes me. But I can't really tell. I can give you his birthday, though, and maybe you can tell me!"

"Uh...uh, sure," Hudson said.

"Awesome," Ellie said, getting distracted by a group of people walking into her house. "Have fun!"

She wandered off to greet the newcomers. Almost before Hudson could absorb this, Logan sat down next to her and opened his sax case. Hudson cast him a sidelong glance. If what Ellie had told her was true, and Hudson had the definite feeling it was, then she needed to figure out what to do about Hillary's unrequited crush.

Logan still seemed intent on ignoring her as he put his saxophone together.

"Do we have a set list yet?" she asked him, in a super-friendly voice.

Logan shrugged. "I guess we're just playing whatever you and Ben want," he muttered.

"No, we're not," Hudson said, confused. "I think we all should talk about it. Together."

"Yeah, just like we all talked about changing the name of the band," he said sarcastically, snapping the pieces of his sax into place. "Together."

"Wait. It's not changed. It was just an idea we had. Who told you that? Ben?"

"Whatever," Logan said under his breath. He slipped the sax onto its stand and walked away.

"Logan!" Hudson yelled, but he didn't turn around. She watched him pick his way through the crowd and disappear toward the kitchen.

She sat on the piano bench, glancing at the crowd to see if anyone had just overheard their fight. This band thing didn't feel right anymore. She felt like an intruder. She'd unwittingly caused a whole slew of problems just by showing up. *I should leave,* she thought. *I can't deal with this guy not liking me.*

But then she remembered: That had been one of her fears, something she'd written down on Hillary's list. *Not being liked.* And here it was, happening right now.

Just as she was about to go find the bathroom and take a timeout for a moment, she saw Lizzie and Carina and Todd and Alex wading through the crowd. She'd never been so glad to see them before. She ran over to them.

"Hey, guys!" she said.

"Hey!" Lizzie said brightly.

"We just walked right in!" Carina exclaimed. "There wasn't even a list or anything!"

Hudson had noticed that, too. In the city, the news of a party always spread dangerously fast. It wasn't rare to see the doormen of the buildings on Park Avenue holding guest lists and checking off names as they let people through to the elevator.

Alex checked out the crowd, tapping his feet to the music. "Nice playlist," he said. "But where's everyone supposed to dance? There's furniture everywhere."

"What's wrong, Hudson?" Todd asked, looking at her with his alarmingly blue eyes. "You look a little freaked out."

"Oh, nothing," she said, embarrassed. "I think this one guy in the band is a little bit mad at me."

"What for?" asked Carina.

"I kind of suggested we change our name."

"What is it now?" asked Todd.

"The Stone Cold Freaks."

"Oh, yeah," Alex asserted. "Definitely. Not even a question."

Ben and Ellie walked toward them, and Hudson waved for them to join. "Hey, you guys, meet my friends. This is Lizzie, Carina, Todd, and Alex. Everyone, this is Ben Geyer and Ellie Kim. Ellie's the one having the party."

After everyone said hi and spoke for a while, Ben pulled Hudson aside. "I think we better start. But I can't find Logan anywhere.

181

Hey, Gordie!" Ben pulled Gordie over as he walked by. "Where's Logan?"

"Haven't seen him." Gordie shrugged.

"I think he's mad at me," Hudson said. "You told him about the new name for the band, right?"

"Just for a second," Ben said. "I didn't tell him it was a done deal or anything."

"Let's try to find him," said Hudson, leading the way to the kitchen. Ben followed.

They looked everywhere. He wasn't in the kitchen or the dining room, or out on the back patio, where a group of kids hung out in the cold. Finally they spotted him in the laundry room, talking with a small group of people. "Can I talk to you for a second?" Hudson asked. She looked back at Ben and Gordie. "Alone, if you guys don't mind."

"No problem," Ben said, and he and Gordie retreated.

"What?" Logan asked, his eyes narrowed. The group of people he'd been hanging out with quietly walked back into the kitchen.

"I just want you to know that I'm sorry if you feel like I've come in and turned things around, because I haven't," she said. "Maybe Ben did speak a little too soon at the bar mitzvah, about having me be the lead singer, but then he gave you guys a chance to talk it out. And this whole thing with changing the band name — that was just something I mentioned to Ben for, like, two seconds. It's not a done deal."

Logan looked past her, fidgeting to get away.

"I know there's nothing I can do to make you like me," she went on, "and I really don't care if you do or not. But what I *do* care about is this band. And I don't want there to be drama before it's even started."

She had no idea where these words were coming from. This wasn't how she usually talked, and she'd never spoken to anyone like this before. Logan darted his eyes around the room, as if he were physically unable to make eye contact. And then he said, "Forget it. There's no drama. Are we going on now?"

"Uh, yeah," Hudson said. "Let's go."

They walked back into the kitchen, where Ben and Gordie waited for them beside the four-layer dip. "We're ready," she said simply, and the four of them walked back to the living room.

"What's going on?" Carina asked, brushing her blond hair back behind her ear.

"Just a little band drama," Hudson said, smiling. "Wish me luck."

"Break a leg, Hudson," Lizzie said, then leaned her head on Todd's shoulder. She looked like she was blissfully in love.

Hudson walked over to the piano. A few feet away, Gordie snapped his high-hat cymbal on above the snare.

"I say we start with the song you wrote, Hudson," Ben said. "Then 'My Baby Just Cares for Me,' 'Fly Me to the Moon,' and 'Feeling Good.'"

Hudson nodded and sat down at the piano.

Ellie called everyone into the living room. "Okay, you guys!" she yelled. "Here we go...the moment we've all been waiting for! May I present...well...Ben's jazz band! Take it away, guys!"

Hudson felt her heart leap into double-time as people quieted down. *You can't freak out now,* she thought. *Not now.* Her hands shook, but she still found the opening chords.

Nobody knows you here, she told herself. *Nobody expects you to be good.*

She started to play. After a few moments, she slipped into her music trance. Soon Ben joined her on his bass, then Gordie. And when she got to the bridge, and Logan started to play, he actually restrained himself. She didn't dare look up from the keys as she sang, but it didn't matter. Her voice was strong and elastic, hitting every note. And somehow, her talk with Logan in the laundry room had only filled her with more confidence.

When she reached the last chord, there was a moment of silence. And then the room broke into applause.

Hudson glanced back at the rest of the band and then, awkwardly, they all rose from their seats and took a small bow. *This is me*, Hudson thought, bowing. *This is what I'm good at. Like it or not.*

"Woo-hoo!" some guys called out.

The twins Hudson recognized from rehearsal jumped up and down.

"Hudson!" Carina called out. "We love you!"

At the end of their set, after they'd played four more songs and rocked every one of them, the Rising Signs, or whatever they were called, linked arms and took their final bows. Hudson locked eyes with Ben over Gordie's and Logan's heads and they traded an ecstatic smile. Their first official gig hadn't just been good. It had been great.

chapter 20

By the time they got off the "stage," it was almost time for Hudson and her friends to get in Carina's car and go back to the city. But Hudson wanted to linger just a little bit longer—especially because Ben and Ellie's friends kept coming up to her and telling her how much they'd loved the set.

"You have a really pretty voice," one girl said sweetly. "It's really strong."

"Where do you go to school?" asked another. "Do you live up here?"

"Hudson goes to Chadwick, in the city," said Ellie, who was now standing right next to Hudson in an almost proprietary way.

"Do you want to sing for a living?" asked one of the twins, who'd sidled up beside them.

"I don't know," Hudson said. "I think so."

"When's your next show?" Ellie asked excitedly. "Oh, and

Hudson, could you take a picture with me and my friends?" she asked, handing her iPhone to one of the twins.

Hudson looked at the camera. Getting her picture taken — and having it possibly be posted on someone's Facebook page, where a tabloid could find it — just wasn't worth the risk. "I can't. I look awful," she fibbed.

Luckily, Carina and Alex rushed over before Ellie could react. "You were amazing, H!" Carina said. "Just amazing!"

"When's your next show?" Alex asked.

"I don't know," Hudson admitted. "I don't think we have one booked yet."

"H, I think we gotta get back," Carina said. "My dad'll have a conniption if I get home after midnight."

"Okay. There's just one thing I still have to do," Hudson said, turning to look at Logan, who was talking with Ben and Gordie. She'd made a promise to Hillary, and she couldn't leave without at least trying to get some information for her.

"Hey, guys," Hudson said, approaching them. "Great show tonight."

"Everyone's asking when we're playing next," Gordie said, walking up to them. "What are we thinking?"

"I think I might be able to swing something at the Olive Garden," said Logan. "They sometimes do live entertainment."

"Um, Logan?" Hudson asked. "Can I talk to you for a moment?"

Logan ran a hand through his blond hair and glanced quickly at Ben.

"It's about something else," Hudson said. "Not the name of the band."

"Fine," he said.

She pulled him over toward the piano. "Um, so you know Ben's cousin, Hillary, right?"

"Yeah," he said, already looking both wary and confused.

"So, um…she's a really cool girl. And, well, I think you guys would, um…" *Oh, God, this is awful,* she thought. *Just say it.* "What do you think of her? Do you like her?"

Logan looked at her like she'd suddenly sprouted a third head.

"Because, um, I think, well…" she hedged.

Logan folded his arms. "*No,*" he said. "And please tell her to stop calling me."

He stalked off, leaving Hudson in shocked silence. *Oh, Hillary,* she thought. *This guy is such a jerk. He doesn't deserve you.*

Later, as Max, Carina's driver, drove them back to the city, Hudson tried to erase Logan's comment from her mind. She had no idea how she was going to tell Hillary about this. The old Hudson would have just decided not to tell her at all. But now Hudson wondered if it was such a good idea to spare Hillary's feelings.

"So when do you guys think you'll do another show?" Lizzie asked, holding Todd's hand in the backseat.

"I'm not sure, but someone mentioned the Olive Garden," Hudson said.

"You guys should play at Violet's," said Alex.

"Violet's?" Hudson asked. "How would we even get in there?" Violet's was a legendary music club in the East Village. It had been around for at least thirty years and everyone from Blondie to the Ramones had graced its small, dingy stage.

"This guy I work with at Kim's Video knows the booker," Alex said. "I'll have him talk you guys up. But if you put some songs on MySpace, then I think you have more than a shot at it."

"Really?" Hudson squealed. "You really think we have a chance?"

"If you're okay with being the opening-opening act," Alex said.

"C?" Hudson asked. "Can I hug your boyfriend?"

"Go ahead," Carina said.

Hudson leaned over her to Alex and hugged him. "Thank you!" she exclaimed.

"Well, don't thank me yet," Alex warned. "Let me talk to the guy first."

Hudson leaned her head on Carina's shoulder as they drove across the Triborough Bridge. In the distance the skyline of New York twinkled and glittered in the cold night. This was all so unreal. Everything was falling into place. Maybe the Rising Signs — because that's what they were to her now — actually had a shot at Joe's Pub, after all.

At eleven thirty, Carina's car pulled up to Hudson's house. "Here you go, Hudson," Max said in his gruff voice. "Last but not least. Have a good night."

Hudson scooted out of the backseat. "Thanks, Max."

He waited while she unlocked the front door and slipped inside. The lights were still bright in the kitchen, but from the relaxed, hushed feeling inside the house Hudson knew that her mom was still out. She waved to Raquel, who sat at the kitchen table by herself eating her dinner, and walked up the stairs. As she headed to her room, her iPhone dinged with a text. She pulled it out of her bag. It was from Carina.

Sorry in advance but thought you'd want to see this.

And then there was a link.

She hurried into her room, and clicked on the link.

It took only a second. Soon she was staring at the garish purple and yellow home page of a celebrity gossip site. And there was the headline, lurid and underlined and not at all surprising:

HOLLA'S GORGEOUS NEW GUY

Underneath it was a photo of her mom and Chris on a red carpet earlier that night. Holla stood next to Chris, her toned arm encircling his waist. Chris's blue eyes squinted at the camera in a sexy way as he pulled Holla in close to him. Hudson stared at the image for a moment. Up until now, their relationship had been something that existed only in her mind, a gross and annoying story to tell her friends. But now it was real. And it hurt, even though she knew that she and Chris would never have had a future.

She texted Carina back:

Looks like he might be my stepfather after all. Taking bets now.

Then she went to signsnscopes.com — now would be a good time to check her horoscope, she thought. But just before the page opened she closed her laptop. She thought of the car ride home with Alex, and Violet's, and how maybe she and the Rising Signs had a possible future after all. Whatever the future held for her, whatever was headed her way, maybe it was time to just let it surprise her.

chapter 21

The next morning her alarm went off at eight, but Hudson turned it off. The idea of running downstairs for yoga class seemed a little ridiculous. And ever since their fight in the studio, Hudson had been doing her best to stick to her room whenever Holla was home. So she closed her eyes and drifted pleasantly back to sleep. At ten, she opened her eyes with a start. She'd never, ever slept this late on a Saturday morning, except when she was sick. She jumped out of bed and got dressed.

When she got to the kitchen, Lorraine was washing her hands and Raquel was folding towels. "You're just getting up?" Lorraine asked. "Are you sick?"

"No, just tired," Hudson said, opening the fridge. "Do we have any bacon?" she asked.

Lorraine and Raquel both stopped what they were doing and looked at her. *"Bacon?"* Lorraine asked in disbelief.

"That's okay," Hudson replied. She opened the refrigerator and took out a quart of fresh-squeezed orange juice. "I was just in the mood for it."

Hudson poured herself a glass of juice and then made herself a bowl of oatmeal topped with berries. Then she walked over to the neat pile of daily newspapers and chose the *New York Post*. Holla mostly tuned the tabloids out, not bothering to read them or surf them or even acknowledge them. The *New York Post* was her one exception. It was in the kitchen every morning, stacked right next to the *Times* and the *Wall Street Journal* and *Women's Wear Daily*. Hudson wasn't sure why the *New York Post* was okay when all the other ones weren't, but then again, her mom was full of contradictions.

"Well, someone's finally up," Holla said as she glided into the kitchen in her workout clothes. Tendrils of sweat-soaked hair curled around her face. "Lorraine? Niva would love an açai smoothie before she leaves."

"Coming right up," Lorraine said, going straight to the blender.

Holla wandered over to the kitchen table. Hudson kept her eyes on her newspaper. "So what's wrong with you?" Holla asked. "Why'd you miss yoga?"

"I was just tired. I didn't think you'd really miss me."

Hudson looked up to see her mom peering at her. Hudson could see that she was trying to keep her patience. "What play did you see last night?"

"Play?" Hudson asked, unsure what her mom was talking about.

"Didn't you see a play last night, with Jenny?" Holla asked, puzzled.

"Oh, yeah," Hudson answered confidently. "*American Idiot.*"

Holla seemed to expect more of an answer. "Did you like it?"

"Yeah. And Jenny's really psyched about the party, by the way."

"How's Jenny doing?" Holla asked, sitting down across from her. "Is she settled in finally?"

Hudson got up from the table and carried her bowl to the sink. She couldn't lie right to her mom's face. "I think she's doing better."

"Is she seeing someone?" Holla asked.

"Nope," she said, running water over her bowl. "By the way, I saw the pictures of you out with Chris last night."

Even though Hudson had her back turned, she could feel her mom stiffen at the mention of Chris's name. "Yeah, I took him to the Jay-Z documentary. It was fun."

"Why?" Hudson asked, turning around.

"Why?" Holla said, taken aback.

"I just thought that you had rules about this kind of stuff," said Hudson. "You know, waiting a month to take someone to a public event. That's what you always told me." Holla's rule about boyfriends was how she and Lizzie and Carina had come up with their own rule in the first place.

"Sometimes it's okay to break rules," Holla said. "And you're very opinionated these days."

"Opinionated?"

"I guess I'm not used to you being so...vocal," Holla said, as Lorraine placed a glass of coconut water in front of her.

"I just don't want to see you get hurt again," Hudson said.

Holla tilted her head, as if she didn't quite get what Hudson was saying. "Don't worry," she said with an edge in her voice. "Everything's going to be fine."

Hudson wiped her hands on a dish towel, then balled it up. She

192

knew that she didn't quite believe Holla, but she didn't have any real reason for it. "I gotta go," Hudson said. "I'm meeting a friend at Kirna Zabete."

"If you see anything there that's cute, can you pick it up for me?" Holla said. "A dressy, third-date kind of top?"

"Sure, Mom." She started to walk out of the kitchen.

"You should really try to get something that's a little more fitted," Holla said, reaching out to touch Hudson's waist. "You have such a cute figure — why are you always trying to hide it?"

Hudson stepped out of her grasp.

"Hudson."

Hudson turned around.

"Please don't worry," Holla said, almost as if she were pleading with herself not to worry. "About Chris. Please, don't."

"I won't," Hudson said and walked out.

*

"Hey, superstar!"

Hillary was almost half a block away, but her high-pitched voice sounded loud and clear down the narrow SoHo street. Hudson waved her arms. "Hey!" she yelled back, trying hard not to laugh.

"I heard you rocked last night!" Hillary said, her face getting lost in her bulky pink knit scarf as she jumped up and down. "Ben said you guys totally killed."

"We did okay," Hudson admitted. "We didn't embarrass ourselves."

"Oh, come on!" Hillary said, as if that were the most ridiculous thing on earth. "I heard it was awesome. And Ellie worships you."

Hudson remembered what Ellie had told her about hooking up with Logan. "Well, she really likes you, too," she offered, opening the door to the boutique and walking inside.

Hillary unzipped her puffy down coat, and Hudson saw that she was wearing skinny dark-rinse jeans and a gray cashmere sweater. Her hair fell straight to her shoulders, and it looked magically thick and static-free. There were no plastic barrettes in sight.

"Wow, you look good," Hudson said.

"Thanks," Hillary said, blushing. "I think today I really need shoes." Hillary headed over to a shelf of shoes and picked up a suede bootie that looked like a cage for the foot. "So, what did Logan say? Did you ask him about me? I hope you weren't too obvious. Were you obvious?"

Hudson ran her hand over a strapless top with a fringed neckline. "I don't know if Logan is the best guy for you, Hil, to be perfectly honest."

"What do you mean?" Hillary asked.

"He got really mad at me for, like, no reason at the party, and..." Hudson hesitated. "I think he might be hooking up with someone."

Hillary dropped the bootie on the table with a thud. "Who?" she demanded, her eyes narrowed.

"I don't know," Hudson said. "Just someone."

"How do you know? Did he tell you that?"

"No," Hudson said. "Not really."

"Then how do you know?"

Hudson looked away and cringed. She should never have stepped into this. "I just think he's not even worth your time."

"*Who* did he hook up with?" Hillary demanded.

Hudson bit her lip and turned to face her. If she told Hillary the truth, then it might get back to Ellie. Or even to Ben. "I don't know," she said miserably. "I really don't. But the point is that he's just not that great a guy. You deserve so much more than him."

Hillary looked down at the floor, lost in thought. She shook her head. "I thought you were my friend," she murmured.

"I am. Of course I am." Hudson took a step toward her.

"You're not acting like it." Hillary zipped up her coat. "The least you could do is be honest with me. After everything we've been through."

"Fine. He said for you not to call him anymore," Hudson said bluntly. "That's what he said."

Hillary's already pale face turned even whiter.

Hudson felt an instant stab of remorse. "Hillary, I'm sorry," she said. "But that's what he said. You wanted to know."

Before Hudson could say anything more, Hillary turned and walked out of the store, letting the door swing shut behind her.

Hudson ran out of the store. "Hillary!" she yelled after her. "I'm sorry!"

But Hillary didn't turn around. She didn't stop. She trudged up the street in her gigantic puffy coat as if she couldn't get away from Hudson fast enough.

"Hillary! You wanted to know!" Hudson yelled.

Hillary picked up her pace, and when she reached the corner she hung a right and promptly disappeared.

Hudson went back inside and bought her mom a pretty floral-print Stella McCartney top that she would probably hate. She felt terrible. She wasn't the girl who didn't mince words; that was

195

Carina. And Carina probably wouldn't have thought that what she'd said to Hillary was that rude. So just to make sure, Hudson called her.

"Oh my God," Carina said. "She said she wanted to know."

"I know," Hudson said, crossing the cobblestone street. "And believe me, she would have said it to me."

"Don't even worry about it," Carina said. "You need to be a little more blunt. This is progress. And by the way, Alex says that his friend can definitely hook you up with a show at Violet's."

"What?" Hudson said, coming to a stop. "Are you serious?"

"Now you just need to create a MySpace page so they can hear you. Like, now."

Trembling with excitement, Hudson hung up the phone and called Ben.

"Violet's?" he asked. "Isn't that the place where the Ramones used to play, before they were the Ramones?"

"Yes," Hudson said. "And my friend can probably get us booked there. If we put up a MySpace page. And record some stuff for it."

"What are you doing tomorrow?" Ben asked.

"Nothing."

"Then come up here and let's get this done!"

*

The next day she told Raquel that she was going over to Carina's house, then she let Fernald drop her in front of Carina's building. As soon as he was out of sight she took a cab to Grand Central. On the train up to Larchmont she tapped her toes and sang her songs under her breath, getting ready. She knew that they would have to record mostly original songs for their MySpace page, and she knew just the ones she wanted: "For You," "Heartbeat," and a new song she'd just written.

She took a cab from the train station to Ben's house, and when she got there, Ben, Gordie, and Logan had Ben's mammoth laptop already set up. They recorded their songs on Ben's computer, and when they were finished, Ben fine-tuned the songs in GarageBand. It was impressive watching him work. Hudson could see that he definitely had a future in music.

"I think we're done," he finally said. "Wanna hear it back?"

He played back the three songs. The music sounded perfect, and her voice was as sultry as ever.

"Put it up," Hudson said. "I'll tell Alex's friend it's there. And I'll give them your number. Cool?"

"Absolutely," Ben said.

*

On Tuesday, just after Geometry, Hudson got the text from Ben: They were booked at Violet's to be the opening, opening act for a Monday-night show in a little less than a month. February twenty-third.

"We're booked!" Hudson shrieked in the hallway.

Mr. Barlow stepped his long, lanky frame out of his office and zeroed in on Hudson with his glacial blue eyes. "And I'm gonna be booking you in detention if you don't keep your voice down, Miss Jones."

"Sorry," Hudson said, running down the hall to tell her friends the good news.

chapter 22

During the days leading up to the Violet's gig Hudson could barely concentrate. She could already see herself and the band on Violet's notoriously small, crooked stage, playing their songs surrounded by the ghosts of rock-and-roll legends. Playing at Violet's meant that she was no longer in a high school band — she was in a *band*. She practiced her piano every spare moment. And at least once a week now, as she sat in Spanish or History or English, a song would come to her. After school she'd go home and head straight to her room, and for several hours she'd work on the song, letting it take shape as her hands slid over the keys.

She managed to escape up to Larchmont a few more times, using Aunt Jenny as her alibi. Whenever she was alone with Ben before or after rehearsal, she'd sometimes think about telling him who she was. It seemed a little weird to have "Hudson Jones" on their MySpace page. Someone, at some point, was going to figure out who she was. *Just tell him, already*, she'd think. *He deserves to know.* But Ben wasn't a boyfriend. A boyfriend deserved to know. Ben was just her bandmate, and if she told him about Holla Jones, he would probably want her to get her mom involved in the band. She remembered what he'd said that night about connections. And right now they seemed to be doing just fine the way they were.

Meanwhile, Holla spent long hours in the studio, putting the finishing touches on her album. She wouldn't get home until late. At night, Hudson would lie in bed, listening to the photographers rushing to snap the SUV as it drove into the garage. It was a relief to have a little break from her mom.

Hillary was someone else she barely saw. In fact, their friendship seemed to have dissolved altogether. Hillary no longer sat in the library in the morning, doing the crossword. Every once in a while Hudson caught glimpses of her trudging up the stairs to the Middle School. Hillary's fashion evolution still seemed to be in full swing. Her messy ponytail had been replaced by carefully blow-dried hair, and her pink knit scarf was gone, along with any hint of bright color. Her sweaters were blue, gray, or black, and even her pink and blue square backpack seemed to have been trashed in favor of a black messenger bag. It was as if her separation from Hudson had only made her more chic and fashionable.

And then there was her mom's ongoing love affair with Chris. When they weren't working in the studio, they took yoga classes together or and hung out in the prayer room, listening to music and talking about her tour. If she passed him on the stairs, he'd ask her a question: how she was, if she wanted to listen to any of her mom's tracks, if she'd had a good day at school. It seemed that after eavesdropping on her fight with Holla in the recording studio,

Chris was determined to be her friend. Sometimes she thought about telling Chris about her band. She wanted him to know that she hadn't completely given up on her music. But it seemed too risky, especially because he seemed surgically attached to Holla.

Sometimes it was a relief for Holla to have someone else to focus on. But it felt strange to be a third wheel in her own house, so soon. It had taken Holla weeks to allow her last boyfriend to spend any time at the house.

On the Saturday before the Violet's show, Hudson woke up late. The sun peeked through the crack in her velvet curtains, and it looked like one of the first days of spring. She got out of bed, showered, and dressed in a long-sleeved purple and gray striped dress layered over black tights and black ankle boots. She would need a new outfit for the Violet's gig, and today seemed like the perfect day to get something.

Down in the kitchen, Holla and Chris were digging into spelt pancakes and drinking kale–green apple smoothies. They were sweaty and flushed, and Hudson could see that they'd either been having a steamy makeout session or an intense power hula-hooping class. Or both.

"Hi, baby," Holla said casually. "You want some breakfast?"

"I'll just grab a muffin," Hudson said, going to the platter of them on the kitchen island.

"We missed you in yoga," Holla added. "Someone here has no idea how to do scorpion pose."

"Come on, do you really want me to be good at that?" Chris asked, as they played footsie under the table.

"So...how's the album?" Hudson asked, doing her best to ignore the lovefest.

"We finished last night," Holla said, clinking her smoothie glass with Chris's. "I think it turned out okay. The label's listening to it over the weekend."

"Just okay?" Chris asked, leaning in to kiss the top of Holla's nose. "I beg you to restate that."

"Okay, *great*," Holla said, kissing him back.

"Awesome," Hudson said, counting the seconds until she could leave.

"So, Hudson, I was thinking of stopping at Jeffrey today to get something for the party tonight," Holla said.

"Party?" Hudson asked.

"Jenny. I'm throwing a birthday party for her tonight. Remember?"

Hudson almost dropped her muffin on the floor. Today was February twenty-first. And then she remembered: Jenny was in Buenos Aires. In all her excitement about the Rising Signs and the Violet's booking, she'd completely forgotten to tell her mom that Jenny was going to be out of town.

"Raquel and Sophie have done an incredible job with the invitations," Holla was saying. "And everything's set. It's going to be about fifty people, most of them my friends, of course," Holla said to Chris. "My sister's social circle is...well, let's just say that it's not quite the kind of crowd you invite into your house."

Hudson couldn't move. The muffin still lay in her hand, dry and crumbly. She couldn't think straight.

"And tell me what you think of this," Holla said to Hudson. "You know how much Jenny loves macaroons. Well, I had about three hundred flown in from Ladurée." In answer to Hudson's blank stare she said, "They make the best macaroons in the world. They're a famous café in Paris. Don't you think she's going to love that?"

"Uh…uh, sure," Hudson said uncertainly.

"Just tell Jenny to be here at six. She doesn't need to help me set up." Holla noticed that Hudson was zoning out. "Hudson? Are you all right?"

"I'm fine," she said. "I'll be right back."

She ran up the stairs to her bedroom, where she'd left her phone. Maybe Jenny hadn't gone away after all, she thought desperately. Maybe her trip had been canceled. She called and waited. One ring. Two rings. Three rings.

Answer, she pleaded silently. *Please pick up.*

Finally she got Jenny's voice mail.

Hey! It's me! I'm out of the country but leave me a message or call me back later!

Hudson hung up and ran to her laptop. Trying hard to keep calm, she pounded out a note to Jenny over e-mail.

Forgot to tell mom about your party being moved. It's happening tonight. Can you come back in time for it?

She hesitated for a second and then added:

Can you call me ASAP?

She clicked Send, her stomach in knots. Her heart was beating so fast that she had to hold the edge of her desk and take deep breaths. She knew that there was the option to just go downstairs and calmly tell her mom the situation — that she'd forgotten, plain and simple, and that Aunt Jenny wasn't in town — but then Holla would want to know why it didn't come up when they went to see the Broadway play. And then Hudson would have to tell Holla that there'd been no play. And then Holla would start asking questions and find out about all the other times Hudson had lied about seeing Aunt Jenny. And then Holla would find out where she'd really been all this time... Hudson grabbed her purse and coat, left her room, and went down the stairs, still unsure of what to say. But only Chris was sitting at the kitchen table, wolfing down another plate of pancakes.

"Hey!" he said. "So what's the latest in the life of Hudson Jones?"

"Where's my mom?" Hudson asked.

"Oh, she rushed out of here. Had to go talk to a florist or something," he said.

"Oh." Hudson slung her coat over her shoulders. "I have to go out for a little bit."

"She's got her BlackBerry with her," Chris offered.

"That's okay," Hudson said, heading to the door. *Just call her right now and tell her the truth*, she thought. *Just tell her that you screwed up, that you're in this band, that you've been saying you're hanging out with Jenny as an excuse.*

But she pushed the thought away. She couldn't do it. Something about messing up that big in front of her mom made her want to run out of the house, head up to Grand Central, and leave the city for good.

She thought of calling her friends, but she knew that they

would make her fess up, and she just couldn't. Instead, she had Fernald drop her off at the Museum of Modern Art, where she walked through the halls of the permanent collection, barely registering the art on the walls. *Just call her,* she'd think, reaching for her phone. But if she did, she'd be saying good-bye to the Violet's gig. And she couldn't do that. Not to herself, and not to Ben.

That night Hudson watched, a smile frozen on her face, as the party guests arrived. Votive candles flickered in every corner of the living room, and black-jacketed waiters passed around platters of hors d'oeuvres. Holla weaved through the crowd, looking glamorous in a one-shoulder crimson dress that swept the floor. Hudson kept her eyes glued on her mother like a traffic accident, unable to look away. Holla was gracious and calm, the perfect hostess, but she glanced at the door repeatedly, waiting for the guest of honor to arrive. Finally, at six forty-five, she walked up to Hudson, who was still standing off to the side, contemplating a vegan dumpling but too filled with dread to eat it.

"Where's Jenny?" Holla demanded, one hand on her hip.

Hudson just shrugged.

"Call her right now and tell her to get down to this house," she snapped.

"No problem," Hudson said, and went up to her room. She sat down at her desk, trying to think. She'd known this moment was coming, of course. And she still didn't have any idea of how to resolve it. She opened her laptop. Jenny still hadn't written her back yet — not that that would have helped anything. Hudson bit one of her fingernails. It was awful to make Jenny look like even more of a flake than she already was, but her mom was used to this, after all.

Jenny had done worse things to her over the years. She'd even dated one of Holla's boyfriends right after Holla broke up with him. So blowing off her own birthday party almost wasn't that bad.

Hudson went back down to the party after a few minutes had passed. "She's not there," she said to Holla with as straight a face as she could.

Holla's eyes blazed. "What do you mean she's not there?"

"I mean, she's not answering her cell phone," Hudson said, cringing inside as she said it.

Holla shook her head as if she didn't quite understand, and then one of her party guests tapped her on the shoulder and drew her back into the crowd.

Hudson retreated into the corner. She reached for a mini veggie burger and popped it into her mouth even though she felt nauseous.

Holla asked Hudson to call Jenny again at seven, at eight, and then, one last time, at eight thirty. Each time Hudson went up to her room and just sat there, staring at the phone for a few minutes. *Just tell her the truth*, she'd think. But it was almost too late.

"She wasn't there," she'd say when she returned, as her mom's expression changed from disbelief to fury to quiet, enraged acceptance.

At the end of the night, after the last party guest had thanked Holla and wished her well, Hudson watched her mother shut the front door, then walk around the living room, blowing out each votive candle.

"Mom?" she asked, thankful for the gathering dark. "Are you all right?"

Holla didn't say anything.

"Mom? Are you okay?"

Her mom turned to her in the dark. "I don't want you to ever see her again," she said evenly. She left the room, leaving Hudson with an untouched tray of pastel macaroons.

chapter 23

"You go on at eight o'clock, you play six songs, and then you have two minutes to get off the stage," said Bruce, the manager and head booker at Violet's, wagging one thick, gnarled finger at them. He had watery blue eyes, a graying beard, and a very suspicious manner. "And no drinking. Do not go near the bar. You want some soda, you come ask me. You got that?"

"Don't worry. They won't be drinking," said Mrs. Geyer. Mrs. Geyer had agreed to be the band's official chaperone for the evening. Hudson was becoming more and more impressed with Mrs. Geyer every day. She'd helped the boys haul in equipment and then parked the car in a nearby garage. Now she sat in the corner with her handbag in her lap, quietly reading a magazine and doing her best to melt into the background. Hudson couldn't imagine her mom doing one of those things, let alone all of them. If Mrs. Geyer still had reservations about Ben's music career, she seemed to be getting over them.

"And anyone asks how old you are, just say eighteen," Bruce continued.

"That's no problem, sir," said Ben, with his usual politeness.

Bruce stared at him with narrowed eyes. "Don't be fresh with me," he said, pointing his finger. Then he walked out, leaving a trail of bad vibes behind him.

"For a guy who booked the Ramones, he seems a little uptight," Gordie said, adjusting his glasses.

"Dude has a killer beard," Logan observed.

"Anyone hungry?" Mrs. Geyer asked, reaching into her purse. "I've got beef jerky and Fruit Roll-Ups."

"Mom," Ben said, shaking his head. "I can't believe you brought Fruit Roll-Ups."

Hudson got up and paced around the small, cavelike dressing room. She'd heard and read so much about this place: famous brawls in the dressing room, police raids on the bathrooms. Of course, these days it was much tamer. The only reminder of Violet's wild past seemed to be here, on the dressing room walls, which were covered in mostly illegible graffiti.

"Hey, does anyone have a pen?" she asked.

Ben walked over and pulled one out of his back pocket. "You gonna add something of your own?"

"We have to leave our mark," Hudson said. She took his ballpoint pen and crouched low, careful not to let the hem of her flouncy burgundy chiffon dress get dirty. She pushed the pen into the peeling paint. *THE RISING SIGNS*, she wrote. And then the date.

"Hudson, is your mother coming?" Mrs. Geyer asked.

"Oh, she can't make it," Hudson said.

"Really?" Mrs. Geyer asked, surprised. "She can't?"

"She's out of town." She'd told Raquel to tell Holla that she was going over to Lizzie's house to study. It was a bit of a sloppy lie, but it was the best she'd been able to come up with, now that her mom and Jenny were so clearly on the outs. And Aunt Jenny was still out of the country. Every time she thought about Aunt Jenny she got a terrible knotted feeling in her stomach. But standing here now in this dressing room, she knew that she'd done the right thing by not telling her mom the truth.

"Your mother *does* know about all this, doesn't she?" Mrs. Geyer asked, trying not to sound too concerned.

"Oh, yeah, she's fine with it. Hey, do you want to come with me to the deli?" Hudson asked Ben. "I think I need some lozenges for my throat."

"Sure."

"Hurry back," said Mrs. Geyer. "You go on in twenty minutes."

As they walked out into the main room, Hudson realized that this was the first time she'd ever been in a real music club; her mom hadn't played places like this since before Hudson was born. Violet's was just one room, hardly any bigger than her bedroom at home. A cluster of tables stood on the floor, just a few feet from the stage. The bar on the side was barely longer than the island in Holla's kitchen. Above the bar hung a collection of old photographs. And there, against the far wall, was the small, cramped stage, bathed in soft reddish light.

"Wow," Ben said, looking around. "You have to thank that guy Alex for me. This is incredible."

"I know." Hudson laughed. "I can't believe we're here."

"I was thinking," Ben said, scratching his un-pomaded curly hair, "It might be kind of crazy, but we should try to get booked at Joe's Pub. What's the worst that can happen? They say no? Big deal."

"Right. I think we should."

They left the club and started walking to the corner. *Just tell him*, she thought. *It would be so easy.* Drops of rain were just starting to fall. A city bus wheezed its way up Bowery Street. Reggae music came from a taxi at the corner. Next door, a restaurant had just opened up. There was a velvet rope set up in front, manned by a large bouncer, and a throng of paparazzi jostling nearby, snapping the people walking in and out.

"I have this theory," said Ben, "that a velvet rope is basically all you need to make a place cool. That and a few weird guys with really big cameras just hanging out in front."

"I think you're right about that," Hudson said.

"Yeah. I mean, people will believe anything if they see a bouncer in front of a place —"

"Hudson!" someone yelled.

Hudson looked. It was a photographer. Before she could move he'd aimed his camera at her.

SNAP! The camera flash exploded in her face.

"Hudson!" another photographer yelled.

CLICK! went his camera as another flash blinded her.

"Where's your mother?" another one yelled. *SNAP!*

"What's going on?" Ben asked. "Why are they taking your picture?"

"Come here," she said, grabbing his arm and leading him into the deli.

210

"Do those people know you?" asked Ben. "How do they know your name? Why are they asking about your mom?"

She ran into the deli and down an aisle of potato chips and bags of mini-pretzels. She couldn't look at Ben. She looked at the potato chip bags, the shelves of candy, anywhere but his face.

"Hudson?" Ben asked. "What was that?"

Finally she met his worried gaze. "My mom is Holla Jones, Ben."

Ben blinked for a few moments. It was as if she'd just said she were a martian.

"Are you serious? Why didn't you tell me?"

"I should have," she said. "But I haven't told her about you guys yet, either."

"What?" Ben asked. "Why not?"

"Because I was supposed to put out my own album this spring."

"You *were*?" he said.

"And she'd never understand why I'm now in a jazz band up in Westchester."

"Thanks," Ben muttered.

"Sorry, that didn't come out right," Hudson said. "Look, I don't want my mom anywhere near this. She just takes over. She takes over everything. She took over my album and changed everything. She turned all my songs into this crazy sampled pop stuff, stuff I couldn't even recognize. It was awful. And then I tried to sing one of the songs in front of this big party and it was a disaster. And I figured that was a sign that it's just not meant to be after all. So I just decided to stop."

Ben nodded slowly, trying to understand.

"But then I found you guys," she said. "And you helped me

remember why I want to do this. Why I love music. And that I need to play the kind of stuff *I* want to play. No matter what." She shivered in the cold. "And being up in Larchmont, being in your basement, hanging out with Ellie, it's like I'm finally just me, you know? I'm not Holla Jones two-point-oh. For once."

Ben smiled. "Hudson," he said, stepping closer to her, "I know we don't know each other very well. But you're talented, okay? *Seriously* talented. And sometimes I feel like you don't really believe it. It's like you're embarrassed by it."

Hudson fidgeted with the bags of chips.

"And now I get it," he said. "I can't imagine having everyone in the world know my mom. And being compared to her. That would suck." He reached over and grabbed a pack of Ricola drops. "But you have to take up your own place in the world. And feel like you deserve to."

Hudson looked up at Ben. He gave her the Ricolas.

"And as far as not wanting your mom involved, that's fine, but think about the position you're in: You don't have to pound down doors. You don't have to stalk someone to listen to your tape. And there's nothing wrong with that."

"I know," she said, readjusting some pretzels on the rack. "I just didn't want you guys to expect that."

"I don't," Ben said. "But if this is what you really want to do, why are you making it so hard?"

She thought about that for a moment. "It's just how I want this to be right now."

Ben nodded. "Well, can I tell the rest of the guys?" he asked. "Would that be okay?"

"Not yet," she said. "Maybe later. But not now." She walked to the register.

"Okay." He touched her shoulder. "And Hudson?"

"Yeah?"

"Thanks for telling me the truth."

"You're welcome." She paid for the Ricolas and they walked out of the deli.

"So, are you gonna get your picture taken again?" he joked.

"It doesn't matter," Hudson said. "They don't usually end up anywhere." She watched the paparazzi milling around outside and was relieved to see that most of them had their backs to her. And then a couple walked out of the bar, past the velvet rope, and onto the sidewalk in front of them. They held their heads down and walked quickly by the paparazzi, who didn't seem to notice them. The guy was tall and skinny and his hair looked reddish-blond in the dim orange light of the street lamps. He held the hand of the woman with him. She was tiny and thin, with long brown hair that fell over the hood of her shearling coat.

Hudson watched as the man leaned down, kissed her, and then reached into the back pocket of his Levi's and pulled out a blue knit hat.

Hudson felt a shiver run through her. It was Chris Brompton. With another woman.

"Oh my God," she said.

"What?" Ben asked. "What is it?"

She watched Chris and his mystery woman cross the street.

"Hudson? What's going on?"

"I know that guy," she said, pointing, unable to say more.

"We gotta go," said Ben, glancing at his watch. "We have a show to play, remember?"

She stared at the man's back as he walked away. It could have been someone else. After all, she hadn't seen his face. But she knew with a sick certainty that it was him.

She was so distracted that she didn't even notice the bouncer in front of Violet's when they walked back inside.

"Wait. How old are you kids?" he asked.

"We're playing tonight," Ben explained, and showed the bouncer his bracelet.

They pushed through the crowd and headed toward the stage. The room had filled while they were gone. They reached the dressing room just as Gordie and Logan were about to walk out. "Where've you guys been?" Logan asked.

"Sorry!" Hudson said, digging in her purse for a comb and some lip gloss.

Bruce walked in, waving his arms. "What are you waiting for, kids? You're on!" he yelled. "Get out there!"

Hudson threw her things back in her purse and ran after her bandmates out onto the stage.

"Hey. We're the Rising Signs," Hudson said into the mic as she sat down at the piano.

A cheer rose up from the tables. A few people even whistled. Hudson pushed the image of Chris Brompton out of her head, leaned into the mic, and, thinking, *You're here, you're actually here,* she started to sing.

chapter 24

I have to tell her, Hudson thought as she lay in bed, staring at the ceiling. *I have to tell her what I saw last night.*

It was early — so early that her alarm clock hadn't even gone off yet. Outside her velvet curtains she could hear the whine of a garbage truck stopped outside their house. It was a school day, but Hudson felt too exhausted to even get up. She'd barely slept last night after the gig. The show at Violet's had been unbelievably and wonderfully great. The crowd had loved the songs, and even Bruce had seemed impressed. They'd even had some requests for CDs, even though they didn't have any yet.

But she couldn't get the picture of Chris kissing that woman out of her mind. It was clear that she had to say something. If she didn't, Holla would fall deeper in love with him. But if she *did* tell her mom, she would have to explain being in the middle of the East Village last night instead of at Lizzie's apartment.

"Don't say anything," Carina had warned her over the phone,

after the show. "Just pretend you never saw it. That's what I would do. No *way* do you want to get in the middle of that."

"You have to tell her!" Lizzie argued when Hudson called her after speaking to Carina. "Wouldn't *you* want to know?"

"But if I tell her, she's gonna want to know where I saw him," Hudson explained.

Lizzie seemed to be thinking. "Just say that you saw him near my house."

"But why would *we* be out on the street?" Hudson asked.

Lizzie didn't have any response to that.

"Ugh," she said into her pillow, remembering the conversation now, just as her vintage sixties alarm clock rang.

Hudson reached up and slammed the clanging bells with her hand. Then she grabbed her iPhone off the floor and, out of habit, checked her e-mail.

Jenny had finally written her back. Holding her breath, Hudson opened it.

Hey, Hudson, just got your message. I'm really shocked to hear about the party. I told you that I was going to be out of town. I was wondering why I never heard from you again. Guess you only needed me for an "alibi." I will be calling your mom as soon as I get home.

Jenny

With a piercing sensation in her chest, Hudson saw that Holla had been cc'd on the message.

Hudson threw the phone to the floor and walked to the bathroom on shaky legs. She was in serious trouble. Now her mom knew almost everything. Like a zombie, she showered, dried off, and put on her school uniform. When she opened the door, Matilda was there, excitedly circling her feet. Hudson picked her up. "I'm in trouble, Bubs," she whispered into the dog's ear. Matilda licked Hudson's nose almost sympathetically. Hudson walked down the stairs, passing the kitchen. If her mom were home, she knew where she would probably be, and there was no sense in dragging this out.

Hudson put Matilda down at the glass doors of the yoga studio. Inside, she could see Holla's pierced and dreadlocked hula-hooping instructor, Che, swiveling a hoop around her waist. Holla stood in the corner, conferring with Sophie, with her back to the door.

Hudson opened the door. *Here goes*, she thought. "Mom?" she asked.

Holla turned around before Hudson even finished speaking. Her eyes were dark and seemed even bigger than usual. Her chest heaved up and down.

"Mom, I saw the e-mail from Jenny —"

"You're grounded," Holla said. "Do you understand?"

"Mom, I'm sorry," Hudson said, feeling tears come to her eyes. "It was just a mistake."

"Oh, really? A mistake? Sophie?" Holla said, sounding like she was just barely keeping herself under control.

Hudson saw that Sophie held a rolled-up newspaper. It uncurled just enough to show the front page, and the *New York Post* masthead.

"Look at Page Six," Holla said.

Sophie handed Hudson the newspaper, without looking her in the eye. With shaking hands, Hudson found the page.

It was a photo of her with Ben. One of the photos that had been taken the previous night when they walked to the deli. And underneath was the caption:

Hudson Jones, daughter of icon Holla Jones, leaving
Violet's, where she wowed the crowd last night with her
own jazz- and soul-inspired songs.

"It's one thing if you're going to lie to me," said Holla, her voice eerily cool and controlled, "but your record label is gonna want to know why someone with crippling stage fright is singing at Violet's."

"I was gonna tell you," she began. "It's just this band I joined. Up in Westchester."

"In *Westchester*?" Holla exclaimed. "You've been going to *Westchester*?"

Hudson didn't say anything.

"Well, that's done," Holla said. "I'm calling your label today and telling them you're back on track. Do you understand me?"

Hudson didn't speak. She knew that her mom meant this.

"And about Jenny," Holla said in a withering voice. "Do you know how that made me look? In front of everyone? How could you let me be humiliated like that?"

Hudson swallowed again. "I'm sorry. I just didn't know what to say."

"And why would you want to play dumps like Violet's when you could be playing Madison Square Garden?" Holla asked, her voice ringing against the studio walls. Behind her, Che and Sophie seemed to cower. "When you have a finished album just sitting on the shelf? What's wrong with you?"

"I just wanted to do something myself," Hudson said feebly.

"Because I'm that horrible. Right? I'm that terrible." Holla shook her head. "I've done nothing but help you. I've given you music teachers and voice coaches and studios. And you throw it back in my face. Just like my sister."

"What if I don't *want* to play the Garden?" Hudson exploded. "What if I don't *want* to do things exactly the way you do?" Her voice was getting louder and louder. "What if I don't need to be a total egomaniac to be happy?"

Holla's face went slack. "You're done with that band. Today. And starting right now, you don't go anywhere but school and back. Do you understand me?"

Hudson turned and ran to the door, choking on her tears. She'd forgotten to tell her mom about Chris. But Holla didn't deserve to know. And when Holla did find out, Hudson wouldn't be there. She'd never be there for Holla again.

chapter 25

"Hudson, it's okay. Really. It's okay," Lizzie said, smoothing Hudson's hair with the palm of her hand.

"Come on, you're gonna make *me* cry," Carina pleaded, reaching out to pat Hudson on the back.

They weren't supposed to be inside the ladies room off the Chadwick lobby, because technically it was for visitors only. But Lizzie and Carina had pulled Hudson in there the moment they saw her, and Hudson had been only too grateful to follow them. She now stood with her head pressed up against Lizzie's shoulder, sobbing so hard she thought she might hyperventilate. As soon as she could breathe normally again, Carina wet a paper towel under the faucet and handed it to her.

"So what happened?" Lizzie asked. "Just tell us."

Hudson blotted her face with the paper towel. "My mom found out about the show. It's on Page Six. And I have to quit the band. *And* my aunt officially hates me."

"That sucks," Lizzie said.

"And now it's all over. Everything. After a great show last night, too." She sniffled, wiping her nose with the back of her hand.

"She was just angry," Carina reasoned. "Wait until she sees you at a show. She'll totally change her mind —"

"No, she won't, not now. That's all finished." Hudson grabbed a dry paper towel and wiped at her eyes. "It's like there's no talking to her. There's no reasoning with her. She said because I signed a contract I should pick up where I left off. But that album just isn't me. It's not even my music."

"Why don't you tell her that?" Carina asked. "Just say that. Tell her you want to make an album that reflects *you*."

"I tried," Hudson said. "That day when you guys were in the studio last fall. Remember how well that worked out?"

"Look, you've been brave, and you've put yourself out there, and you've gotten out from under your mom's thumb," Lizzie pointed out, her hazel eyes calm and reassuring. "And that's more than anyone else could do in your shoes. Maybe you can rejoin the band in a little while. After things calm down."

"And why does your aunt hate you?" Carina asked. "I mean, not to make things worse, but that part I still don't get."

"My mom threw her a party, and I knew my aunt couldn't be there, and I forgot to tell my mom. You know how controlling she is about stuff. I just couldn't tell her. I couldn't say that I'd made a mistake."

Her friends looked at her gently. "She's your mom, H," Carina said. "She doesn't expect you to be perfect."

"Yes, she does," Hudson said, feeling the tears start to come again. Hudson glanced in the mirror. Big red blotches spread out from her green eyes down to her cheeks, and her lips were swollen. "She can't be normal," Hudson said. "She can't eat like everyone else. She can't relax for a second. It's all about being the best, the biggest, the most amazing person in the world. She wants me to be like that, too. It's like I'll be some loser if I don't end up a superstar."

"Do you believe that?" Lizzie asked.

Hudson swallowed. "No."

"So then why does it bother you when she says that?" Lizzie asked.

Hudson played with the hair elastic around her wrist. "I guess a little part of me is afraid she's right," she said quietly.

Carina looked at her watch. "Oh, *shnit*. Madame Dupuis's gonna have a French cow if we don't get up there." She put her hands on Hudson's shoulders. "You okay?"

Hudson sniffled one last time and then splashed her face with more water. "God, I love school," she groaned, and then cracked a smile.

As they walked out of the bathroom, Hudson tried to believe what Lizzie had said. She *had* been brave. She'd tried to do her own thing. For just a few short weeks, she'd just been Hudson onstage. And it had been wonderful.

But that was all over now. And the sooner she accepted it, the better.

chapter 26

All day Hudson watched the clock. In every class, during every free period, she kept tabs on the time. Twelve o'clock. One o'clock. Two. Every minute that brought her closer to the end of the school day only increased her sense of dread. Spending the evening under the same roof as her mom was pretty much unthinkable. Right now she never wanted to look at or speak to Holla again. She almost asked Lizzie or Carina if she could sleep over. But whatever was waiting for her at home, she knew that she needed to face it. At least the worst seemed to be over.

When she walked out of school, the black SUV was waiting right at the curb, directly in front of the school doors. Holla had meant what she'd said about tightening her grip on Hudson's comings and goings.

"Bye, guys," she said to Lizzie and Carina as they hovered by the side of the school building, shielding themselves from the rain. "Say a prayer."

"You just have to get through tonight," Carina said.

"Maybe your mom will reconsider the band thing," Lizzie put in.

But as the SUV inched its way downtown, Hudson doubted it. For all she knew her mom had already booked her time in the studio to finish the album and get it released by summer. When she got home she took the service elevator up from the basement and walked into the kitchen, holding her breath.

"Your mother's upstairs," Raquel said sternly, arranging a spray of white flowers. "She wants to talk to you."

Hudson felt an even bigger wave of dread. "Thanks," she said listlessly, then took the elevator to the fourth floor, which belonged entirely to Holla's suite of private rooms. Hudson walked down the hall, past the pale peach-colored bedroom and gym, where Holla ran on the treadmill and lifted weights in the afternoons. Then she turned into the closet. She slipped off her boots at the entrance — Holla didn't like the idea of dirt so near her clothes — and entered.

Holla was standing on a pedestal in a magenta bandage dress, flanked by mirrored closet doors that magnified her reflection over and over, so that it looked like there were at least a hundred Hollas in the room. Kierce, her stylist, sat on a tufted ottoman to one side. He had a long black ponytail, ghostly pale skin, and a permanent, disapproving squint. Even though he wore only black, he was always trying to get Hudson to wear bright colors.

"We're looking at stuff for *Saturday Night Live*," Holla said curtly. "What do you think?" She twirled around on the pedestal with her hands on her waist, showing off the dress, which hugged every curve. "You like the color?"

"The color is not even a *question*," Kierce put in.

"I like it," Hudson said, relieved to talk about fashion.

"I don't know. I don't like what it does here," Holla said, gesturing to her flat stomach. "It gives me a pooch."

"No, it doesn't," Hudson said. "It looks really nice. I swear."

"And Kierce has a few things for you."

"For me?"

With a glum stare, Kierce took several clothes bags out of a cabinet and handed them to Hudson. "There's some Rodarte in there," he said. "Don't even ask me what I had to do to get that."

"But what is this for?" Hudson asked, giving Kierce a weak smile as she took the clothes.

"*Saturday Night Live*," Holla announced. "You're doing it with me. It's all set. March seventh. Two weeks." She turned to Kierce. "Would you unzip me, please?"

The bag of clothes slid out of Hudson's hands. "What?" she asked, her voice barely above a whisper.

"If you can try things on now that would be best," Holla said. "Kierce can take back whatever doesn't work."

"But, but…" she stammered. "Why am *I* doing *Saturday Night Live*?"

Kierce unzipped her dress. "Because I sent them one of your tracks," Holla said, "and they called back this afternoon saying they wanted you."

"So this was *your* idea?" Hudson asked, panicked.

"Honey, your label's thrilled. And I think in light of everything, this is the best thing for you." She stepped out of the dress and into the royal blue shirred silk dress that Kierce held open for her. "Most people have to wait 'til they have a huge hit to get on *Saturday Night Live*. But they want *you* now."

Her heart was pounding. "Mom, I can't," she said.

"Hudson..." Holla warned.

"I'm in a band now," she said bravely. "I need to be there for them. They're my priority."

"That's over," Holla snapped, turning her back so that Kierce could zip her up.

"It's not. I made a promise to them. And they like my music. They like me for me."

"Really?" Holla asked, turning around. "Are you sure about that?"

"What?" Hudson asked, picking up on her mom's sarcastic tone.

"Sophie heard from the publicist for Joe's Pub today," Holla said, suppressing a grin. "Apparently they'd been told — *promised*, actually — that I'd be playing a show there. In exchange for booking your band."

Hudson blinked. "That...that can't be right," she said.

"Sounds like a real loyal bunch of people," Holla said thickly. She assessed her reflection and turned back around. "Unzip me again," she said to Kierce.

Hudson stood there motionless. She didn't believe it. She *couldn't* believe it. But then she remembered what Ben had said that night in front of Ellie's house, about how getting ahead was ninety percent connections...and she started to feel a rumble of anger down deep inside of her.

"They're using you, honey," Holla said, stepping out of the dress. "I just thought you should know."

The sour taste of anger filled Hudson's mouth. "And your boy-friend's using *you*," she shot back. "I saw him leaving a bar with some woman. Holding her hand. And kissing her."

Holla froze, one leg out of the dress. "What?"

"I saw him last night," she said. "He was with someone. On a date. I saw them leaving some club." She knew she was being cruel, but she couldn't help herself. "Where'd he tell you he was last night?"

Holla still didn't move. "Visiting his family," she said hoarsely.

"Not from what I saw."

Kierce looked appalled. "Didn't you say he was in Poughkeep-sie?" he asked Holla.

"So he's just like all the others, isn't he, Mom?" Hudson asked. "He *really* loves the spotlight. But you? Not so sure."

It was probably the meanest thing she'd ever said to her mother, but right now, the words were flying out of her mouth.

"Kierce, please hand me my phone," Holla said. She remained perfectly still. "I think that's enough now, Hudson. Why don't you just worry about your own life, okay?"

Hudson stormed out of the closet, grabbed her shoes, and went down a flight of stairs. Her heart was beating so fast it was all she could hear. When she reached her room, she pulled out her iPhone.

Ben picked up on the second ring. "Hudson? Hey, what's up?"

"Did you call Joe's Pub and tell them that my mom would play there?" she asked breathlessly.

"What? No," he said. "What are you talking about?"

"Well, someone did," she said. "Remember what you said about connections? How it's all about who you know? How I should use what I have?"

"What?" Ben sounded utterly thrown. "Hudson...what's wrong?"

"This isn't a game to me," she said. "The whole reason I joined your band was to prove to myself that I could do this, alone."

"You're *not* alone," Ben said. "There are three other people in this band besides you. You're not the only one who wants to get something out of this. And what are we all supposed to do? *Not* care that you're the daughter of Holla Jones?"

"So you told the guys," she said. "Great."

"I thought it was important," he said.

"And you told them at Joe's Pub," she said. "You told them who I was."

"It's not like we can hide it," Ben said.

"Thanks," she said. "That's just great. I trusted you."

"Hudson, hold on —"

"Good-bye, Ben," she said.

She slammed her finger on End Call before he could reply, then tossed the phone onto the bed as if it were on fire.

She sat down on the floor with her back to her bed and hugged her knees to her chest. *You did the right thing,* she said to herself. *This all had to end sometime. You knew things would change when you told them who you were. Better to get out now.*

She leaned her forehead against her knees, shutting her eyes against the tears. But she couldn't escape the feeling that she'd just made a gigantic mistake.

Then she got an idea. She stood up and went into the other room, where her laptop waited for her on the desk. She logged in to signsnscopes.com and clicked on Pisces.

Congratulations, little Fish! You achieved a massive breakthrough during the lunar eclipse! Everything you've ever wanted is finally within reach... Now all you have to do is go for it!

Hudson shut the laptop and went straight to bed.

chapter 27

"So, tomorrow's the big night," Lizzie said, picking some burnt crust off her BLT. "You feeling okay?"

"I can't believe you're doing *Saturday Night Live*!" Carina squealed, slamming her foot into the base of the diner table. "This is so cool!"

"I feel fine," Hudson said to Lizzie as she ate a forkful of coleslaw. "It's really not that big a deal." She picked up her Reuben and took a small bite.

"Are you sure I can't come?" Carina asked, grabbing Hudson's hand. "I'll sit in the audience, way in the back. You won't even see me, I *promise*."

"You guys, I wish you could," Hudson said gently. "But it's all part of my master plan: making sure nobody sees this. You haven't told anyone about it, right?"

Lizzie and Carina shook their heads.

"Good. And somehow my mom convinced *SNL* not to promote it," she said. "And I'm not doing any of the commercials with her, either."

"People *are* going to see this, you know," Carina reminded her. "Even if it *is* the first day of spring break."

"Thanks, C. You're really making me feel better."

"Then why did you say yes?" Lizzie asked.

Hudson rolled her eyes. "My mom's been a wreck ever since the breakup, which was basically my fault."

"It wasn't your fault, Hudson," Carina said.

"But I told her about it," Hudson said, taking another bite.

"And it was the right thing to do," Lizzie exclaimed. "Somebody had to!"

"I just wish it hadn't been me," she said.

"We know your mom broke up with some guy, but that's her life, Hudson, not yours," Lizzie said. "You shouldn't do this just because you feel like you have to."

"Well, what's my other option? Being in a band with a bunch of guys I don't trust?"

"So the guy used your name to get a booking," Carina said. "You know how people are. They don't think sometimes. And you really liked that band."

"You guys, please," she pleaded, putting down her fork. "I'm really nervous about this *SNL* thing. Don't make it worse for me, okay?"

Lizzie and Carina traded a look and then went back to eating their meals. Hudson resumed picking at her food. The breakup had hit her mother hard, just as Hudson had feared. Holla had confronted Chris about the mystery woman that same night, and after some denials, he confessed. She was his last girlfriend, with whom he'd never quite broken up. Luckily Holla's album was finished. She called Chris a few choice words and then hung up on him, and despite the frantic voice mails he'd left, she hadn't looked back.

Except Holla descended quickly into Breakup Mode — periods of manic activity followed by utter depression. The day after the breakup, Hudson came home to find Holla padding around the house barefoot, looking lost and remote. Hudson had seen her mom suffer through many a breakup, but she'd never actually been the instigator of one. Hudson told Lorraine to whip up a batch of her vegan chocolate-chip cookies and bring them up to the prayer room, where she and her mom ended up hanging out on the couch, watching *The Devil Wears Prada*. She told her mom that she was better off without Chris, and reminded her that she'd barely wasted any time on the guy. Still, Holla was heartsick.

"The whole time, he was with her," she kept saying, as if she didn't believe it. "The *whole time*."

When Holla eventually brought up the *Saturday Night Live* appearance again, it wasn't even a question that Hudson would do it.

"If you're out there, doing it with me, I'll feel strong," Holla said, squeezing Hudson's hand. "I won't be thinking about him."

"Sure, Mom," Hudson said, squeezing back. It was the least she could do.

Now the show was all Holla could talk about. They'd already had three hour-long rehearsals for a three-minute song. There had been sit-down meetings about hair and makeup with Gino and Suzette. Holla even wanted Hudson to do a dance solo, to which Hudson had reluctantly agreed.

Now Hudson sat with her friends in uncomfortable silence. She knew that she'd made a mistake by saying yes. And there was no way out of it.

"Have you heard from Ben?" Lizzie asked quietly.

Hudson put down her fork and shook her head. "I wonder if he has spring break for the next couple of weeks, too."

"Are they still doing the Joe's Pub show?" Carina asked.

Hudson shrugged. "No clue. I haven't heard from any of them. Not that I would."

"Are you sure you don't just want to call him?" Lizzie asked. "You *did* hang up on the guy."

"Call him and say what?"

"At least hear him out," Carina said.

"I think I know all I need to," she murmured.

"Ben just doesn't seem like the kind of guy who would do something like that," Lizzie said. "Did he seem like that to you?" she asked Carina.

Carina shook her head. "I didn't think so. But people do crazy, selfish stuff sometimes. Hey, speaking of crazy," she said, glancing over at the corner. "Is that Hillary coming over here?"

Hudson looked up from her plate. If the girl gliding toward them had ever been Hudson's eccentric, fashion-challenged friend, it was now impossible to tell. This was an astonishingly elegant stranger, wearing silver ballet flats, a leather backpack falling artfully from one shoulder, and dark lipstick. She'd traded her sequined sweaters for a silk camisole and a cropped black blazer — both against the school's uniform code — and her once-dowdy Chadwick kilt had been rolled up at least five inches. She even wore jewelry: a silver cuff bracelet and silver leaf earrings that caught the light as she walked.

"Did *you* do that to her?" Lizzie asked Hudson.

"I don't think so," Hudson said.

"Hey, you guys," Hillary said as she approached.

"Hi...uh...hi," they murmured, all of them in awe of Hillary's new look.

Hillary's gaze zeroed in on Hudson. "Can I talk to you for a sec? It's kind of important." She drummed her fingers on the strap of her book bag, and Hudson noticed that her nails were French-manicured. Almost like Ava's.

"Uh...sure," Hudson said, still a little stunned. "I'll be right back, you guys." She followed Hillary outside onto the street.

Hillary walked down the block and planted herself in front of Sweet Nothings, Carina's favorite candy boutique.

"So, what's up?" Hudson said.

"Why'd you quit the band?" Hillary asked, point-blank. "Ben told me you quit. He also told me you hung up on him, but we'll get to that later. Why'd you quit?"

"That's between me and Ben."

"You know how much this Joe's Pub show means to him," Hillary said. "How could you do that?"

"Is he still playing the show?" Hudson asked cautiously.

"Of *course* they're not playing. They can't do anything without you."

"Hillary, this might be hard to believe," Hudson said, "but I think Ben did something really gross."

Hillary put her tiny fists on her hips. "*What* are you talking about?" she asked snippily.

"I think he told the people at Joe's Pub that if they booked us, my mom would personally show up and do a few songs there."

Hillary just stared at her.

"My mom got the call. And this was after I'd finally told him everything — who my mom was, all the reasons I wanted to be in his band, and why I didn't want her involved," she went on. "He totally destroyed my trust in him, okay? That's why I quit. That's why I hung up on him."

"Ben wouldn't do that," she said.

Hudson shrugged. "He did it. He practically admitted it to me."

"No. I know my cousin. And I know that this is something he would never do." Hillary pulled her phone out of her book bag. "Call him up right now and apologize."

"Hillary! No," Hudson said, backing away from her. "I'm not apologizing!"

"But you have to," Hillary said. "I know he didn't do this. And maybe it's not too late to save the Joe's Pub show —"

"It *is* too late," Hudson said. "I have another show tomorrow night. With my mom. I'm doing *Saturday Night Live*."

"With your *mom*?" Hillary asked, aghast.

"Yeah. With my mom. Why are you looking at me like that?"

Hillary shook her head. "I'm just..." Hillary was quiet for a moment. "What about all the work we've done together?" she finally said. "What about doing stuff your own way?"

"I tried that," Hudson said, stepping away from her. "It didn't work."

Hillary went quiet again.

"I'm not the one who did anything," Hudson added. "This is all his fault. So if it's okay with you, I have to get back to my friends."

Hudson wheeled around and walked quickly up the block, not looking back. She was so angry that her chest hurt. None of this was Hillary's business. And she had no right to take her phone out like that and push it in Hudson's face.

Carina and Lizzie watched her carefully as she made her way back into the diner and to the table. "Everything okay?" Lizzie asked.

"Yeah, everything's great," Hudson fibbed, reaching for her bag.

"What happened?" Carina prodded.

"She's mad that I got into a fight with her cousin," Hudson answered. "She said that it wasn't like him to do something like that."

"Maybe she's right," Lizzie said.

"Well, she still had no right to get mad at me," Hudson said. "She's just upset with me about other stuff, too."

"What other stuff?" Lizzie asked.

"Nothing," Hudson murmured.

"I think you just got a text," Carina said, gesturing to Hudson's bag.

Hudson pulled out her phone. It was from her mom.

Rehearsal today at 4—don't be late!

"You guys, help," Hudson pleaded.

"What?"

"I really don't think I can do this. How do I get out of this?"

Carina and Lizzie looked back at her, stricken. Hudson knew what they were thinking: *Sorry, H. It's too late.*

chapter 28

"Now, just stand very still for a second," said Paula, the wardrobe lady, as she pulled Hudson's silvery purple dress tighter around her back. "You're so tiny, but this should do the trick."

Hudson stared in the full-length mirror as Paula secured the pin and the dress magically shrank a size. It was, Hudson had to admit, beautiful — metallic and sparkly and belted, with short sleeves and a V-neck. She'd actually bought it online, and Holla had taken one look at it and had decided to wear something in almost the exact same color.

"Okay, I think that should do it," Paula said, squinting at Hudson in the mirror. "You're going to look *adorable* next to your mom out there."

"Thanks," Hudson said, stepping off the pedestal. "Do you need me to send her in here?"

"She looked fine to me during dress rehearsal, but I'll check on her. And I think it's better if I go to her," she said, grabbing her sewing box.

Hudson followed Paula out of the wardrobe room and into the main hallway of the *Saturday Night Live* studios. It was jammed with people — writers, producers, NBC pages dressed in uniform and scurrying around in the five minutes before air. A few cast members ran by, already in makeup and costume for the opening sketch. A college-aged intern pushed a wardrobe cart up the hall, and a PA wearing headphones led some people into the green-room. At the end of the hall was a set of double doors, and behind that was the studio, where the *SNL* house band was grinding out "Mustang Sally," warming up the audience. Through the doors Hudson could hear them clapping and hooting. Even though she'd been terrified of this night, now she looked around her in awe. It was hard not to get swept up in this.

Paula turned left at the double doors and then right, into Holla's dressing room. Hudson followed her but almost bumped right into Little Jimmy, who had been edged out of the room.

"Too many people in there," he said and pointed at the crowd spilling out of the narrow doorway and into the hall. Hudson had never seen most of these people before, but she could tell from their suits and dead-serious expressions that they were from Holla's label. Hudson pushed her way inside.

At the far end of the room, Holla sat in a director's chair in front of a mirror framed by tiny white bulbs, her head thrown back and her eyes closed, letting Suzette and Gino do their work. Suzette applied fake eyelashes while Gino ironed Holla's hair, which hung straight down on either side of her head, perfectly smooth. Her bangs — newly cut — just skimmed her thickly lined eyes. Her strapless, bandage-style dress in the same purple-gunmetal metallic sheen as Hudson's glinted under the lights.

Brendan, the music producer she'd met at the rehearsal, approached Hudson through the crowd. He was dressed in jeans and beat-up sneakers and held a folder under his arm. He was cute, with short, rumpled-looking black hair, but Hudson tried not to notice. "So we'll be coming to get you around ten after twelve," he said, "but before that someone'll come by to mic you and your mom."

"Great," she said, forcing a smile.

"I know you didn't want to rehearse, to keep everything under wraps," he said, "but we just have to know in advance . . . Are you all set? It *is* live television."

"I'm fine," she said, trying to sound like she went on *Saturday Night Live* once a month.

Brendan looked at Hudson just a bit longer than necessary, as if he were trying to figure this out himself. "Okay, I'll see you out there," he said, checking his watch. "Have a great show."

The TV looming above them in the corner of the room flickered, and a blue screen came on.

"What's that?" Hudson asked.

"It's the live feed from the studio," Paula explained. "As soon as the show starts, you'll be able to watch it in here." Paula approached Holla. "Just want to make sure you're okay with wardrobe?"

Holla held up her hand. "It's all good. But let me see you, Hudson," she ordered. "Come over here."

240

Hudson dutifully pushed her way up to her mother's chair.

Suzette and Gino moved aside and Holla beamed at Hudson in the mirror. "Adorable," she said, holding Hudson around the waist. "Just *adorable*. Look at us. This is *brilliant*." They practically looked like twins in their matching silvery purple dresses.

Kierce walked up to them and gave Hudson a sweeping head-to-toe squint. "It's perfect!" he decided.

"Hey, the show is starting!" somebody yelled. Hudson glanced up at the TV. A hush fell over the crowd as the screen went black, and the opening sketch began.

"Honey." Holla grabbed Hudson's wrist and pulled her in closer. Hudson almost collided with Suzette's mascara wand. "You *are* ready for this, right?" she asked.

The crowd in the room laughed uproariously at the TV.

"Do you remember the dance moves?" Holla asked, sounding impatient. "Shimmy, then double-turn, then head thrown back?"

"Yeah," Hudson said. "Of course." At least she thought she did. It would be hard to forget something so embarrassing.

"Good." Holla narrowed her eyes. "If you feel yourself getting anxious, just remember what I always say: *No negativity.*"

"Right," Hudson said.

Holla released her grip, and Hudson stepped aside to let Suzette apply Holla's mascara. As she tried to make her way to the sofa, she repeated those words back to herself: *No negativity.* They did nothing to quell the feeling of doom that was starting to over-take her.

"Okay, people!" Sophie cried. "Holla would like everyone who doesn't need to be here to please move into the greenroom! Now!"

Reluctantly the men in suits started to head to the doors. Hudson sat on the leather sofa, staring at the yellow and red diamond-patterned carpet. Did she need to be here? This was a mistake. Maybe an even bigger one than the Silver Snowflake Ball.

"Good luck, Hudson," someone said to her, patting her on the shoulder. "We'll be watching."

She looked up. It was Richard Wu, her record label executive.

"We're so excited you're back. And we've got a great tour lined up for you already," he said with a smile. "If tonight goes well, we'll even get your mom to come out with you onstage a few times." He squeezed her shoulder. "Now just go out there and have fun."

He walked out the door before she could say anything. *My mom?* she wanted to yell. *On my tour? Come out onstage with me?*

And then she realized: Her mom didn't just want Hudson to be a mini-Holla, the perfect daughter following in her mom's footsteps. She wanted a way to keep reaching younger fans.

She had to get out of this. If she walked out onto that stage and did this show, it would kick off a chain of events that she would never be able to stop.

Minutes later, a knock on the door made her jump, and then a bearded PA walked in, holding a couple of mics and sound packs.

"I just need to get these on the two of you before we go out there," he said. He walked over to Hudson first. "This'll only take a second."

Hudson stood still as the PA looped the mic around the back of her dress. She hoped he couldn't hear her pounding heart.

"Okay, now you," he said to Holla.

Holla took her time getting out of her chair, never taking her eyes off her reflection as she fixed her hair. "Okay, fine, go to it," she said, and the PA clipped the mic to her dress.

Brendan walked into the room. "Okay, how're we doing? We all ready to go?"

"Just a second," Holla said, turning around in front of the mirror to check for any unsightly bulges. "I'm ready," she said.

"Mom?" Hudson suddenly asked. "Are you planning on doing more duets with me? You know, if I go on tour?"

Holla frowned. "What are you talking about, baby?" she asked, looking back in the mirror.

"Just what I said," Hudson said evenly. "Are we going to be doing this again? Is this something you talked about with my label?"

"Let's talk about this another time, shall we?" Holla said sternly.

"No," Hudson said, blocking her way. "I need you to tell me now."

Holla folded her arms. She looked more glamorous than Hudson had ever seen her, with her Cleopatra bangs and dramatically dark eyes. She took a deep breath, as if she were trying not to lose her temper. "We don't have time for one of your moods right now, honey. We have a show to do." She pushed past Hudson and began walking toward the door.

"Just follow me," Brendan said, trying to still sound excited.

Hudson followed them, quietly furious at being cut off. Of course it hadn't been great timing, but her mom could have answered her question. Brendan led them out of the dressing room and into another hallway, which seemed to be the entrance to the stage. Hudson spotted two or three *SNL* cast members, in costume, waiting to go on.

"Okay, we're going to have you wait out here," Brendan said, leading them up to another door.

Beyond it Hudson could hear the band playing. The show had to be at a commercial break. In just a few moments they would be back, and it would be time for her to walk out onstage.

She tried to picture what it might be like in there. The cameras moving around silently like ghosts on the studio floor. The people in the audience. The stage manager motioning for them to wrap it up, that time was running out...

She started to breathe fast. Her vision got darker. It was as if someone were pulling a blindfold over her eyes.

And then a small voice rose up inside of her: *This isn't right, Hudson. Don't fight it anymore.*

"Okay, here we go," Brendan said, grabbing the door handle and pulling the door open.

Hudson grabbed her mom's arm. "No. I can't."

Brendan and Holla turned around. "Hudson, come on," Holla said, trying to smile.

"I can't do this," Hudson said. "I can't be you. This isn't me. It never will be. As much as you want it to be. I just can't do it."

"Hudson," her mom warned, stealing a look at Brendan.

"I'm not quitting," she interrupted. "I'm saying no. I totally respect what you do, Mom. But this isn't what *I* do."

Brendan pulled the door open. Thunderous, earsplitting applause poured in. "I'm sorry, we've got to go," he yelled. "Now!"

Holla didn't move. Something rippled across her face — a

moment of understanding, of acceptance. Or maybe it was just that she couldn't argue anymore. She touched Hudson's cheek. "She's not coming," she said over her shoulder to Brendan. "Let them know out there."

Brendan pulled up the mic on his headset. "It's just Holla. The daughter isn't coming. *It's just Holla.* You got that?" Brendan pressed on his earpiece, then nodded, satisfied. "They're ready for you," he said to Holla. "Let's go." Then Holla turned and followed Brendan into the studio, and the doors swung shut behind them.

"Her tenth album comes out this Tuesday," she heard the guest host announce, "and she's here for the fourth time. Ladies and gentlemen...Miss Holla JONES!"

As the studio erupted in applause, Hudson looked up at the monitor hanging in the corner. Her mom stood on the stage, shimmering in the sparkling purple dress. It had only been a few seconds, and already she owned the room. She pulled the mic out of the stand and executed a perfect turn as the song started. On her first note, goose bumps rose along Hudson's arm. Hearing Holla sing this song wasn't weird anymore. Her mom was a star. She could sing anything. This was what she'd been born to do. She would always be a star first and a mother second. And maybe, Hudson realized, that was how things were meant to be.

chapter 29

"I need to ask you something," Hudson said carefully. "And I just want to say, in advance, that if I offend you or something, I'm really sorry."

Across from her, Jenny frowned slightly and rested her chin on her wrist. "Okay. Go ahead. Offend me."

Sitting across from Jenny at her wooden kitchen table, Hudson thought her aunt looked just as beautiful as ever. Her eyes were a little puffy from sleep, but her cropped hair had been highlighted with warm caramel streaks and her lips shone with clear gloss. When she'd called her that morning, Hudson hadn't expected an invitation for homemade crêpes suzette and tea. But Aunt Jenny had been incredibly gracious under the circumstances.

"First, I want to say I'm so sorry about the party," Hudson said. "I should have just told my mom in the first place that I forgot. I don't know why I didn't. I'm so sorry."

Jenny nodded, and then spooned some powdered sugar onto her

crêpe. "Obviously, it was worse for your mom," she said. "I can't believe you did that to her. And I can't believe I missed all those macaroons."

Hudson didn't say anything.

"But at least your mom and I started e-mailing again because of it," Jenny admitted. "And we're having lunch next week."

"Really?" Hudson asked, impressed. "You are?"

"Not at your house; at a restaurant," Jenny said, holding up one hand as she cut into her crêpe with the other. "Neutral territory. Of course we'll probably have to close down the restaurant so she doesn't get mobbed," she added.

Hudson smiled and then took a small bite of her crêpe. "Oh my God," she said. "This is incredible. You're a really good cook, you know that?"

"Thanks. But don't tell your mom I fed you white flour," Jenny said in a mock whisper. "So, what did you want to ask me?"

"When you decided not to audition for Martha Graham the second time," Hudson said carefully, "it was because you didn't want to compete with my mom, right?"

"*That's* what you want to know?" she asked.

Hudson nodded.

"Ye-es," Jenny said. "But I also don't think I wanted it bad enough. I didn't want that life."

"But don't you regret it?" Hudson asked. "Don't you wish you'd at least tried?"

Jenny reached across the table and took Hudson's hand. "Is this about what happened last night?"

"I told you how my mom changed my album because she said it wouldn't sell?"

Jenny frowned again and nodded.

"And at first I didn't care if it sold or not. I just wanted it to be my thing. *My* vision. But to my mom, it's like there's no point in even trying if you're not going to be huge."

Jenny nodded. "Right."

"And sometimes I think there's a part of me that believes that. I joined this band, up in Westchester, which you probably realize," Hudson said, embarrassed.

"Yeah, I got that," Jenny said knowingly.

"And I was finally doing my own thing again. But my mom found out and she's hurt. She thinks I'm crazy for wanting to be in some high school band and play these tiny clubs. She doesn't understand why I don't want what she has. We're all supposed to want that, right?"

"Oh, Hudson," Jenny said, shaking her head as she looked down at her plate. "I wish I could have been there for you a little more. I really do. It's my fault I wasn't." She leaned so close that Hudson could smell her fig-scented perfume. "Your mom is an amazing person. She's accomplished a lot. But you know how you're scared of being in the spotlight? She's scared of being *out* of it. She's been doing this since she was ten. It's all she knows. And sometimes having thousands of people love you from a distance is easier than living in the real world, where people can reject you and leave you and *see* you. And I don't think your mom knows how to be seen. As a real person. I think that scares her. More than anything else in the world."

Hudson bit her lip. It hurt to hear these things about her mom, but she knew that they were true.

"So my question is, do you really want to be like that?" Jenny asked. "Does anyone?"

Hudson shook her head.

"You don't have to be like your mom," Jenny said. "Not even if you want to do what she does. That night you got stage fright? That was your inner self, telling you that what you were doing didn't feel right. And so you ran off that stage. That was the bravest thing you could have done."

It had never occurred to Hudson that running off the stage at the Silver Snowflake Ball had been brave.

"We're living in a time where we're all told we're nothing if we're not famous," Jenny said. "Sometimes it's easy to forget how crazy that is."

"But you're the one who told me that it's in my chart, being famous," Hudson said. "You're always telling me that."

"I should have just said successful," Jenny said. "When you were little, you used to love to hold your mom's awards and sing her songs. I thought that's what you wanted. But there are many kinds of success. You can play music and put all your passion into it, but it doesn't have to be your whole life. There's a middle road out there, Hudson. Your mom had no idea what she was getting into, and now she's stuck. She doesn't have a choice. But you know what that life is like. *You* have a choice."

Hudson looked at the glass vase of early spring daffodils on Jenny's kitchen table. *A middle road.* She had never thought of it that way.

"Sometimes I wish I could talk to my dad about this stuff," Hudson said.

Jenny nodded. "I know. But you can always come see me if you need some reminding."

"And you'll have to let me know how lunch with my mom is."

"Well, one thing's for sure," Jenny said, taking another bite of her crêpe. "It's going to be very, very healthy."

Hudson smiled and picked up her fork. A middle road. She liked how that sounded.

chapter 30

"Well, you *almost* did *Saturday Night Live*," Carina said later that afternoon as she dug her spoon into her pomegranate Pinkberry. "And how many people can say that? Seriously?"

"Thanks for looking on the bright side, C," Hudson said. She took a small bite of her yogurt with blueberries, lost in thought.

"*Go you*, that's what I think," Lizzie said, wagging a spoon of plain topped with mochi. "You totally listened to yourself, you spoke up to your mom, you realized that it wasn't right for you in the end —"

"And you may have finally cured her of her mini-me obsession," Carina added. "How is she now?"

"She's actually great," Hudson said. "This morning she seemed totally normal. I couldn't believe it."

She'd been expecting a stony glare, or at least a lecture on sleeping in so late when she walked into the kitchen that morning.

But her mom just gave her a warm smile and started talking about the awesome after-party at the Standard Hotel.

"Everyone *loved* the song. It's probably going to be a big hit. Shows how much I know."

Hudson looked out the window. Couples strolled up Bleecker Street in the sun, their coats open to the mild late-winter day. Everyone looked so happy that spring was almost here. "I know I did the right thing," she added. "I just wish the band wasn't over. First the album was over, now the band is over —"

"Wait," Carina interrupted, leaning forward. "What about the first album? The one you loved? What happened to that?"

Hudson shrugged. "I don't know. It still needs to be mastered, but the tracks are all done."

"Then why doesn't your label just release that one?" Carina asked, shaking her blond ponytail. "Just go in there and tell them that's the album you want to release. You could go out there and promote that one, right?"

"Exactly!" Lizzie exclaimed, hopping up and down in her chair. "Go in there and tell them that's your true sound and always has been!"

"And you'd be totally fulfilling your contract," Carina pointed out.

Hudson tapped her foot under the table to the beat of the music playing over the store's speakers. Why had she never thought of this idea before? For just a moment she pictured Ben onstage with her, but blocked it out. "I will," she said. "That's a great idea."

"I think that's the best idea I've ever had," Carina said proudly, polishing off her yogurt.

"But what about my mom?" Hudson asked.

"I think by now you probably have her blessing," Lizzie said gently, licking her full lips. "And there's no way you're ever going to do this totally on your own. Your mom will always be a part of it. You're just going to have to accept that."

Hudson nodded; she knew her friends were right. Maybe she'd been a little unrealistic this whole time: There was no way she could ever stop being Holla Jones's kid.

When they walked out of Pinkberry and onto Bleecker Street, Hudson heard her phone chime with a text. She pulled it out of her bag. It was from Hillary Crumple.

Hey can u meet me at Kirna Zabete? Need to talk to you.

"Who is that?" Lizzie asked.

"Hillary," said Hudson. "She wants to go shopping again."

"Personally, I don't think that girl needs any more clothes," Carina put in.

"I think she's still mad at me about the stuff with Ben," Hudson said, texting to Hillary that, yes, she'd meet her. "But maybe you guys are right. Maybe I shouldn't have gotten so angry at him."

"Guys," Carina said ruefully, shaking her head. "I will never, ever, understand them."

"Except Alex, of course," Lizzie said.

"No, even him. He wants to dye his hair blue. Can you believe it? If he does it, I'm gonna kill him."

"They set the court date for Todd's dad," Lizzie said quietly. "Todd's really upset about it. He didn't want his dad to have to have a trial. He wishes he would just fess up and go to jail. He thinks that's almost less humiliating."

"But you guys are still okay, right?" Carina asked.

"Yeah, he's not acting weird around you or anything, right?" Hudson asked.

"We're great," Lizzie assured them. "I just feel bad for him, that's all."

"Don't feel *too* bad for him," Carina said. "Guys don't like it when you feel sorry for them."

As Hudson listened to her friends talk about guys, she couldn't help but feel a little left out. It wasn't that she really wanted a boyfriend; right now her life felt full enough without one. But *not* having a boyfriend made her feel a little behind. She was technically the oldest of the three of them, but now she felt like the baby of the group. Both her friends were going out with guys and having experiences that she just couldn't relate to. Sometimes she found herself wondering if she ever would.

"Well, you guys, I gotta go meet my dad at his office," Carina said. "He wants me to look at this proposal for a new networking site or something."

"So you're giving the Metronome thing another try?" Lizzie asked.

Carina shrugged. "He begged," she said, grinning. "What was I supposed to do?"

Hudson smiled. She knew that things had changed between Carina and the Jurg — so much so that now when he asked her to do him a work-related favor, she actually did it.

"So I think I'm gonna go meet Hillary," Hudson announced. "Thanks for letting me vent, you guys."

"Congratulations, Hudson," Lizzie said, tucking a red curl behind her ear. "I mean it. Even though I'm not your official life coach, you should know what a big deal last night was."

"Thanks, Lizbutt. I know it was."

"Be proud of yourself for that," Lizzie said.

Carina waved good-bye to Hudson, and then she and Lizzie started walking up Sullivan Street toward Washington Square Park. Hudson tilted her face up to the sun and soaked in the feeble winter rays. Her old album was still out there. It hadn't disappeared or gone away. All this time she'd thought of it as gone forever, when it was still intact, and waiting for her to return to it. It didn't matter anymore what her mom thought of it. And maybe she could take the middle road to it, just like Jenny had said.

She wrapped her chunky knit scarf closer around her, and started walking to SoHo.

chapter 31

Hillary stood outside Kirna Zabete, tapping the toe of her tiger-striped ballet flats as Hudson walked up Greene Street. Hillary looked incredible — maybe too incredible. She'd traded in her puffy down coat for a belted swing coat with a fake-fur collar, and she'd pulled her hair back in a chic ballerina knot. Her bag looked like a knockoff of the Lizzie bag by Martin Meloy — bright white leather and gleaming silver buckles. And in her hands was a cluster of shopping bags.

"Hey," Hudson said, walking up to her. "Do you want to just get some coffee? I'm not really in the mood to shop."

Hillary shrugged and they started walking back toward Prince Street. Hudson didn't say anything; she was still a little scarred by Hillary's tongue-lashing the other day, and she didn't want to have another fight in her favorite store.

"So I noticed you weren't on the show last night," Hillary said as she maneuvered herself, shoulders first, past the tourists. She still walked as if she wore that gigantic backpack. "What happened? Did they cut you out at the last minute?"

"I decided not to do it," Hudson said, ignoring Hillary's slightly cruel remark. "It didn't feel right to me."

Hillary's shopping bags smacked against a lamppost. "Well, I think you seriously messed up with something else," she said. "I spoke to Ben, you know."

"Of course you did."

"And guess what? He *didn't* call Joe's Pub and make that deal." She shouldered her way past a dog walker. "But he found out who did."

"Who?" Hudson asked. But before Hillary spoke, she already knew who it was.

"Logan," Hillary said softly.

They stopped at the corner of Broadway. The signal read WALK but Hudson just stayed on the curb. "How did Ben find out?" she asked.

Hillary waited with her at the corner. "I guess Ben told Gordie and Logan who you were."

"Even though I told him not to."

Hillary sighed as if she wished Hudson wouldn't interrupt. "They promised to keep it to themselves. But Logan made some comment about Ben being lame for not trying to use your mom to get some gigs. And after you hung up on him, Ben found out that Logan had called Joe's Pub and promised them your mom. So Ben kicked him out of the band."

"He kicked him out?"

"Yep," Hillary said. "And they've been friends since, like, kindergarten."

Hudson winced. "What about the band now?" she asked cautiously. "Is it over?" Without a pianist and a saxophonist, how could they still have a jazz band?

"I don't know," Hillary said. "His parents are kind of happy it's over, I think. Come on. Let's cross the street."

Hudson followed Hillary across Broadway as the words *it's over* knocked around inside her head. It was bad enough that she'd kept Ben from playing at Joe's Pub. But now it seemed that she was responsible for the total demise of the band itself. Not to mention Ben's dream of being a jazz musician.

"So, the other thing I guess I need to say to you," Hillary said, turning around to face her, "is that you were right. As much as I hate to admit it."

"Right about what?" Hudson asked. So far it hadn't felt like she'd been right about much.

"About Logan being kind of a jerk." Hillary looked at Hudson and there was a flicker of sadness in her yellow-green eyes. "He hooked up with Ellie and then he hooked up with one of the McFadden twins, too." She wrinkled her nose with distaste. "But he really did give me his number back in January. Just so you know."

"Oh, Hillary," Hudson said, and without thinking, put her arms around her. "I'm so sorry." She squeezed Hillary's tiny frame. Eventually Hillary let her shopping bags drop to the ground and hugged Hudson back.

After a few moments Hillary pulled away and wiped her eyes with the back of her hand. "Whatever. It's not that important."

"Is he the reason you changed your look?" Hudson asked gently.

Hillary looked down at the sidewalk and nodded. "Why? Do you think that's lame?" she asked.

"Not at all," Hudson said. "I just think that I liked the old Hillary Crumple better."

Hillary looked up. "You *did*?" she asked.

"Yeah. Maybe she wasn't the trendiest girl on the face of the earth, but she was a true original. And this Hillary..." Hudson gestured toward Hillary's clothes. "Well, she looks nice and everything, but she's definitely not original."

A tentative smile spread across Hillary's face. "Yeah, I guess it's not really me," she said. "And God knows, it's expensive."

"Is Ben's family going away for spring break?" Hudson asked suddenly, changing the subject.

"Just for a couple of days," Hillary answered. "They go down to see his grandparents in Florida."

"When are they leaving?" Hudson asked.

"I think their flight is tonight."

Hudson checked her watch. It was almost two. "Hold on one second," she said, taking out her phone. She dialed Ben's number. It rang and rang and rang.

"Are you calling him?" Hillary asked.

"Yeah," Hudson said.

"Oh, he's not gonna answer," she said. "It's the Westchester chess championships today."

"Where are they?" Hudson pleaded.

"At the high school in White Plains," said Hillary.

"How long will they last?" Hudson asked.

"What are you gonna do? Just barge in there while he's playing chess?" Hillary asked in reply.

"Yep," Hudson said. She glanced back at the N and R subway station on the corner.

"So, no shopping?" Hillary asked with a wry smile. Then she laughed and said, "Just kidding."

Hudson leaned down and hugged Hillary. "Have a great spring break. And thank you. For everything."

Hillary hugged her back. "Good luck up there. Say hi to the nerds for me."

Hillary pulled out of the hug, picked up her shopping bags, and almost knocked down a small child as she headed off down Broadway.

chapter 32

Hudson stared out the smudged train window at the parade of school buildings and churches and budding trees on the way to White Plains. *Stupid, stupid, stupid,* she thought. Of course Ben wasn't the one who betrayed her. Of course it had been Logan, who'd had it in for her from the beginning. And she'd hung up on Ben, on top of it. She flinched just thinking about it.

She owed Ben Geyer everything. He was the reason she was going to go back to her old album. He was the reason she'd finally discovered music on her own terms. And in return, she'd accused him of something terrible and hung up on him. Oh, and kept him from realizing his one dream in life: playing at Joe's Pub. *Great,* she thought. *Way to really screw up.*

By the time the train lurched to a stop at the White Plains station, Hudson was on her feet. She stepped onto the platform and headed toward the line of idling black cabs.

"The high school, please," she said as she opened the back door and threw herself into the seat.

White Plains was more of a city than Larchmont was. The car took her through downtown and then veered off into a more residential neighborhood. It finally pulled up in front of a large, squat brick building that looked shuttered and empty. "Can you wait here for a sec?" she asked, pressing a ten-dollar bill into the driver's hand. Then she took off at a run.

She threw open the main door of the school and ran down the empty hall. It smelled strongly of lemon soap, and her sneakers squeaked on the shiny linoleum. Being in school on a weekend always felt strange. She passed classroom after classroom until she came to the end of the hall and a pair of double doors. With all her might, she pulled one open.

She was in the school cafeteria. At least ten pairs of faces looked up from their chessboards. First Hudson saw Ellie, her hand poised over a pawn. And there, at the next lunch table, his brow knit in concentration, was Ben.

He looked up at her. "Hudson?" he said slowly. "What are you doing here?"

"Excuse me!" yelled the proctor. A tall, extremely thin older man with a bow tie and round, delicate glasses stood up from another table. "We're in the middle of a tournament here. Please wait outside —"

"I need to talk to Ben Geyer," Hudson managed to say, panting. "Please. Just for a second."

"You may absolutely *not*," said Mr. Bow Tie.

262

Hudson ignored him and ran down the aisle of tables to get to Ben.

Now Ben and Ellie were both staring at her openmouthed.

"Hillary just told me the truth," she blurted out. "She told me that Logan was the one who called Joe's Pub and promised them my mom. I'm so sorry, Ben. I never meant to hang up on you. And I never meant to screw up the Joe's Pub thing. I'm so sorry."

Ben shook his head. "O — okay," he stammered.

"So I'm here to ask you to take me back," she said. "Or, actually, not that. I want you to be in my band now. I'm going to put out my first album. And I want you to play shows with me. Would you be my bassist? Please?"

"Excuse me, young lady, but you're going to have to leave!" the proctor yelled, walking up to her.

Ben looked at her and then at the proctor. He seemed utterly at a loss for something to say.

"But if you don't want to be in my band, I totally understand," she rambled. "If you don't want to be my friend anymore, I get that, too."

"Just so you know, Hudson, I don't do stuff like that," he finally said. "You're my friend. I don't betray my friends. Ever."

"Okay." She exhaled.

"And as far as being your bassist," he said, breaking into a smile, "I'd love to."

"Really?" she asked, her heart pounding. "And wait a second. I can't believe I never asked you this before, but what's your sign?"

His eyebrows shot up. "Virgo," he said. "Why?"

"I'm a Pisces, which means we're, like, a perfect match!" She looked over to see the proctor's face turning purple with rage. "Sorry. I guess I should go."

"Yeah, good idea," Ben said, glancing at the proctor. "We have a few more minutes, and I'm totally about to win this."

Awkwardly, she leaned down to hug him, and then stuck out her hand. He shook it. "I can't say we're still going to be called the Rising Signs," she said.

"The Hudson Jones Trio is fine with me," he said.

"Hudson Jones Trio," she said, mulling it over. "I like that."

She walked out of the cafeteria and back into the hallway, ignoring the glare from Mr. Bow Tie. So Ben didn't hate her, after all. And even if the Rising Signs were over, she had something even better in place now. As she pushed the school doors open, she realized that she even had a possible name for her album.

Hudson Jones: The Return.

chapter 33

"Do you want to do the talking or should I?" Holla asked as Fernald navigated the late-afternoon traffic on Fifty-seventh Street. April rain pattered against the windshield.

"I'll do it," Hudson said.

"You start, and I'll come in at the end," Holla suggested.

"Mom, let me be in charge of this, okay?" Hudson replied.

Holla put her hand on Hudson's back. "Fine, but sit up straight."

Fernald double-parked in front of the smoke-colored skyscraper that held the offices of Swerve Records and leaped out of the driver's seat with an umbrella.

Upstairs, the receptionist picked up the phone. "Richard, they're here," she said quietly and hung up. "You can go right in," she said. "Last office on the right."

Hudson and Holla walked down the hall as Little Jimmy walked behind them. At each open door they passed Hudson could see people at their desks, craning their necks to get a good look at them. Or rather at Holla, who once again had the top single on the *Billboard* charts.

At the end of the hall they made a sharp right, into the corner office. Several executives sat on the long gray couch. Richard Wu stood up from his chair and walked over to greet them. He took Hudson's hand first. "Hi, Hudson," he said.

"Hi, Richard," she answered.

"Hello, Richard," Holla said, bringing him in closer for a kiss on the cheek.

"Congratulations on the single. To both of you," he made sure to add.

"Thank you," Holla said. "She's not bad, huh?" she asked, circling an arm around Hudson's shoulders.

Richard introduced them to the other Swerve executives, including the man whose office they were in. Hudson shook everyone's hand, and then she and her mom made themselves comfortable on the couch.

"So, I have to admit, Hudson," Richard said, "I was surprised to hear from you. We all thought after *Saturday Night Live* that you'd decided not to do this anymore."

"I know," she said, looking each of the four men in the eye. "I'm sorry about that. But I've changed my mind. I want to put out my album. My *first* album."

"But I thought you and your mother agreed that you wanted to go in a different direction," Richard said smoothly.

Hudson looked at Holla, who gave her a quick nod of encouragement. "I've changed my mind," she said. "And so has my mom. We think the first album is the better one."

The record executives traded surprised glances. "I don't know," said one of them, a man with a shaved head and a fat gold ring. "We spent a lot of money redoing it to your exact specifications."

"To *my* specifications," Holla said in a throaty voice. "It was my idea to change it. But," she said, gazing at her manicured hands, "I've since realized I was wrong."

The phrase *I was wrong* echoed through the office. Two of the executives looked at each other, as if to say, *Did I just hear that?*

"Whatever it costs to finish the first album," Holla said, "I'll pay for it myself."

Hudson watched as there were even more surprised glances around the room.

"So you're sure you want to do this, Hudson?" Richard prompted. "You want to put out a smaller, more intimate album that's going to be marketed in a very different way? Not on the scale of anything we would do with your mother — not even close."

Hudson nodded. "That's what I want," she said. "And that's the one you guys signed me to do in the first place."

"I know," Richard said, "but we believe there's potential for you to be a much bigger star."

Holla held up her hand. "This is what my daughter wants. And may I remind everyone that she wrote the number one song in the country?"

The executives traded more glances.

"I want it to be real music, real musicians, all of us recorded together," Hudson said. "And no stadiums, no big venues. I want to do small, intimate shows and work my way up. No TV appearances — only live gigs. I want to sing my songs the way I want to sing them."

Richard cleared his throat. "How soon can you go back in the studio?"

"June," Hudson said. "So I can finish school first."

Richard nodded. "I think that sounds good to us. We would plan on a Christmas release if that's the case."

"Great," Hudson said. "I've already written a few more songs, too. But I just have to ask you guys for one thing. One thing I'd like you to promise me."

"Sure," Richard said, steepling his hands under his chin.

Hudson took a deep breath and looked at Holla. "Mom? Can I speak to them privately for a sec?"

Holla eased out of her chair. "Sure, honey," she said, smiling encouragingly. "I'll be just outside."

Hudson waited until her mom was gone. As soon as the door shut, there was a palpable relief in the room. One of the guys even loosened his tie. The executives looked at Hudson expectantly.

"What is it, Hudson?" asked Richard.

"From now on, I want you to think of me as Hudson Jones, not Holla. Not even her daughter. Just me. Just another one of your artists. And if I do well, great. If I don't, you can drop me."

The men looked at one another across the room yet again. Richard fiddled with his watch band and swallowed hard, as if he were suddenly embarrassed by something. "Sure, Hudson," Richard said. "I think we can do that."

"And there's just one more thing."

Richard sat back down in his chair. "We're listening," he said.

"Is there any way we can set up a gig at Joe's Pub? Something this summer, maybe?"

Richard looked at the other executives. "I'll see what we can do."

When Hudson walked out of the office, Holla was sitting in the lobby while Little Jimmy stood guard, reading a magazine while people walking in and out of the elevator openly gawked at her. It was the first time Hudson could remember her mom waiting for her in a public place. "How'd it go?" she asked, putting down the magazine. "Did you say everything you needed to?"

"Yup," Hudson said.

"Did they listen?"

"Yes."

Holla smiled. "I'm proud of you, honey." She brushed some hair off Hudson's forehead. "Honey, do you ever wear any eyeliner? A little purple liner would really bring out your green eyes —"

"Mom?" Hudson said, taking her hand.

Holla pressed her lips together and smiled. "Sorry. So how do you feel about ditching the car and just taking a walk in the rain?"

"Are you serious?" Hudson asked in disbelief. "We can't do that."

"I've got dark glasses, an umbrella, and *him*," Holla said, pointing her thumb at Little Jimmy. "I think I can walk down the street."

Hudson pushed the elevator button. "That sounds great, Mom."

chapter 34

Hudson leaned close to the mirror and applied one last coat of mascara to her lashes. She stood back and fluttered her eyes open and closed. She wasn't wearing purple liner, but her sea green eyes shone, anyway. Her mom would have been proud.

She ran her hands through her wavy, barely styled hair. The black silk halter dress still fit perfectly. Wearing it again could have been a bad idea, but she was glad she'd chosen it. No matter what happened, tonight was going to be a better experience than the Silver Snowflake Ball. She knew that now.

She zipped up her makeup bag and headed to the bathroom door. A sign beside the door read JOE'S PUB — CALENDAR OF EVENTS. There, under today's date, June tenth, was THE HUDSON JONES TRIO, 8:00 P.M. She had to read it a few times to really absorb it: *The Hudson Jones Trio*. It had a nice ring to it. And she couldn't have asked for a better way to celebrate the last day of ninth grade.

She stepped out of the bathroom and back into the dressing room. Ben and Ricardo, the drummer, sat together over a miniature chessboard. "Checkmate," Ben said as he knocked Ricardo's queen off its square. "Sorry about that."

"Are you crushing my drummer?" Hudson asked him.

"Hey, I'm not being crushed," Ricardo said. "And those just came for you." He pointed to the extravagant arrangement of red roses in a glass vase on a dresser.

Hudson walked over to the flowers. The card was in a tiny envelope on the dresser. Hudson opened it and read:

To Hudson,
Good luck tonight. We miss you on tour. London isn't the same without you.
Love, Mom

Hudson folded up the card and slipped it into her purse. She never would have expected it, but she actually missed her mom. Her first gig at Joe's Pub wasn't going to be the same without Holla there.

There was a knock on the dressing room door, and then a voice asked, "Is it weird if I'm back here?"

Hudson turned around and saw Hillary standing on the threshold. She wore her dark-rinse jeans, but her pink shell and sweater set had embroidered hearts all over the front of it, and her hair was back to its usual messy ponytail, slightly tamed by plastic barrettes.

"I just wanted to wish you luck," she said in her small, rapid-fire voice. "Or tell you to break a leg and fall down some stairs. Whatever."

"Thanks, Hil," Hudson said. "And I have to say, you look great."

"Really?" Hillary said, looking down at her outfit. "It definitely took a lot less time to get ready. You were right about those clothes, by the way. They weren't me. And they weren't gonna make some guy like me, either."

"A guy not worth your time," Hudson added. "I hope you remember that part."

Hillary rolled her eyes. "Yeah, well, everyone's entitled to a bad crush, right?"

"Hey, nerd," Ben called out. He got up and checked his chunky black watch. "Nice of you to drop by, but I think we need to start."

"Don't embarrass the family," Hillary said to him, punching him in the arm. "See you out there." Then she left and walked back out to the restaurant.

Hudson turned to look in the mirror one last time. "So how do I look?"

"Really pretty," Ben said shyly.

"Thanks," Hudson said, turning to look at Ben. "I'm ready if you guys are."

"Let's go," said Ricardo.

As she and Ben and Ricardo walked down the hall toward the stage, she could feel the old butterflies start to flit around her stomach. But she let them do their thing. She knew that they couldn't hurt her.

"Can you believe we're here?" Ben whispered in her ear.

Hudson shook her head. "No. Not one bit."

"So, ladies and gentlemen, without any further ado," said the announcer, "we introduce the Hudson Jones Trio!"

The three of them walked into the room and up onto the stage. There, at the tables nearest them, so close she could practically touch them, were all of her friends: Lizzie and Katia and Bernard; Carina, the Jurg, and Alex; Ellie Kim and her mom; Mrs. Geyer and Hillary. Everyone clapped and someone hollered, "Hudson!"

She made her way to the piano, praying she wouldn't trip. When she looked out at the room, past the stage, she could see people at the two-top tables. At one of them was Richard Wu, sitting with a colleague. He gave her a little wave, and Hudson smiled at him. This was nothing like the scary darkness of the Pierre Hotel's ballroom. She had friends here, people who were rooting for her. And as for the people she didn't know, they were probably here for the two acts that followed her band. In which case Hudson wasn't going to worry about what they thought.

"Hi, everyone," she said into the mic. "Thank you so much for coming. We're the Hudson Jones Trio, and we're going to start off with a song I wrote called 'For You.'"

She felt her heart flutter and the adrenaline shoot through her arms. But tonight she knew that she was going to be okay. She looked over at Ben. He smiled and nodded to say he was ready when she was.

She smiled back, took a deep breath, and started to sing.

acknowledgments

First off, I would like to thank my agent, Becka Oliver, for her unswerving support and encouragement. She is the best advocate, and friend, a writer could ask for.

I would also like to thank the following people: my wonderful editors at Poppy, Elizabeth Bewley and Kate Sullivan, who gave me valuable advice, suggestions, and feedback; Cindy Eagan, whose enthusiasm for this series makes me so happy; Matt Piedmont and Ethan Goldman, for schooling me in the basics of jazz; Janet Siroto, for her knowledge of Larchmont; JoAnna Kremer, for her impeccable copyediting; and Tracy Shaw, for her eye-catching cover design for this series. I am also indebted to John Lahr and his excellent article on stage fright, "Petrified," in *The New Yorker* (August 28, 2006.)

And, of course, endless thanks go to Edie, my family, and to Ido Ostrowsky, the coolest Gemini I know.

Meet Emma Conway, the daughter of a powerful presidential hopeful and the black sheep of her family.

Facing pressure to be the perfect First Daughter-in-training, Emma must learn to speak up for herself and for what she believes in. Thankfully, she has her new friends and fellow daughters—Lizzie, Carina, and Hudson—to help her along the way.

Turn the page for an exclusive introduction to New York City's newest Daughter. . . .

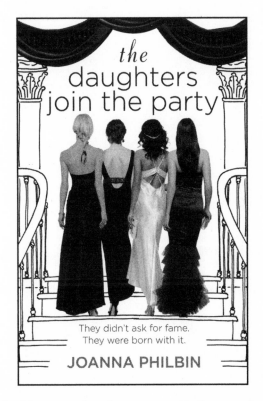

the **daughters join the party**

They didn't ask for fame.
They were born with it.

JOANNA PHILBIN

Available in bookstores November 2011

"I'm going to ask you one more time," said Mr. Moyers, tapping his meaty fingers on his desk blotter. With his pale face, hangdog eyes, and rainbow-striped necktie, the headmaster of Rutherford looked like a very sad clown. "Who were you trying to see in Flanner Hall last night? And be honest, Emma. For both our sakes."

Emma shifted in the leather wing chair across from his desk. She could easily just tell him. Jeremy Dunn hadn't shown up for breakfast, and when she'd passed by him on the quad on the way to first period, he'd actually looked right past her. But she wasn't a tattletale. "Nobody. I was having trouble sleeping, so I just felt like taking a walk."

"A walk," Mr. Moyers repeated doubtfully. The afternoon sun poured in through the tall window behind him. Through it Emma could see two girls walking to the Art Building past the massive elm trees. She wished she were with them.

"I couldn't sleep," Emma said. "Doesn't that ever happen to you?"

"Emma, do you like being in this office?" Mr. Moyers asked, leaning forward. "At this point, I feel I have to ask."

She took in the framed degrees in education from Yale and Columbia, and the cheesy poster of a rainbow with a quote that read: *There is nothing impossible to him who will try. — Alexander the Great.* And of course the electric guitar leaning against the wall, which Mr. Moyers supposedly used for "jam sessions" with some of the faculty members. Just thinking about that made her cringe. "I guess it's kind of cozy," she said. "Though you might want to think about redecorating soon."

"Emma." Mr. Moyers sighed. "We're going to have to discuss your future here at Rutherford."

"My *future*?" she asked.

"Yes," he said soberly. "Your future."

Those ominous words still hung in the air when a brisk knock on the door made her jump. "Yes?" Mr. Moyers called out.

His assistant, Kathy, stuck her gray, permed head into the room. Emma always got the impression that Kathy was secretly listening on speaker to everything that went on in Mr. Moyers's office. "Senator Conway is here," she announced. "And his wife."

"My *parents*?" Emma exclaimed, sitting straight up in her chair. "But they're on vacation. At Lake George. Nuclear fallout wouldn't get them to leave."

Mr. Moyers coolly flapped his rainbow necktie. "They didn't seem to have a problem coming in. Especially when I told them the gravity of the situation."

A shiver ran through her as she gripped the chair's armrests. She wasn't going to just be getting detention. That much was clear. "Can I speak to them first?" she asked, getting to her feet.

Mr. Moyers blinked, surprised.

"They're my parents. Isn't that my constitutional right?"

"Go ahead," he said with a resigned shrug.

She opened the door. Her dad was talking to Kathy. He held a miniature bronzed football that he'd picked up from her desk, and his large green eyes were lit up, the way they always were when he talked to a voter. "You said your husband's a Giants fan?" he asked her, a faint New York accent curling around his words. "Well, you tell him from me that I think they're going to have a terrific season. And if they don't, I will *personally* —"

"Dad?" she interrupted.

His expression went from folksy to furious. "Hello, Emma," he said soberly. He put down the football and crossed his arms over his barrel chest. Adam Conway was just over six feet, but he could suddenly appear several inches taller if he wanted to, especially if he was annoyed. "I take it you're here to plead your case?" he asked.

Kathy stood up from her chair. "I'll just leave you two alone," she said, and ducked out the door.

"Where's Mom?" Emma asked, looking around. Mr. Moyers's waiting room was permanently dim, even in the middle of the day.

"She's in the ladies room," her father said. He cocked his head to the side. His thick, wavy brown hair had yet to go gray, but it seemed to be getting lighter at the temples. And it was always strange to see him out of a suit, and in a blue polo and khakis.

"First of all, this has gotten *way* blown out of proportion," she said. "It was barely anything. I didn't even make it into the dorm. Nothing happened."

"Whatever happened, it was bad enough to get your mother and me in a car at eight thirty this morning."

"I'm just asking you to have an open mind. The way you would if Remington got into trouble."

Her dad gave her a searing look. "Your brother doesn't get into trouble," he said, just as the door to the office opened and Emma's mother entered.

"Hello, honey," she said, reaching out her slender arms. Even in a crisis, Carolyn Conway could be counted on to look good — no, impeccable. She wore a yellow silk top and navy blue capris with gold ballet slippers, and she'd pulled her thick black hair back into a casual but chic ponytail. She didn't wear makeup, and she was too practical to indulge in jewelry. But she did like handbags. Today she carried a bright pink Kelly bag in the crook of her arm, and it banged against Emma as she gave her mom a hug.

"Hi, Mom," Emma muttered, getting a noseful of citrus-gardenia perfume. "Sorry about this."

Carolyn pulled out of the hug and frowned at Emma. "So. You snuck into a boys' dorm."

"I *tried* to sneak in," Emma said. "Huge difference."

Her mom seemed about to say something when she noticed Emma's T-shirt, silk-screened with Edie Sedgwick's face, and her black skinny jeans.

"Sorry I'm not decked out in J. Crew," Emma said.

"Nice earrings," Carolyn said. "Skulls really send a great message."

"Okay, let's get this over with," said her dad, heading toward Mr. Moyers's office. Her mom followed.

Emma trailed behind them with a sinking feeling in her chest. She had a strong hunch that this wasn't going to go very well.

When they walked inside, Mr. Moyers almost leaped out of his chair. "Senator, Mrs. Conway! It's so nice to see you again," he said, approaching them with his hand extended.

"Same here," said Senator Conway, shaking Mr. Moyers's hand. "And please, call me Adam."

"Then call me Jim," Mr. Moyers said, so excited that his eyes seemed about to bulge out of his face. "Mrs. Conway," he said, turning to Emma's mom.

Carolyn shook his hand. "Hello, Mr. Moyers," she said in her brisk lawyer's voice. Unlike her husband, she had little talent — or use — for chitchat. She sat down next to Adam on the couch.

"Emma?" Mr. Moyers said. "Do you want to join your parents?"

Emma realized that she was still standing by the door. She perched herself on the arm of the sofa and winced. Her butt still hurt from last night's fall.

"So, uh, Jim," her father said. He leaned forward so that his elbows rested on his knees. She'd seen him sit this way in some of the photos on his Senate Web site. SENATOR ADAM CONWAY CARES ABOUT NEW YORKERS, read the banner at the top of the page. "What can we do to help?"

"Well, I believe you know what happened here last night," Mr. Moyers said, settling into his chair. "Leaving one's room after lights-out, and then trying to enter another dormitory, is a serious violation of the Rutherford student code."

"So what's the punishment?" asked her mom. "This can't be the first time someone has done this."

"It's the first time someone has violated as many codes as your daughter has," Mr. Moyers said.

"How many are we talking about?" Emma's father asked, casting an alarmed glance in her direction.

"Well, let's see here…" Mr. Moyers picked up the file on his desk. "January tenth, Emma showed up in homeroom with purple hair."

"What?" her mother exploded. "She *dyed* her hair?"

"Yes. Purple."

"Burgundy," Emma cut in.

Mr. Moyers gave her an annoyed glance. "February fourteenth and twenty-first, she cut first and second period to sleep in."

"I was sick," she argued.

"When the RA went to her room," Mr. Moyers said, "she found Emma watching a movie on her laptop."

"Which was for class," Emma said.

"Emma," her father warned.

"March fifth," he went on, "Emma was caught in the pool, with a boy, after hours."

Emma let that one pass. Her dad sighed deeply and looked at the carpet.

"April seventeenth," said Mr. Moyers, "Emma started a food fight in the dining hall."

"I flung a piece of bread at someone," she said.

"Which hit Miss Wilkie, the math teacher," Mr. Moyers added. "May tenth —"

"Okay, we get the picture," Adam interrupted, holding up his hand. "And then last night —"

"Our head prefect heard Emma first try to scale the boys' dorm, and then fall on the ground." Mr. Moyers closed the file. "Which leads me to conclude that this might not be the best place for your daughter." He cleared his throat and swallowed. "We think it best she explore new possibilities for the coming school year."

Her parents looked dumbfounded. "Are you saying you don't want her to continue here?" her mom asked.

"I don't believe Emma wants to be here, Mrs. Conway. And I think she's doing everything she can to let us know that."

"You know she's dyslexic," her mom pointed out, in a way that made Emma cringe.

"We have plenty of other students with learning disabilities who don't have the . . . behavioral issues that Emma has." Mr. Moyers swallowed again. He seemed uncomfortable. "Emma's bright. She has the capacity to be an excellent student, despite her learning disability. But she doesn't take school seriously. In fact, she doesn't seem to take anything seriously."

"That's not fair," Emma argued. "What about my A in Swimming? And Photography? And the social service I did at the animal shelter?"

"Emma," Adam said sternly.

Carolyn reached over and put her hand on Emma's arm.

"I'm sorry," said Mr. Moyers. "But we think it's best that you find Emma another school."

Emma fumed silently. *Come on, Dad,* she thought, staring at the carpet. If he could get the Republicans and Democrats to agree on a health-care bill, he could get Mr. Moyers to keep her here. But instead of saying something persuasive and charming, her dad simply looked at her mom and held up his hands.

"All right, then," Carolyn said, reading his signals. "We'll take her home."

Emma got to her feet. "It was Jeremy Dunn," she confessed. "That's who I was trying to see last night. He's on the second floor of Flanner. Summer student, from Boston. Just ask him —"

"Thank you, Emma," Mr. Moyers said, scribbling something on a pad. "And good luck."

"That's it?" she asked. "I just gave you a name."

Mr. Moyers sighed. "Good-bye, Emma."

She went straight to the door, not even waiting for her parents. This was a joke. If this school wasn't going to give her a second chance, if it was going to kick her out for *attempting* to sneak into someone's room, and if it wasn't even going to give her a break for naming names, then she didn't want to be here anyway.

She hurried past Kathy, who she knew had probably heard every word, and threw open the door to the hall. All she wanted to do was run back to her room, slam the door, and try to think. She just needed to be alone. Even though she knew that would be impossible. Behind her she heard her parents walk into the hall.

"Well, I guess we shouldn't be too surprised," Emma heard her dad say. "It was a matter of time."

"You're the one who thought she was ready for boarding school," her mom replied.

"I just said we should try it," he said. "I didn't say it was going to be the perfect solution."

Emma whirled around. "Can you stop talking about me like I'm not here?"

"What would you like us to do?" her father asked. "You're walking ten paces ahead of us."

"You didn't even try to talk him out of it!" she said. "You didn't even defend me."

"Defend you?" Her mother's voice was uncharacteristically loud. "For dyeing your hair purple? Causing food fights?"

"Of course you'd believe all that," Emma muttered.

"Are you aware of what's going on with your father these days?"

"No, I have no idea," Emma said sarcastically.

There was no way she couldn't know. For the past six months, whenever she walked by the huge flat-screen TV in the student lounge, he was all over the news. *If Conway runs for president… Senator Conway put in another appearance today… The crowds showing up for Conway today were in the thousands… Sources close to the Senator say he is definitely eyeing a run…* She'd see a snippet of her dad making a speech in front of a crowd, or being applauded as he walked from his town car into a building, and it would all feel like she was watching someone else. It was too surreal. But ever since he'd won the Democratic New York seat for the second time, he'd practically become a celebrity.

First there'd been the health-care bill that he'd shepherded through the Senate, the one that nobody thought would get passed. Then there'd been his book, *Bridging the Divide,* about his plans for a *"united* United States of America," which had hit the *New York Times* bestseller list the day it was released and hadn't dropped off since. Then there'd been the interview on *60 Minutes,* where, when Morley Safer asked him about his plans for a campaign, he said, "I definitely haven't ruled it out," which only got every on-camera pundit and political blogger more obsessed over whether he might run. She would've had to have been trapped under a rock not to know what was going on with her dad. "Of course I know," she said.

"Well, there's more," her mother said. "When we get home —"

"I'm not going to live at home."

"Emma, your mother is trying to tell you something," her dad said somberly.

"And I am *not* going to Chadwick," Emma added. "You are not going to make me go to Remington's school. I *refuse.*"

She turned and headed for the door that led out onto the quad. She needed to get some air. *Expelled,* she thought. It was such an ugly word.

She pushed through the doors and there, on the veranda of the administrative building, stood a man talking on a cell phone. "Yeah, we had a quick change of plans this morning," he said in a raspy voice. "Now we're at their daughter's school." His slicked-back, dark hair was beginning to thin on top, and he wore an expensive-looking black suit. He looked up and saw her. "Lemme get back to you." He clicked off the phone. "You must be Emma," he said, holding out his hand. "I'm Tom. Tom Beckett."

Emma shook his hand. There had always been people hovering around her family — mostly anxious men in their twenties, who were always waiting to ferry her dad to appearances or to hand him a speech. But none of them had ever seemed this confident or well-dressed, and none had ever come with her parents to her school. "Hi," she said uncertainly.

Just then her parents came through the doors. "Who is this?" she asked them, turning around.

"This is Tom, my chief strategist," said her father.

"Chief strategist for what?" she asked. "You just got reelected last year."

Her dad paused for a moment. "I'm running again, honey."

Emma blinked. "You're running again? For what?"

"For president."

For a moment the words didn't compute. She watched as he put his hand on Tom's shoulder. "Tom here is the best," her dad went on. "Came highly recommended to me by Shanks. Where is he, by the way?"

"Out by the car, on the phone," said Tom. "He's lining up that Parks Department event for you tonight."

Emma tried to think of something to say. Anything.

"It all just happened," her mother put in. "Tom came up to the house yesterday for a meeting with a few people from his team. We were going to tell you when you came home next week."

"Come on," her father said. "Let's go pack up your things."

Emma began to follow them across the quad. She was supposed to be leading them, but she was too distracted to do anything but put one foot in front of the other.

Tom Beckett slipped on a pair of black wraparound sunglasses that made him look like a cross between an alien predator and Tom Cruise. "Everything okay?" he asked her parents.

"Not exactly," her father said, giving Emma a disapproving glance. "But then again we're all a little used to that by now."

What if a beautiful vintage dress
could take you back in time?

What if the gown you just slipped on
transformed you into a famous movie starlet
aboard a luxurious cruise ship a hundred years ago?

What if her life was filled with secrets, drama,
and decadence?

The Time-Traveling Fashionista is a stylish and adventurous
new series about a girl who adores fashion, proving
that some clothes never go out of style.

AVAILABLE NOW

Where stories bloom.

poppy

Visit us online at
www.pickapoppy.com